The Bachelor

The Bachelor

a novel

ANDREW PALMER

HOGARTH
London / New York

Published in the United States by Hogarth, an imprint of the Random House Publishing Group, a division of Penguin Random House LLC, New York.

Grateful acknowledgment is made to Farrar, Straus and Giroux for permission to reprint excerpts from "Message" and "Tea" from *Collected Poems: 1937–1971* by John Berryman, copyright © 1989 by Kate Donahue Berryman. Reprinted by permission of Farrar, Straus and Giroux.

Library of Congress Cataloging-in-Publication Data
Names: Palmer, Andrew, 1981 August 4– author.
Title: The bachelor : a novel / Andrew Palmer.
Description: First edition. | New York : Hogarth, 2021
Identifiers: LCCN 2020056621 (print) | LCCN 2020056622 (ebook) |
ISBN 9780593230893 (hardcover) | ISBN 9780593230909 (ebook)
Classification: LCC PS3616.A338824 B33 2021 (print) |
LCC PS3616.A338824 (ebook) | DDC 813/.6—dc23
LC record available at https://lccn.loc.gov/2020056621

Printed in Canada

9 8 7 6 5 4 3 2 1

First Edition

Book design by Jo Anne Metsch

For Liza

Much is repulsive.
But I am taken with a passion for reality!

—GEORGE MEREDITH, *Diana of the Crossways*

The Bachelor

1

NOT LONG AFTER I MOVED INTO THE MOSTLY EMPTY house of a friend of my mother's in northwest Des Moines, near the dead end of the street I grew up on, in order to reset my life or retire quietly from it, I discovered on the satellite television service channel 665, "home of *your* Chicago Bulls." I started tuning in to every game. I didn't ask myself why I watched. I watched because for the two and a half hours it took for the forty-eight minutes of each game to elapse, I knew exactly how to feel: removed from myself into hope and joy when the Bulls were winning, full of almost comforting anxiety when they weren't. These automatic responses took root further back than I can remember; they're as much who I am as anything. My family never had cable when I was a kid—my parents once told me they would have gotten it but they knew if they did I'd lose my childhood to ESPN (they were right, as usual)—so the occasional Sunday afternoon NBC telecast was all I could watch of the Jordan-Pippen-era Bulls, from whom I learned everything I know about heroism. When I started watching Bulls games again at my mother's friend's house, after living without a TV for more than a decade, those distant, wide-open afternoons returned to me, and, though I would soon be a thirty-year-old man, I felt something of the annihilating sweetness of childhood. This sensation was no doubt heightened by my familiarity with the telecasters, Stacey King and Neil Funk. King had been a mediocre but enthusiastic reserve on the Bulls' first three championship teams, whose radio broadcasts, called by Funk, I used to love to listen to, lying on the bristly orange living-room carpet in front of my parents' enormous speakers, or probably enormous only in memory, whenever an especially meaningful game failed to reach our little TV screen.

And so it was strange to reencounter Funk and King allied in this new way, but before long their partnership grew to seem natural, and I came to look forward not only to watching the usual miracles of semi-choreographed human movement, but to listening to Funk, in his grating Chicago accent, ooze derision toward the Bulls' opponents ("Is it me or does something *stink* in this gym?"), and to King shout his silly catchphrases ("Pressure bursts pipes!"). They were terrible telecasters. Several times each game their narration of a play would be contradicted by the footage itself: "That right there is a clean block," for example, as I witnessed what was plainly a heinous mauling; or "Inbound on the baseline," as a player inbounded from the sideline; or—more than once—"Short," as a shot flew long. It was as if they and I were watching different games.

In any case, by January 2011 the Bulls were among the best teams in the NBA for the first time since Jordan left them for good in '98, and I could root for them again with the assurance that more games than not I'd be rewarded with a brief respite from my malaise. From time to time it unnerved me, though, to see these unfamiliar men in the red and white jerseys that had loomed so large in my childhood dreamscape, and I couldn't shake the sense that these new Bulls were impostors.

Sometimes as I sat there in front of the vast flat-screen, I felt as though I'd fallen out of myself, free to watch this solitary man reclining on an overstuffed couch in a stranger's house, sinking so deep into its forest green cushions he seems on the verge of disappearing into its softness, never to be seen or heard from again. Watching myself watch *my Chicago Bulls,* a great sense of release coursed through me, as though my body were ridding itself of some previously undetected foreign object, something hard, jagged, and compact that had been lodged deep within me for many years. I felt wonderfully susceptible, calm, almost content. That I felt almost miserable doesn't mean that I couldn't also feel almost content. I waited for the almosts to drop away. The smallest action, the slightest change of mind or mood, just might be the door through which would enter some big definitive feeling or idea. In this way my life was full of suspense.

At first I didn't change the channel during commercials, whose strategy of tricking me into buying things via immaculately crafted thirty-second comedy skits struck me as terrifying and hilarious, a lot funnier than the skits themselves, but they soon lost their novelty and I started switching over to PBS, bow-tied antiques dealers or Peruvian birds of paradise or actors reading Andrew Jackson letters with echo effects. One early January evening I was watching the Bulls play the Toronto Raptors at the United Center in Chicago, where my father and I used to drive once a year to see a game when I was a teenager. Chris Bosh had left the Raptors the previous summer to join Wade and LeBron in Miami. Everyone hated him for this but he seemed thoughtful and kind and everyone should get to decide where they live, and so I felt defensive on his behalf, vaguely. Without him the Raptors were very bad. Their players hailed from seven different countries. Toronto is a city that takes pride in its multiculturalism. Ashwini, my ex-fiancée, though we were never actually engaged, whose parents grew up on premodern farms in unimaginably lush southern India, grew up in a northern suburb of Toronto, and I was trying not to think about the three months I'd just spent with her on the outer reaches of Nova Scotia. The Bulls were up big, Stacey King was trying out new catchphrases, Neil Funk was yelling at the Raptors for being awful. The game went to commercial and I changed the channel to PBS, Custer's Last Stand, the Battle of Little Bighorn, Sitting Bull was a hero, Custer was a monster who was made into a hero, he and his band of palefaces desecrated Lakota burial grounds, they deserved their fate. About three minutes seemed to have passed and I pressed the PRE CH button on the remote, except I must have pressed a different button because instead of the Bulls game I was watching a man who looked a little like Brad Pitt talking to the camera in a slight southern accent about the ways in which he'd *grown emotionally* in the past three years. He'd spent a lot of time thinking, self-analyzing, changing. He had struggled, he wasn't ashamed to admit, with trust and commitment issues. Thanks to Thomas Parker, PhD, he'd traced these back to his father's absence from his childhood. "I don't know if I've ever let someone know the real me," drawled the beautiful man. "When I give my all to somebody and I'm let down, I revert back to that feeling of when my dad told me he was comin' to pick me and my brother up for ice cream and . . . yeah, he never came. And after that"—he lowered his eyes and pursed his lips—"after that I didn't hear from the guy for five, six years."

He had forced himself to face up to his past. He had done a lot of soul-searching. Finally, after all these years, he was ready to fall in love.

The Bachelor is a heartbreaking reality TV show on which twenty-five single women in their twenties or early thirties compete for a lifetime of sex and companionship with a conventionally handsome and successful man. Each episode, the Bachelor takes some of the women on "dates," many of which involve helicopters and/or rooftops and/or leaping from high places, so that he might gauge their suitability as wives. The bachelorettes are made to live together in a gaudy mansion outside L.A. in order to exacerbate the tensions between them inherent in the show's competitive premise. Each episode ends with a Rose Ceremony, where the Bachelor dramatically hands out roses to the women he wishes to remain in the competition, tacitly eliminating the ones who aren't on the show for the *right reasons,* or have failed to *open up.* When the rejected women are interviewed immediately after the Rose Ceremony they cry, smudging their dark eye makeup. "I should've put myself out there," they say, or, "I can't believe I put myself out there like that." They say, "I'm tired of being alone." They wipe their tears. "I would've been a good wife, a good mother." Then they say, "It's his loss."

Who are these women? Where did they come from? How did they get here? They are executive assistants and apparel merchants and operations managers and food writers and nannies and dancers and dentists and dental hygienists and insurance agents and sales directors and sales consultants and publicists and models and aestheticians, although many of them, as they stress to the Bachelor to convey that they're on the show for the right reasons, have quit their jobs so they can be here. They are Madison and Raichel and Lacey and Britt and Britnee and Keltie and Marissa and Shawntel. They're Ashley H. and Ashley S. They're from America's biggest coastal metropolises and the beautiful beige suburbs of its most authentic heartland, but mostly they're from California and Florida. They're the type of people like, "This is me. This is who I am." Their faces glow. They're all about family. They love a good love story. They're totally huggers. Most of them harbor some deep, secret hurt, the revelation of which constitutes their *opening up.* Many, like the Bachelor, have father issues. All are losers in love. All, too—how could they not be?—are aware of the show's ridiculousness, and all who make it deep into the competition express surprise at how quickly that ridiculousness has become just another condition of their existence, to be transcended or at least ignored, so that they can allow their relationship with the Bachelor to seem to mean something. "I didn't expect to feel this way," they say. They always say, "I didn't expect to feel this way." And their self-awareness, imperfect as it is, makes them almost complicit with you.

Still, I struggle to understand, these many years later, what made my first encounter with *The Bachelor* seem so enriching and deep. I've watched every subsequent season of the show—and also its fascinating mirror version, *The Bachelorette* (not to mention the irredeemable spin-offs, *Bachelor Pad* and *Bachelor in Paradise*)—and while usually I find something to be interested in, I've never been gripped like I was that first season. Along with untold millions of co-viewers, I had chosen to invest some twenty-five hours, rationed almost cruelly across twelve weeks, in the romantic fate of a man I would never meet and likely would have little to say to if I did. Was it just that I loved a good love story? Maybe. Everyone loves a good love story. And maybe since I'd all but renounced romantic love, my interest in the Bachelor's quest, I mean *journey,* took on a heightened vicarious quality. Maybe a part of me wanted to *be* the Bachelor. Of course a part of me wanted to be the Bachelor. I'm not sure that's the right way to put it. In this case, as in so many others, my desire felt somehow separate from me, as if it belonged to someone else and had strayed by accident or sinister design into my defenseless body.

Probably what pulled me in that first episode had something to do with my ignorance of the show, which seemed to strategically take for granted a certain amount of familiarity in its viewers. It was its own world, with its own laws and logic, fraught with history, self-reference, and myth. I sensed I was missing some essential information; actions and speech seemed full of obscure significance. The narrative that constituted the Bachelor's identity was rounded into fullness by way of suggestion and omission. The Bachelor had a whole world inside him; he had, if people have these, a soul. I quickly came to understand that this wasn't the Bachelor's first time on *The Bachelor:* he'd been the Bachelor a few seasons ago, but instead of proposing to one of the two finalists, per the rules of the competition, he confessed to both that he wasn't in love, then sent them to their limos to weep in their finery, leaving himself once again all alone. "For this Bachclor," narrated the show's kindly host, "nothing would ever be the same." Now, a changed man, he was back for the most controversial *Bachelor* ever. It was a new beginning. He had the sincerest intentions. Near the start of the first episode he sits in his Austin apartment—where he has spent, presumably, thousands of unfilmed hours, dusting and doing push-ups and microwaving Hot Pockets and masturbating—and watches a slightly younger version of himself tell two women he'd after all only recently met that he's sorry, he wishes he felt differently, but he doesn't want to spend the rest of his life with either. "I can't look you in your eye and tell you that I love you," I watched him watch himself say. Those words struck me as brave and honorable, and I sat up a little straighter on the couch.

After his initial season aired, though, the Bachelor sank into a deep depression. He tells us this over footage of himself re-enacting his depression: the Bachelor sitting at his kitchen table eating a bowl of cereal; the Bachelor sitting on a concrete floor watching rain fall over his city; the Bachelor sitting at his computer reading *Bachelor* forums, on which fans of the show release their venom toward him, the Bachelor. But the fans were right, he can now admit. He was closed off for so long. He put up walls. He made a habit of hurting women before they had a chance to hurt him. This time, he promises, things will be different. "I truly believe my wife is sitting in that room," he says before entering the bachelorette living room to meet his second batch of pursuers. "I really do."

The Bachelor often punctuates his statements in this way: "I think you're one in a million. I really do." "I'm so sorry I kept you waiting. I really am." It adds to his air of impossible earnestness, which he has the ability to convey even without words. His shoulders are broad, his jaw square, his eyebrows thick, his eyes an intriguing silver blue. He has a five o'clock shadow and high cheekbones. He takes long shirtless runs on beaches at dusk. His chest is smooth and shapely. On his back: a tattooed cross. He is solid. He has presence. He is a Real American Man. When he speaks he furrows his brow and gives intermittent little nods. He's convinced himself he's the role he is playing, or else—which may amount to the same thing—doesn't believe he's playing a role at all. This, it struck me with the force of an epiphany, must be how what is called character is formed.

At first, and this may have been another part of the show's appeal, the Bachelor seemed so remote from me that I could hardly believe we shared a language and country. Sometimes I could hardly believe we belonged to the same species. It wasn't just that the Bachelor was on TV and I wasn't. It went beyond his superhero physique. There was his accent—no state comes closer to a foreign country than Texas—but it went beyond that as well. It even went beyond the depressing sterility of the Bachelor's meticulously staged environment, all those thornless blood-red roses, all that bluish light. The Bachelor's foreignness, I've come to think, was rooted in the *certainty* he exuded: certainty about how beautiful he was, certainty that marriage was the endpoint of love, certainty that America was the greatest nation in the world, certainty that Jesus Christ was the Son of God and that one day He'd return to Earth and whisk the Bachelor up to Heaven, trailing clouds of rose petals. The bachelorettes, while presumably as devout as the Bachelor—the show generally avoided religion—for the most part seemed to lack this certainty. Who wouldn't be consumed by self-doubt in their positions? They made up for it, though, until the moment they were rejected, with an impressively relentless cheeriness—a cheeriness that seemed to serve basically the same function as the Bachelor's certainty: to camouflage a deeper, maybe more existential, uncertainty (so I hoped, so I consoled myself). The Bachelor and his cheery band of bachelorettes, in any case, came to occupy for me a sort of shadow world, a world whose weekly dispatches I watched with a blend of bafflement, boredom, sympathy, delight, sadness, horror, and longing.

I was pleased to note, as I watched the first episode, a small puncture in the Bachelor's Bachelorness: he runs funny. I noticed it as he was taking one of his shirtless sunset beach runs: there's a slight but undeniable awkwardness to his stride. His knees bend too deeply, his feet are splayed—he's gawky. The Bachelor is gawky. And this physical imperfection brought the Bachelor a little closer to my world. It called to mind a younger version of him, pre–protein drinks and personal trainer, an awkward, acned, resentful adolescent. And after adolescence? A year in college, a year out, two years of pulling himself together, finding God, then back to college, business school, gyms, hair products, drinking buddies, the downtown condo? Or was it L.A., commercials, an aborted modeling career, semi-famous friends, piles of coke, something gone wrong at a hotel in Malibu, the shameful return to Texas? The show had a way of planting these seeds in your brain, which grew into stories that should have competed with one another but instead bled together, forming an underlayer of hypothetical realities. Even as you sense the gulf between yourself and the Bachelor, you start to feel you know him as you know people in real life, or at least as you know characters in books and movies.

My favorite bachelorette that first episode was an intelligent-eyed high school teacher from Charlottesville, Virginia, but she didn't get a rose and wept and wiped her tears and said it was the Bachelor's loss and I switched back to the Bulls game. The fourth quarter had just started, the Bulls were up big, their coach had inserted the second team. "I mean, it was like he shot that *blindfolded,*" said Neil Funk. "Can I get some butter with that roll!" yelled Stacey King. I found myself, as I often did that winter, focusing my attention away from the ball, toward the players trying to shed their defenders or help their teammates shed theirs. It was strange to watch these glossy men scamper across the glossy floor. They spread their legs wide and covered their crotches with their hands, or pressed their backsides hard into the muscled fronts of their defenders, or took off at full speed in one direction only to suddenly stop after a few strides and sprint back to where they started. There was a constant squeaking of sneakers on hardwood, louder than crowd or commentary. On the bench the Bulls' starters whispered hilarious things in each other's ears and cheered their backups in a jokey way that I hoped didn't hold the hint of condescension it seemed to. Joakim Noah, the Bulls' manic French-speaking ponytailed center who'd broken his hand a few weeks earlier, sat at the end of the bench in a powder blue suit and purple bow tie. I'd seen him once, on a quiet street in Greenwich Village, walking and laughing with a group of normal-sized men, and now I wondered if he and I might be friends if only we had a chance to get to know each other. The screen switched to a shot of the Raptors' bench: everyone was solemn, no one spoke. Soon they'd board a charter plane back to Toronto, then drive their Benzes to their mansions in the suburbs. Probably Ashwini, at that moment, was sitting on her love seat in her dark apartment, grading or preparing for a class. Pausing, now, to listen to the rain. In Halifax it was always raining. My first week there I discovered the spot where I would propose to her, a clearing on top of a hill in the wooded park on the city's peninsular southern tip. In spite of my skepticism of the rituals surrounding marriage, I'd nevertheless kneel, my back to the ocean. She would laugh and wipe tears from her face. "What movie are we in?" she'd say. A month and a half later I lay next to her in the dark of our bedroom and, as she said probably accurate things about me, felt as though I were shrinking to an infinitely small size, then being placed by a disembodied hand into a wooden box, then lying in the box as it was dropped into the ocean and sank. The last time we had sex Ashwini was on top of me when she gradually slowed her movements, then stopped and put her hands on my chest and, faintly smiling, said, "Let's just look at each other for a while. We never just stop and look at each other," and she sat upright and arched her back a little and folded her arms beneath her breasts, and we looked at each other and who knows what she saw but she laughed in what I chose to interpret as happiness, and I laughed back. In a week we would fly to London, then Mumbai, then train down the coast to Alappuzha to spend the holidays with her extended family; and at that moment, after several days of dreading the trip, I felt a surge of renewed optimism.

A week later, as I sat at my gate in the Halifax airport, waiting for the first of the series of flights that would deliver me not to Mumbai but Des Moines, I was alarmed to detect a strong vibration moving up my thighs and into my stomach and chest, where it lingered for a moment before I realized its source was external to me, an airplane landing or taking off. On my flight to Detroit a long-standing feeling, which I'd lacked the space or courage to examine in Halifax, hardened into a resolution: I was done trying to write my novel, done writing novels period. One was enough. One was one too many. Like so many others at around this time—as if we'd all come down with the same sickness—I had begun to doubt the value of making up stories in the service of some hoped-for truth. Now that I'd decided to stop trying, I felt relieved. The work had not been going well.

My flight from Detroit to Minneapolis was canceled due to snow. I was wheeling my suitcases to an information desk to ask about hotels when I remembered I knew someone in town I could probably stay with, a poet who'd moved to Detroit from New York with a group of other poets and art school grads in order to live for practically nothing in one of the city's abandoned mansions, where they could practice their respective arts and have sex with one another and urban farm all day. I'd been surprised when I heard Maria was leaving New York; the city seemed to suit her. She'd stood out among the cool kids and strivers as someone who would rise to the top (of what?) without any apparent effort, without pain, by force of remaining quietly herself. Meantime everyone envied her job, personal assistant to a famous mystery writer, since it paid ridiculously well and demanded virtually nothing—the dream. She was, I'd always thought, *genuinely* cool—one of the coolest people I knew. Her coolness had nothing to do with irony or distance or disaffection. She loved what she loved without embarrassment.

I hadn't seen or spoken to her in a few years, and we'd never been especially close, but she seemed excited to hear my voice and was at the airport within an hour. When she saw me she shook her hands next to her face and pretended to scream, then got out of her car and slow-mo sprinted to the curb and hugged me. She looked different than I remembered, less substantial somehow. Maybe it was only the hooded parka she wore against the upper Midwestern December cold. She told me she'd just returned from an extended visit with her father and I was lucky to catch her.

On the way to her house she asked how things were with Ashwini—they'd fallen out of touch, she said to my relief—and I told her things were wonderful, I was just going to my parents' for the holidays, but later that evening, at a Japanese restaurant, emboldened by the dim lighting and Maria's collarbone and the sake, I confessed to her that Ashwini and I had broken off our engagement. This wasn't true, since we'd never been engaged, plus our official position when I left Halifax had been that we were *taking a break,* but it wasn't hard to convince myself as Maria and I shared a rainbow roll that Ashwini and I both understood, deep down, that this would be one of those breaks that lasts forever. "She had the most perfect facial structure," Maria said, which was accurate but a strange way to commiserate, I thought. She congratulated me on the success of my novel, which I took to mean she either hadn't read it or hated it. (*The New Distance* had almost met its modest sales expectations and had gotten a couple of positive-ish reviews.)

We finished our sake and paid for the meal and, "Wanna get drunk?" Maria suggested, and we walked through the faded city to her crumbling artist house and sat on the thin rug on her bedroom floor, talking and drinking Cabernet Franc from her father's southern Indiana winery. The room was lined with bottles of wine and stacks of books. The wine was surprisingly delicious, and I said so. Maria told me her mother came from a long line of Argentinian vintners. And her father? She gave the beginning of a shrug; her father was born in Argentina to German parents, both of whom died when he was a boy. But he'd been the one who'd seen the possibilities in making wine in southern Indiana, at a time when virtually no one else was doing that, and when he and her mother divorced he'd taken sole control over the vineyard. Why, I wondered, had her parents moved to Indiana in the first place?

"Ever heard of the American Dream?"

"Remind me?"

The sip of wine Maria took represented the act of thought. She seemed about to say something else before she said, "This is it. I'm living it."

"Cheap rent and walking distance to decent sushi?"

"I mean—the rent is *so* cheap. You wouldn't believe it."

I laughed. "You hate it here, don't you?"

"No!" Her voice sounded almost pleading.

"You love it here."

"I mean . . ."

"Tell me again why you moved here?"

"I mean, why does anyone move anywhere?"

I thought for a moment. "Religious persecution. Political oppression. Gold rushes. War. Grad school."

"All of the above," Maria said nonsensically, and then she tried to explain at some length her ambivalence toward her current living situation. What was amazing about it, she said with apparent reverence, was that she had all this *time,* so much time, she'd never been in a place so full of time (hadn't she had plenty of time in New York?). She was reading more than she'd ever read in her life, and what's more she was reading *better,* more deeply, she didn't know quite how to explain it, she said; in New York reading had always felt like an escape, whereas here it felt like a *return,* if that made sense. As for the rest, the obligatory twice-weekly dinners and working in the garden and the endless parties and gatherings and meetings and teaching at the experimental preschool—all that was fine, but not essential. For her, Maria said, it all felt like a game, and sometimes it was fun and sometimes it wasn't and it was always a little ridiculous. Listen. She tilted an ear toward the floor; I did the same. Over a just-perceptible rumble, I made out faint shrieks, irregular stomping, and what sounded like choppy synthesizer music. Her housemates were putting on a show in the basement, Maria explained, a combination of skits and monologues and videos and musical performances whose quality was purposely a little shitty, for all the other twenty-something transplants in town who'd allowed their ambitions to be absorbed into the seductive fuzziness of a *sense of community.* I asked Maria what her ambitions were, and she laughed and said she'd never had any. I asked if she didn't value a sense of community, and, in a gesture both awkward and graceful, she waved her arm toward the stacks of books surrounding us, and/or the bottles of wine.

I don't have a clear memory of much of what Maria and I talked about the rest of the evening, but I vividly remember the sheen of saliva at the top of her bottom lip, and the occasional appearance there of the tip of her tongue, and I was able to connect this appearance with something I'd never noticed in her before: a slight lisp, which either was becoming more pronounced the more we drank or only seemed so because of my new awareness of its reality. Nothing is sexier than a lisp. Maria burnt popcorn in a frying pan and we ate it. Early New Order emanated from her laptop. We talked about New York, old friends, books. I or she opened another bottle of Indiana wine. I asked how her poetry was going and she laughed and said it had been years since she'd written poetry. To retaliate she asked what I was working on these days, and I said I was almost done with a novel based on the memoirs of my grandfather. Then, to balance my lie with a truth (I'd abandoned the novel less than halfway through a draft), or who knows why, I told her Ashwini had recently sold her debut; it was due out next spring. She's so talented, Maria said, and I agreed, though I was basing that judgment on a handful of stories: Ashwini had forbidden me to read her book until it was published and everyone could read it. "You know it'll be about you," Maria said.

We woke up fully clothed and holding each other in her bed, and then she was up and had made blueberry-banana smoothies. While she was showering I found a biography of the confessional poet John Berryman in one of her stacks. That is how I thought of him then: "the confessional poet John Berryman." For several years I'd confused him with Wendell Berry, the righteous Kentucky farmer-poet. Now I knew the difference but couldn't remember if I'd actually read any of Berryman's Dream Songs or only read about them. Either way I had the feeling of liking them, their springy intensity, their schizoid exuberance. I examined the biography. Dark-suited, hands in pockets, reclining against a weathered wooden fence, a slender, young-looking, black-and-white Berryman gazed out at me from the cover, his narrow, handsome, half-shadowed face tensed in an expression of defiance or reproach. Beneath a thick mustache his lips parted as if to say something and without thinking I opened the book. "Berryman came over to see Miriam," I read,

> chatted with her, read her some of his Dream Songs, and was soon boasting of his sexual prowess. In spite of her protests, he began chasing her around the room. When she told him to get out, he suddenly became contrite and downcast and promised to be good if only he could stay. After a short while, however, he started again, until he finally browbeat her into letting him spend "ten or fifteen minutes reverently caressing her feet, while reciting poetry." Then, realizing that the house had windows and that someone might be watching, Berryman recovered himself, hailed a taxi, and went home.

The anecdote strained the limits of credibility, and I found myself wondering where it had come from, whether Berryman or Miriam, whoever Miriam was, or else some absent third party. I checked the back of the book for notes: there were none. *Realizing that the house had windows.* The sound of water against Maria's body had stopped and I tucked the biography into my carry-on. Confessing my theft could be a good excuse to stay in touch with her, I thought vaguely.

As Maria drove me back to the airport, she asked what I was working on these days. I paused to see if she'd remember asking me the night before, but when it became clear she didn't remember, I told her I was finishing another novel. About my grandfather. Like I'd told her the night before. "Oh god, did I ask you that last night?" she asked, in a voice that conveyed both exaggerated fear and sincere anxiety. "You didn't forget the entire evening," I said, "did you?" and while I hadn't meant to imply that we'd had sex, I discovered on my plane to Minneapolis (where forty years earlier, I was soon to read, Berryman had jumped from a bridge to his death) that I wasn't displeased with the implication. For a moment I hoped she thought we might have. It thrilled me to imagine Maria thinking of me as someone who would sleep with another woman—her!—just days after breaking off an engagement, even if that wouldn't have accurately characterized me if we actually *had* slept together. But no, no, it would be awful if she thought that, it was awful for her not to know what happened, what didn't happen, last night. I composed a clarifying text; I'd send it as soon as the plane touched down. Still, as I gazed through the faintly streaked window, I felt a little mysterious to myself, unmoored, a little dangerous. The places I had left seemed muted and distant. The snow-covered grid of the upper Midwest was blinding in the sun. I lowered the shade, closed my eyes, and thought about how lucky I was to live in an age of human flight. I fell asleep.

2

THE HOUSE OVERLOOKS A BRUSH-FILLED CANYON STUDDED with golden and pinkish gray outcrops whose jagged edges soften in the California sun. From above, its cruciform layout is clearly visible, as are the hot tub and pool and lawn and various outbuildings and rows of evenly spaced cypresses. Its roof is low and flat, its lines are clean, its walls are the color of rust or Mars. It's too big for one person, only it's not, since just one person will live here. And maybe he'll need all that space, all those rooms, maybe he'll fill them with his thoughts. We zoom closer. Concrete, stone, horizontally aligned wood, columns of gray and cream-colored brick. Everything tasteful, modern, clean. The floor-to-ceiling windows that must let in such nice light reflect the close sky's warming haze.

The Bachelor emerges barefoot in a black T and charcoal cargo pants. He slips his hands into his pockets, crosses a stream of pebbles, and steps out onto a lovely swath of dense green grass or Astroturf.

"Waking up in L.A. today, all of this became so real."

The voice is the Bachelor's but his lips don't move: he is narrating his own experience again. The Bachelor is always narrating his own experience. Shots of him moving through time and space alternate with shots of him speaking to a never-seen interviewer, significant candles flickering in the background. Often this secondary, narrating Bachelor is telling us, in the present tense, what the primary Bachelor thinks and feels. "I'm a little nervous, but I could not be happier." "I know I'm the luckiest guy in the world." A psychological dimension is thus introduced; there's more to the Bachelor than sun-flattened surfaces. Before long, story becomes inextricable from commentary, and the two Bachelors, one acting, one struggling to make sense of action, merge almost imperceptibly into one.

He takes a few deliberate steps, then stands and surveys his pristine property—its cypresses, patios, boulders, mulch, its low bushes and tall grasses and cacti like artichokes. The sleeves of his T-shirt hug his biceps at their latitude of greatest circumference. The Bachelor considers his remarkable situation. "Never in a million years," says his second self, "did I think I was gonna be the Bachelor again." Somewhere nearby, a house full of women dream of becoming his wife. In spite of this, as he walks to the edge of the lawn toward a football (where did it come from? did he bring it? was it planted?), he permits himself a moment of self-doubt. "I didn't find love before," we hear him think. "What if it happens again?" Has he forgotten his sessions with Thomas Parker, PhD, all that deep emotional work? He got so vulnerable with Dr. Parker. He's not the same closed-off Bachelor he was before.

He bends from the waist to pick up the football, balancing for a moment on his bare right foot, his left leg extending with balletic grace behind him. He gives the ol' pigskin a familiar slap and tosses it once, twice, a foot or so in the air, flicking his wrist to generate a slight spiral. Not a trace of gawkiness now: just expertly casual American masculinity. Of *course* he will meet his wife this time. Of *course* she will bear his children and prepare his meals and run her hands up and down his chest and eight-pack in wonder and affection and loving submission. He is the Bachelor. He was silly to doubt himself. "I want to find somebody," he reminds himself and us, his voice insistent, certain. "I wouldn't be here if I didn't." To *find somebody*: every love story is a quest—a knight on horseback roaming the countryside, searching for maidens in distress. Only in this story the knight stays put, bides his time, and waits for the maidens to come to him.

The Bachelor turns around, strolls back to the lawn, tosses the football one more time, then cradles it in the hollow between his neck and shoulder, a perfect fit. His gaze is downcast, contemplative. It's serious business, being the Bachelor. What task more serious than *finding somebody*? He lifts his head to look out over the canyon that falls away from his big backyard. Beyond the canyon's distant opposite rim, barren land stretches to a ridge on the hazy horizon; beyond the horizon lies the conjugal happiness that awaits the Bachelor and his wife-to-be.

Des Moines in winter: grimy, faded. Dead leaves scratching across sidewalks and driveways. Crows keeping watch from telephone poles. Dirty snow piled high against curbs. Fresh snow falling on dirty snow. Iowa Hawkeye and Iowa State Cyclone flags fluttering wanly on front-porch poles. Thin sunlight turning, as if before your eyes, the primary colors of plastic backyard jungle gyms (glimpsed, inevitably, through chain-link fences) to pinks and grays and mottled off-whites.

My mother's friend's house was at the opposite end of the

block from my childhood home. As a kid I rarely ventured in its direction, a little afraid of the woods the street gives onto, so while it was maybe two hundred yards from the setting of many of my most persistent memories and dreams, I sometimes had the feeling the winter of my return that it wasn't in Des Moines at all but rather in some notionally similar city, Indianapolis or Omaha or Peoria. It was a tan two-story brick-and-aluminum bungalow. My mother's friend had emptied it of all furniture and appliances save the bed and dresser in the master bedroom and the TV and couch in what I thought of as the family room, plus a small wooden table and two chairs and a clock and printer and toaster in the kitchen. In effect it was a multi-room one-bedroom apartment, and my rent was around what I'd considered paying for a standard Des Moines one-bedroom (or approximately a third of the rent for the room Ashwini and I had shared for two years on the extreme periphery of the then most recently gentrified neighborhood in Brooklyn). I had enough money from my novel to live in Des Moines for a year and a half, maybe two, not that I planned to stay that long, not that I planned to do anything else. In any case I didn't know how long I'd be allowed to hang on in my mother's friend's house: she'd moved with her family to lower Manhattan a few months earlier but was keeping a home in Des Moines for a while so she'd have a place to sleep and toast bread and print documents and watch satellite TV when she returned to attend her central Iowa art-world events; there was one the last week in January.

I hadn't been to Des Moines for six years. My parents had retired north, to Duluth. My childhood friends, like me, had fled the city, or weren't my friends anymore. My first few days there, I moved through the house's rooms as if afraid of disturbing some sleeping person or animal or spirit. The clock's ticking seemed to issue from inside my skull, so I removed it from the wall and put it in the garage. Sometimes I felt as if I were in a church, other times the set of a sitcom. The emptiness made the house seem huge, and as I crept over its carpets I felt what I remember as a sort of weightlessness or substancelessness, as if my body had sublimed so that it could fill and partake of this hugeness. It was a feeling I knew only from reading and dreams. At first I attributed it to the sudden change of setting and the quiet of the neighborhood and my newfound solitude, but after some time I discovered what I suspected was a deeper source: the house had the same floor plan as my childhood house, and differed only in its location on the block, the things it held, the lives it had witnessed, the paint and wallpaper and carpets that covered its surfaces, and the views from its many windows. It had the same open ground-floor layout, the same two rows of upstairs bedrooms, the same closets and staircases and ceilings and walls, the same insubstantial wooden doors. As in a dream, it was and wasn't a place I knew.

It was hard to say why Ashwini and I broke up, I told another ex when she called, though Ashwini and I had technically not broken up and I'd long thought of Laura as a friend.

Laura accused me of being evasive. I knew, she said, I just didn't want to say. I said I didn't want to blame Ashwini for what happened, and yet, if I was being honest, I felt it was mostly her doing.

"*Are* you being honest?"

"I know, it's a dumb phrase."

"How was it mostly her doing?"

Ashwini had started to behave strangely, I said. She seemed . . . angry. At everything and everyone but, most concerningly, from my perspective, at me. I told Laura about the time the Wi-Fi stopped working and Ashwini threw a chair across the living room, shattering a lamp. I'd never seen such violence in her, outside of her writing, and I didn't know what to do. I tried to calm her down but she started yelling at me, vicious attacks whose content I immediately forgot, until I left the apartment.

"You've never liked conflict," Laura said.

"Who does?"

"Sometimes it's necessary."

Maybe, I said, but this particular conflict felt especially disturbing. Anyway, I'd already sensed Ashwini turning away, but after the chair-throwing incident it was almost like I didn't exist to her. She'd go to campus early in the morning and stay there till late at night. She must have been napping in her office sometimes, because when she got home we'd stay up even later fighting about who knows what. She started talking about the possibility of visiting India without me. She said it would be best if I left Canada for a while; I never should have come in the first place, she said, even though she'd encouraged me to come when she found out she got her job, an assistant professorship at one of eastern Canada's premier universities.

"It sounds like you both needed some space," Laura said.

"I didn't. I had plenty of space."

"Mmm. You're good at that. Making space for yourself."

"Thanks. Anyway, it's over. I mean, not officially, but it feels final."

"I'm really sorry," Laura said. "It's the worst. You loved each other."

"Mm-hmm." I wondered if she could hear the catch in my throat. "We did. We still do."

After a brief silence Laura said, "Everything happens for a reason."

"Everything that happens will have happened," I said.

"Everything that happened did."

The resurrected routine gave me more solace than anything since I'd arrived in Des Moines. Laura and I had broken up just out of college and since then had remained closer than I could have imagined. She was second-chair cello in arguably America's best chamber orchestra and, in spite of having grown up in one of the most dysfunctional families I'd ever seen, was among the happiest people I knew. Devoted to playing other people's music, she was free, it seemed to me, from the tyranny of big decisions. The past barely existed to her; the future was simply what would come.

Now she was distracting me with stories about former mutual friends—Mindy had been dating a man with an infant son for over a year and he hadn't allowed her to see the baby yet; Paul's wife was pregnant and Paul was depressed; Jane's mother was encouraging Jane to freeze her eggs—and her *yoga-class boyfriend,* whatever that meant (I felt a muted, absurd pang), and her delinquent new co-cellist, and, at some length, her latest fight with her mother, with whom I'd always had a nice rapport in spite of her imperiousness and alcoholism. What happened was that Laura had been in Chicago the previous month to help her sister with wedding preparations, and one afternoon they were trying on dresses and Laura took a photo of her sister wearing their favorite and sent it via text to their mother, who didn't respond. A couple of weeks later Laura was back in the Twin Cities, having dinner with her parents at their house, everyone throwing back as usual glass after glass of Pinot Grigio, when the subject of her sister's wedding dress came up: Laura told her mother she was pretty sure her sister had decided on the one she'd sent a photo of. "You tell your sister if she wears that dress," said her mother, who Laura suspected had been waiting for an excuse to express her disapproval of her daughter marrying a woman, "her mother will not be attending her wedding. Makes her look like a slut."

"So we haven't really spoken for a couple months," Laura said.

"Jesus," I said. "I'm so sorry. How do you feel?"

"Totally fine. I mean—honestly, I'm used to it. But seriously, tell me seriously this time: how do *you* feel?"

"I don't know. Hollow. Like a nonentity."

"What are you *doing*? What's your *project*? Aren't you working on another book?"

For a moment I considered repeating the line I'd delivered to Maria, but instead I said, edging closer to the truth, that I was taking a break from the second book and wasn't sure I wanted a project.

"I think you might feel better if you had one."

I suggested that my project could be to resist well-intentioned suggestions to have a project. This was a joke, but the more I reflected on it the more it seemed like a good idea. All my adult life, such as it was, I'd had projects; I was lost without them. I'd never considered myself an ambitious person but looking back I was forced to conclude I had been. Or maybe it's more accurate to say I was blindly devoted to a certain story about myself, a story I didn't realize, because I couldn't bear to, didn't belong to me. Now, I decided on the phone with Laura, or maybe that evening, or the next day, or the next, I would empty myself of stories. I would wait. Instead of fighting my newfound anonymity, I would embrace it, work with it, see what it could bring me. "Cultivate a radical ambivalence," I wrote in my notebook. "Stop clinging to outworn preferences. Renounce the fantasy of self-determination. Lose control a little." Through my project that consisted of not having a project I would open my story to other stories, open my self to other selves, open those selves to the circumambient world, its gentleness, its indifference. For a moment, at least, I felt fantastic, not fantastic but fantastically unlonely. A little nervous. It was a new beginning.

How did I spend those first few days back in Des Moines? To an observer it might have appeared that nothing was happening. And yet so much is always happening! I ate a lot of packaged pastries, which I bought from the Kum & Go at the end of the street. I ate a lot of Hot Pockets. Presumably I spent a lot of time on the Internet, though I have no specific memory of this. I walked around with Ashwini's absence, spoke to it, tried to ignore it. Mostly I did a lot of sitting and staring. It wasn't long before I discovered a favorite spot: on the thin, pearlescent living-room carpet, my back supported against the bare white wall opposite the grid of south-facing windows that looked out on the quiet dead-end street. From there I liked to watch parallelograms of sunlight make their slow progress from right to left across the floor. Sometimes I'd scoot into the center of the room and stretch out like the drowsy animal I was, and, as I lay there, sleeping and not quite sleeping, the shape the sunlight carved out of the carpet took flight and carried me somewhere else, a shopping mall, a childhood classroom, a lakeside beach in the height of summer, warm and alive with human activity, the sounds of insects and birds, soft breezes—only to drop me off right where I started, in the middle of my mother's friend's living room, alone.

Then I'd get up and wander from room to room, feeling both larger and smaller than myself. The house wasn't as empty as it had first appeared. I discovered drawers still full of stuff—pens and pencils, batteries, power cords, old cameras, business cards, playing cards, keys, flash drives, folders packed with contact lists and instruction booklets and warranties and receipts, a toy car I was sure had once belonged to me, a few wooden blocks, a yellow-and-red-and-orange stained-glass cat. The bathrooms were full of fancy "natural" creams and lotions and soaps and shampoos and body washes and bubble baths. "Free and clear," they said on their labels. A few small dresses and sweaters (lots of cashmere) and blouses hung in the master bedroom's closet. A framed reproduction of a Modigliani—the usual elongated empty-eyed nude gazing out emptily at the viewer—loomed above the dresser on the wall opposite the bed, which I assumed was the bed my mother's friend and her husband slept in, the *conjugal bed,* to use the phrase I involuntarily repeated to myself as I lay in it waiting for sleep to come or go.

I spent a morning mindlessly rummaging through boxes that sat open on and under a Ping-Pong table in the basement. One held nothing but sculpted hands. Another was full of photographs of birds. Another held folders thick with clippings from a wide array of newspapers and magazines, organized by category: Natural Catastrophes, Climate Change, War, Restaurants, Education, Gardening. Another box held a dozen or so small waxy abstract paintings in which the night sky seemed to pulse behind a gauze of oranges and pinks and purples and salmons that suggested drugs or memory. From these and other ephemera in the house, I formed a picture of my mother's friend as a Des Moines type familiar to me from my childhood: an effervescent, vaguely tragic woman of advanced middle age who'd grown up in a small Midwestern town and sublimated her creative impulses in a variety of innocuous and doggedly pursued hobbies, and also in a constant, effortful display of superior taste in clothes, food, and interior decoration. As a kid I had always been drawn to this type—Mrs. Bond, my sixth-grade English teacher; Mary Perkins, the wife of my high school tennis coach; the mother of my friend turned enemy Evan Heinrich, who baked cupcakes for us every time I visited her house to play the barbaric video games my parents wisely denied me.

She called—my mother's friend—to check in on me a few days after I arrived. How was everything going? Had I found the key? Of course I'd found the key. Had I figured out the trick to the washing machine? Did I have everything I needed? She must have picked up on an unintended tone, because the next thing she said was "Did I interrupt you?"

The question struck me as almost funny. "From what?" I said.

"I don't know!" she said.

I apologized, sensing I'd said something offensive. "No—no, you didn't, sorry. Not at all."

"Oh good. I know you're a very busy person." Where had she gotten that idea? "A very *competent* person. I can't imagine there's anything about the house you won't be able to figure out."

I told her I'd be sure to tell her if there was.

"Do! Meantime I'll try to keep myself from asking if you've gotten the remotes to work."

"Is there a secret?"

"Oh yes, mm-hmm. There is a secret. But I'm afraid I can't tell you what it is."

I told her of course I understood, and she told me I should feel free to use the—well, there was no food in the house, per se, but I should feel free to use the spices.

We ended the call and I stayed where I was, stretched out on the living-room carpet. The day was fading, I felt more than saw. My body was the fading day; the steam rising from it was made of moments. I stared at the white plaster ceiling, pocked with shadows, until it became a floor. I walked through the upside-down house in my imagination, hopping over lintels and ducking under chairs, eventually pausing in some other room to lie down on the ceiling and look up at the floor.

The still-young man, newly a bachelor, stands up and goes to the south-facing windows. He presses his nose against the glass. In the windows of the houses across the street he sees a reflection of himself at ten. It's the winter of the Bulls' second championship season, and he's alone in the house—really alone—for the first time. His family is cross-country skiing in Minnesota, the latest in an endless series of *family outings.* They'll be gone the whole day; he can hardly believe it. To choose not to participate in a family outing has never seemed possible until this morning. What changed? I think I'm going to stay home, he'd said, and his mother said, You sure? and he was sure. Almost disappointing how easy it was. And a few minutes later his family was gone—not on a family outing now at all, but something else, something without a name—and at first he felt an urge to run after the green minivan, tell his parents he was only joking, of course he was coming, it was a family outing, it wasn't a family outing without *him,* a member of the family; or they would come back and tell him *they* were only joking, it wasn't that easy to get out of a family outing, family outings weren't things that could be gotten out of: and so he's come here to the windows to watch for the minivan pulling down the street and turning into the driveway. No one stirs in the houses across the street. A few cars pass, a girl with a dog. He is measuring the movement of clouds against treetops when he sees with startling clarity the minivan on the interstate, its inexplicable slow drift toward the shoulder, the green mass hurtling toward the ditch, the flames, the smoke, the mangled bodies, the ambulance—too late: his family is dead and he killed them, he killed his family, murdered them by making a family outing something else, he'll have to live with Brian Leslie's family, and every day he'll shoot baskets with Brian, who will be his brother, on their backyard half-court basketball court, and play video games with him in his big blue basement, and his new parents will let him stay up late on weekends to watch *Saturday Night Live* and Letterman and *SportsCenter,* and he'll be able to act however he wants because everyone will know his family's dead and who will blame him.

The wave of warm guilt that rushes pleasantly over him restores his family to life. The green minivan, intact, makes its way to Minnesota. The houses across the street return his gaze. He turns from the windows and looks around at the new world opening up to him.

"The art of poetry," I read, "is amply distinguished from the manufacture of verse by the animating presence in the poetry of a fresh idiom: language so twisted and posed in a form that it not only expresses the matter in hand but adds to the stock of available reality." The poet and critic R. P. Blackmur wrote that for *Poetry* magazine in 1936, and it made such an impression on a twenty-two-year-old John Berryman that he'd quote it verbatim in a poem thirty-five years later, by which time he'd added to the stock of available reality some of the twentieth century's most distinctive poetry, *The Dream Songs, Homage to Miss Bradstreet, Sonnets to Chris.* Such recurrences weren't unusual for Berryman; from one perspective they were the defining feature of his life. He held on to things, or they just stuck, or they left for a while only to return in another form, called back by imperatives that remained forever hidden to him or else were revealed through dreams or psychoanalysis or alcohol. He wasn't good at *letting things go*: he wanted too badly to make things matter.

I read the biography of the poet I'd barely read in a handful of long, uninterrupted stretches across what must have been three or four days. I read as I used to read legal thrillers as a preteen—headlong, totally absorbed in the story, almost afraid to close the book. I read for the richness of incident, the *drama*—the turmoil, the heartbreak, the love. My days were empty; Berryman's were full; I filled my days with his. There were fistfights, affairs, family conflicts, divorces, drugs, alcohol, guns. There was war. I read in admiration and disgust, alternately attracted to and repulsed by this man who seemed to court suffering at every turn. And yet it may have also been true that I recognized something of myself in Berryman. I, too, had spent a good deal of my life engaged in the exhausting and mostly thankless battle of trying to *make things matter.* I, if only in my modest way, had added to the stock of available reality. Strange that the reality we're given isn't enough. Continents, oceans, antelopes, skyscrapers, neutrinos, Melville, sex, the Internet, *our Chicago Bulls*—not enough. For Berryman, in any case, nothing sufficed. There was a hole in the middle of his world.

Easy enough to conclude—Berryman did—that the hole opened up outside an apartment complex in Tampa on the morning of June 26, 1926, when his father, cuckolded, out of work, far from home, shot himself in the chest. The boy was eleven. Ten weeks later, his mother married the man whose open involvement with her had precipitated the suicide; his name was John Berryman, and so his stepson, who'd been John Smith, became John Berryman, too. It wasn't until 1947, when he began his regular visits to a psychoanalyst, Dr. James Shea, that the younger Berryman would start to seriously reckon with his father's suicide. He blamed himself: "The Oedipus," he wrote in his journal. "I realize suddenly—I never did before—that I may have wished Daddy's death, and may feel permanent guilt for the satisfaction of my wish." Dr. Shea was thrilled to find a case that fit so neatly into his theories. Berryman was grateful to find a template for his sadness and justification for his bad behavior. Their sessions opened up the world he would explore to its outer limits in the Dream Songs. His life from this point on would rarely be happy, but at least he would feel the intermittent satisfactions of being actively engaged in discovering or creating a self that could pass, at times, for authentic, if only in its constant unhappy passage from one form to another. At least since his father's suicide, he had felt like a stranger to himself.

At prep school Berryman was gawky, sickly, small, ashamed of his intelligence and academic ability, shy, uncertain, superior, retreating, greedy for achievement and praise. He was frequently bullied. He had acne and dandruff and terrible eyesight and often worried his hair was falling out (an anxiety that would last his entire life, though he died with plenty of hair on his head). He read widely, but a preoccupation with grades seems to have outweighed any incipient literary passion. He wanted badly to excel at sports, but when he played hockey he could barely see the puck (his classmates made fun of him for the protective goggles he had to wear over his already thick glasses), and he couldn't play football without getting hurt (gashed forehead, twisted knee, bruised and bloody nose). He was a fast runner, though, at least at short distances: at a track meet in June 1929 he came in third out of twenty-five in the fifty-yard dash. "This may not seem good to you," he wrote his mother, "but I'm proud of it. . . . Not a single one laughed at me when I ran yesterday."

His mother: a radiant, youthful, vain woman who loved her son too strongly and perhaps in the wrong ways. Late in his life he wondered to himself: "Have I been wrong all these years, and it was *not* Daddy's death that blocked my development for so long? . . . Maybe my long self-pity has been based on an *error,* and there has been no (hero-)villain (Father) ruling my life, but only an unspeakably powerful possessive adoring MOTHER, whose life at 75 is still centered wholly on *me.*" Berryman never stopped needing to please her; when, as a graduate student, he won two scholarships, he wrote in his journal: "I vow to achieve her happiness in all ways open to me. May these prizes give me a start."

As a young adult he came to realize with wonder that he was in possession of certain qualities many women found attractive. He was tall and slender, an ardent dancer, an intense listener, and, according to one of his lovers, "capable of prolonging the ecstatic moment almost indefinitely." He pursued the ecstatic moment with purpose. By his sophomore year of college he'd had romantic encounters with seventeen Barnard girls. He made a list. He put check marks next to names of women he'd dated and dashes next to those he'd "necked": Garnette Snedeker, Betty Bolton, Louise Harris, Louise Pearse, Kay Owens, Agnes Leckie, Bobbie Suckle, Barbara White, Vivian White, Bobbie White, Irene Pacey, Peggy Wadsworth, Peggy Vollman, Peggy Howland, Mary Roohan, Yolanda Krajewski. "Man is nothing but an ambulatory penis," he wrote in a letter to a friend. He may have gotten briefly engaged to a woman named Jane or possibly Jean. A breakup caused him such distress he had to drop out of school for a while. When he returned, fortified by his mother's warnings, he rededicated himself to his studies, especially literature. He fell in love with Yeats, Auden, Eliot, Stevens, Hart Crane. He took classes from the poet and critic Mark Van Doren and under his influence began writing poems. One was a forty-two-liner in blank verse whose subject was "that gnarled fantastic lava-land of love."

He won a graduate scholarship to Cambridge, where he read the English canon and got engaged to an actress and brooded and dreamed of becoming a great poet. Two years later he returned to New York in debt and burdened by an affected British accent, "a disagreeable compound of arrogance, selfishness, and impatience," by his own accounting, "scarcely relieved by some dashes of courtesy and honesty and a certain amount of industry." He lived with his mother until he started having "hysterical," probably psychosomatic, fits, then went to Detroit to teach literature at Wayne University. His first semester he taught 131 students divided among four classes, which left him almost no time to work on his poetry. Then his best friend died of cancer and his fiancée broke off their engagement. "Error and waste," he wrote, "betrayal, loneliness, disease, war, failure." More temporary university teaching appointments, more student papers, more rejection, more debt. He got engaged to a woman named

Eileen Mulligan. He married her. Two years later he turned thirty, certain he would never accomplish anything noteworthy. As a student he'd "wept blindly" over Lear's last lines (*No, no, no life! / Why should a dog, a horse, a rat, have life, / And thou no breath at all? Thou'lt come no more, / Never, never, never, never, never!*) and he'd recently begun work on a new scholarly edition of *Lear,* a project he would toil at for years without completing. His nephew drowned in a bathtub. His grandmother was dying. "This happens," he concluded a letter to his mother: "what should be normal life comes to have, transient & tolerable, the air of a vacation, unreal interim. The nightmare shows as real."

Then, in 1947, he had an affair. The woman was the twenty-seven-year-old wife of a friend, a lively, ironic woman named Chris. They met at a lecture by the historian Arnold Toynbee. For her, the affair was a fun diversion; for Berryman, the latest wrenching descent into the gnarled fantastic lava-land of love. He chronicled his deepening obsession in a series of letters, apparently never sent. "After breakfast at Sidney's going off at nine, I came up here to the office and just sat at the desk seeing nothing, wanting you." "You were the whole sky and the whole sea in that one moment, Chris." "The sun makes happy the bloody birds—what's that to me who remembers you and have you not." His love was "a giant band locked about my chest, every breath every moment is difficult, each taken in your relation, I move with weights on me or underwater, so all things are distorted. What can I do for this hopeless longing but be with you?" "It is all but inevitable, but nothing in it is easy, loving another separate all-distinct human being until the separateness and the distinctions dissolve, and we can be together."

If it sounds as if he was rehearsing for poems, that's because he was: as the affair wore on he wrote sonnets about it—the poems in which Berryman starts to sound like Berryman (prickly, ecstatic, erudite, mournful, oscillating violently between irony and candor), and which in 1966, post–*Dream Songs,* at perhaps the height of his fame, would be published as *Sonnets to Chris.* "We are made wrong," he observed in his journal. "Either love should not come, or it should stay."

The last twenty-five years of Berryman's life were a fury of liquor, women, poetry, prizes, lectures, readings, friends' deaths, small acts of grace, books, changes of address, hospitalizations, half-recoveries, resolutions for self-improvement, aborted projects, repetitions, departures, and returns. He wrote in his journal, "I live entirely in the Past (loss, regret, guilt—distance!) and the Future (fear, Death). Naturally I am miserable and drink." He divorced, remarried, smoked three packs a day. He put his hand up Philip Levine's wife's skirt, twice, in full view of Philip Levine, who punched and then forgave him and ten days later found himself hungover with Berryman in Berryman's bed. A fight with Dwight Macdonald at a cocktail party caused Berryman to walk into the ocean with his clothes on. He slipped on a rug and hurt his back. He fell down a staircase and crashed into a glass door. "It was because you did and do not love me that you accuse me of not loving you," wrote his mother. Berryman was the first person in the hospital to notice that Dylan Thomas was dead. He decided the postwar years were the Years of Mud. He analyzed and catalogued 154 dreams and talked about them with Dr. Shea. In Iowa City, he got very drunk and locked himself out of his apartment, and when his landlord refused to let him in he shat on the front porch and was arrested. (At the jail, the policemen pulled down their pants and pointed at him and laughed.) He decided the time had come to quit drinking. He needed to drink to write the Dream Songs. "Have not really slept for four nights," he wrote. He partied with his students, then slept by the pond. He fell in love with Harriet Rosenzweig, Ann Levine, Kate Donahue. On a Monday he gave a lecture on *Don Quixote.* That Wednesday he gave the same lecture, to the same class. He gestured wildly when he talked, he compulsively pushed his glasses up the bridge of his nose. He bought a blue raw-silk jacket that made him feel "three percent more normal." His beard, already long, grew longer. He massaged the feet of a friend's wife while reciting poetry. He wet his bed and watched Bergman films. He won a $4,000 grant. He had a daughter. When a cab rolled over his leg, he wrote, "I feel like a minor character in a bad F. Scott Fitzgerald novel." The "actual world" had become "unreal." He moved into the Chelsea Hotel with his family. He smoked four packs a day. "Dexedrine morning and afternoon," he wrote; "martinis before dinner; nembutal and sherry after midnight." He drank for two days and woke up in the hospital. In Dublin he didn't make a single friend. He made pilgrimages to Yeats's grave, Dante's tomb. He gave a reading with shoe prints on his jacket, probably his own. He won the Pulitzer, the National Book Award, a $10,000 grant. "Try not to be so fucking self-important," he wrote. He fell in the bathtub and twisted his arm. One semester, he taught two seminars, "The American Character" and "The Meaning of Life." He said, "It's terrible to give half your life over to some-one else, but it's worse not to. . . . You've got to try!" Back in the hospital, he quoted Greek poets and sang Bessie Smith songs poorly. He found God. He saw himself not as an actor in an amphitheater but as the amphitheater itself. He taught a class called "The American Nightmare." A bottle of bourbon smiled at him from the counter. "He looked decayed," said Saul Bellow. He'd published thirteen books and wanted thirteen more. He would start by finishing his novel and his Shakespeare book and his book of essays and his new book of poetry. Also a biography of Christ for children. He figured he had ten more years to live. "Nouns, verbs, do not exist for what I feel."

Almost as soon as I finished the biography I put down some of my feelings about it—no doubt refracted through their imagined reception—in a handwritten note to Maria that I enclosed with the stolen book. I was touched by Berryman's devotion to literature, I wrote, or something along these lines, but couldn't help feeling it was a relic of another age, an age when literary heroism still seemed possible and all the old distinctions and hierarchies still held, when T. S. Eliot was a sort of god and Robert Frost probably could've been president if he wanted; pre-postmodernism, pre-MFA, pre-Amazon, pre–reality TV, when literature could still be a kind of religion or at least the best replacement for it. I could almost miss this age, I wrote, though it ended before I was born. Irony had yet to give way to sarcasm, tragedy to nihilism. Newspapers still had book review sections, people *read,* books *mattered.* (That many had been lamenting along the same lines for decades—that Berryman and his cohort made the same lament—should amplify, not mitigate, our sense of loss, I added.) It was an age, maybe the last, of geniuses and masterpieces and the shared felt presence of an unshakable pantheon of greats to which you might, if you were chosen, gain admittance.

Yes, and also an age of drunks and bloated failures and terminal self-promotion, I continued (starting to get worked up by my own rhetoric), and young men in small rooms all across the country trying in total earnest to write the Great American

Novel, guided only by the failed efforts of their forebears and the throbbing of their perennially unrelieved erections. That was the problem with postwar American literature: it inspired idol worship, a slavish allegiance to the canon, a chilly obsession with ranking the top writers (Berryman's response to the news of Frost's death: "Who's number one? Lowell is number one, isn't he?"); it was obscurely or not-so-obscurely allied to racism and classism and imperialism and misogyny (Berryman also liked to rank the "lady poets"—Bishop, Moore, and Rich, one-two-three), and a blind and crusty and ugly and above all *male* lust for fame. "Resolution," Berryman wrote in an early journal: "to scorn or ignore any honour, any fame, my poems may get in my life. Expect nothing, distrust what comes, work." He had to make such resolutions, I argued, because his desire for fame was so present, so implacable, he had to push against it to be able to write at all; but he could never push it all the way out of the picture, and then when he actually *did* get famous—stories about him in *Time* and *Life;* TV interviews; "fan mail from foreign countries," to quote a Dream Song—he found out firsthand what we all know by now fame does the second it descends on you: it kills you. Strips you of your soul, a living death. Berryman's fame lust was also a death wish, suicide in slow motion, an almost imperceptible dissolution aided by affairs and drugs and liquor and escape into music and literature. What I felt above all toward Berryman, I wrote Maria, was pity—pity mixed with anger. The implication, impossible to miss, was that I was above Berryman's base desires, and as I prepared the package for Maria I was almost convinced it was true.

That evening, though, as I drifted toward sleep, safe in my mother's friend's conjugal bed, I both saw and was myself at eleven, shooting free throws in my driveway on a summer evening, and I was also Michael Jordan, Scottie Pippen, John Paxson, and many other Bulls and even some non-Bulls, Kevin Johnson, Gary Payton, Jeff Hornacek, Reggie Miller. I made ten in a row, twenty-seven, forty. I shot twenty-five without my guide hand, made twenty. I switched to the two-ball dribbling drills I'd learned earlier that summer at Hawkeye basketball camp, then moved into midrange jumpers, three-pointers—first off the self-pass, then off the dribble, then with a pump fake, then pump fake / dribble, making sixteen shots in each category before moving on to the next. I ended my session with ten more made free throws as the sky's blue darkened and seemed to solidify, then went inside and informed my mother that one day I'd play in the NBA, and my mother looked up from the book she'd been reading and said, It's good to have dreams.

3

MY CHRISTMAS PRESENT TO MYSELF WAS A SECOND BOWL of granola. As I sat at the kitchen table and ate I thought of my little sister, a geologist in New Mexico whom I rarely saw or spoke to. When we were kids, our Christmas mornings would begin when I woke her up at three or three-thirty. It always took a few seconds after she opened her eyes before she realized who I was and who she was and why I was in her room and that it was the best day of the year, and even all these years later I could picture that realization registering on her face, the sudden catch in their sockets of her big blue eyes, the beginnings of a smile, that flickery transition from total inwardness to a sense of the reality of the world not her. I remember wishing I could catch my own fugitive mind in the moment of its passing from one realm to another. "It's Christmas!" I'd whisper to my sister. Christmas: the Incarnation.

As I ate the granola with pleasure and regret, I remembered I had a package to open. Every year since I'd graduated from college, my parents had given me the same two gifts: a year's worth of daily disposable contact lenses and an ill-fitting dress shirt from Kohl's or Younkers, which I'd typically exchange for a similar but better-fitting shirt. These presents had never failed to fulfill their apparent purpose: to produce an echo of the joy I used to feel on receiving Christmas gifts as a child. But because it was no more than an echo, they also made me a little sad. My mother had sent the package to Halifax a few weeks earlier, and I'd brought it with me when I left. I'd told her I wouldn't be arriving in Des Moines till mid-January, after I returned from India with Ashwini, to whom, I strongly implied and may have believed, I'd then be engaged to be married. Later I presented the trip's cancellation as the result of a decision Ashwini and I had lovingly arrived at together with the long-term interests of our relationship in mind: it would be best, I told my parents, if I returned to the U.S. for the rest of our engagement so I could find a legitimate job (teaching? writing instruction manuals? repairing refrigerators?), and then in a year or so we could start our marriage as real working adults. Once we were married one of us could move to the other's country more easily. Probably, I told my parents, knowing it would sound true, Ashwini would want to move to America to take the next step in her writing career. (In reality she was aiming for tenureship at the university in Halifax.) Eventually I'd have to tell them the truth, but I wasn't worried about that yet. I finished my granola and opened the package: contact lenses and a dress shirt from Younkers. I tried on the shirt: too big.

A couple of weeks later I took it to a dry cleaners to get it altered. This way, I'd reasoned, I could avoid some small portion of the guilt I knew I'd feel if I exchanged it. My mother's friend had encouraged me to use the Volvo sedan she was keeping in the garage; I'd opted not to tell her I hadn't driven in many years. A lone bumper sticker said SOW ONLY SEEDS OF LOVE. I adjusted the mirrors and started the engine and felt a vibration run through my hands and arms and down my shoulders through my chest. A faint nausea rose up in me and I closed my eyes till it subsided. Then I started to back out, very slowly, checking each of the mirrors several times, obeying a long-standing, dormant habit whose impetus must have been the fear of running over an animal, as my mother had run over our cat Fritz when I was ten. Just two weeks had passed since we'd brought Fritz home from the Animal Rescue League. No one knew how he'd gotten into the garage. I cried a little and my sister wailed and we both petted his bloody and convulsing body as my mother drove us to the animal ER, where a tall man wearing a compassion mask casually injected him with poison. I can still see Fritz sitting on my chest in the middle of the night before he died, pawing affectionately at my face.

One evening a few years after Fritz's death—I've never told anyone this part of the story, but it feels important to put down here—I found myself in my brother's bedroom. He was taking a year off between high school and college to work at a cross-country ski resort in the north Minnesota woods. Without motive or even much curiosity, as if controlled by exterior forces, I went through what he'd left behind. Buried beneath folders full of high school homework, in the bottom drawer of the old oak desk I'd inherit a few years later, was a computer printer box full of single-spaced pages lined with hole-punched, perforated edges. The top page said something like: *Dear Family, and by Family I mean anyone who happens to be reading this: DO NOT READ ANY FURTHER. YOU ARE READING FURTHER. PLEASE, IF YOU HAVE ANY RESPECT FOR MY HUMAN DIGNITY, STOP. THESE PAGES WERE WRITTEN BY ME FOR ME, AND IF I GRANTED THEM CORPOREALITY IT IS ONLY SO I MIGHT RE-*

TURN TO THEM A WISER MAN AND COMMIT THEM TO THE FLAMES. I remember that phrase, *commit them to the flames,* so antiquated and melodramatic, as I must have realized even then. The next page said something like: *I am on my knees, begging you to stop. Proceed if you will, but know that if you proceed you are tearing out my very soul.* I read these top two pages several times. *Tearing out my very soul.* The next page was a journal entry dated three years earlier. It was about how my brother enjoyed talking to a certain friend, but only one-on-one, and only about "ethics and metaphysics," and otherwise found him insufferable, and were these infrequent conversations enough to justify remaining friends with him? Two years' worth of similarly precocious journal entries followed; I stayed up late and went through them all, possessed by an unfamiliar impulse: I wanted to be absorbed into my brother's words. I was angry that I couldn't *become* my brother. I don't think I'd really believed in him before that night—hadn't believed in his existence, I mean.

Most of the journal's content passed quickly from my mind, but one entry has stayed with me all these years. In it, my brother confessed to being the one who failed to close the door that opened onto the garage—where Fritz must have been drawn by the smell of dust and damp newspapers, or by the grass and trees and neighborhood cats beyond—and tried to trace the various interconnected causes for that single fatal act. Was it really accurate to call Fritz's death an accident? What if my brother hadn't been so eager to get to the woods after the humiliation of the "homecoming bullshit" in the high school parking lot? (He didn't elaborate on the nature of this humiliation.) What if Fritz had been asleep upstairs, instead of lurking as he apparently had been somewhere near the garage? The rule in our house was to keep doors closed at all times; did my brother realize as he exited that evening that the door hadn't shut completely? If so, how had he justified to himself, as he headed toward the woods, leaving it open? Did he actually do it, on some level, on purpose? Ultimately, he wrote, it doesn't matter. I am the sum of my actions, good and bad; with free will comes responsibility; guilt and innocence have little to do with intent; I am alive and another soul is dead.

The night I read that I lay awake in bed feeling what I recognized as a new kind of sadness. I think I understood it had something to do with guilt—my brother's for leaving the garage door open, filtered through mine for reading my brother's journal (could *I* somehow have been responsible for Fritz's death?)—and also something to do with writing: the intimation, in my brother's words, of a kind of aloneness that suddenly seemed necessary to honestly confront the world; the mystery that my brother's self-interrogation contained and illuminated: some things were unknowable—unwritable, unreadable—no matter how old you got.

I returned to my brother's journal every day for the next week, reading new passages more or less at random, until he came home from Minnesota for Christmas. In one entry he wrote that a book called *The Stranger* was "the only truly essential novel," the first and last word on how to live, not to mention how to die, and so I found it on his shelf and spent the next two evenings reading it and decided my brother was right. Did Maman die yesterday or today? It didn't matter: because *nothing mattered*. I bought a spiral notebook and copied out my favorite passage—*for the first time, in that night alive with signs and stars, I opened myself to the gentle indifference of the world*—and this became the epigraph for my first journal, in which I transcribed sentences from novels and books of philosophy and tried to work up my nerve to become a writer. I determined to write a short story and filled several pages with notes for it: its protagonist would be a middle-aged, balding, unmarried obituary writer for the *Des Moines Register* who requests and is (yet again) denied a raise from his boss but who continues to move calmly through the tedium of his days and finally hangs himself, because nothing matters, nothing matters in this life. . . . A few years later I made a small but crucial revision to my philosophy: not *nothing* matters, but *everything* matters. I wrote it in my journal to make it stick. Then I wrote, "What's the difference?"—a good question.

I shifted into first and set off for the dry cleaners. The sky was cloudy-bright behind the dusty windshield. Holiday lights still hung from many of the houses, and several lawns were strewn with skeletal white wooden deer in various poses—head bent to the grass as if grazing, neck craned as if listening for predators, staring stoically ahead. Christmas trees lay dead on curbsides. Iowa Hawkeye and Iowa State Cyclone flags hung unmoving from their poles. In one yard a giant inflatable Santa or snowman lay flaccid. Menorahs filled the windows of my childhood home. I drove past the house of T. J. Davis, 1998's Mr. Iowa Basketball, who everyone thought would make it to the NBA (last I heard he was in real estate in Missouri), and turned onto Lower Beaver Road and continued past the Kum & Go that used to be the Kwik Shop where as a kid I'd ride my bike to buy candy and gum and pop and basketball cards. I drove past Lawnwood Elementary, which looked too small to hold the dozens of classrooms I could only assume still lay inside; past the Muslim Cultural Center, new to me and both more and less real than the surrounding buildings—more in that my vision of it wasn't fogged by memory, less in that it lacked the depth and texture memory would have given it. I drove past the redbrick veterans' hospital where my childhood best friend Taylor's father was a surgeon (we used to play H-O-R-S-E and one-on-one on a concrete court on the hospital grounds), then turned south onto Thirtieth Street and headed down what might be the steepest hill in the city. My high school driver's ed teacher had once told me, I remembered, that you know you're a good driver if you can maintain a constant speed as you descend and ascend the Thirtieth Street hill—really more of a ravine—which seemed like a metaphor for something, I thought, and also seemed obviously false, since maintaining a constant speed on a hill doesn't test a driver's steering, traffic awareness, freeway maneuvering, or any number of other skills that make good drivers good. Then I remembered remembering and rejecting my driver's ed teacher's assertion every time I drove down Thirtieth as a teenager. At the bottom of the hill the street was flanked by thick woods, which I was for some reason pleased to remember sheltered a creek that ran east to the Des Moines River.

The woman behind the waist-high pink counter looked between forty-five and seventy. Her body and face were shapeless in a comforting way, maybe in an Iowan or Midwestern way, and her smile was so intimate I wondered if I knew her. She was wearing a red knit Cyclones cardigan over a red-and-"gold" Cyclones T-shirt, and called to mind cross-stitches, doilies, baby powder. We exchanged overfriendly smiles and hellos and I told her what I wanted done with my shirt. She worried that if she did that it would end up being too small—though of course she'd be happy to make whatever alterations I wanted. I told her I liked my shirts relatively tight-fitting, not quite sure whether that was true, and if so by whose standards. Several days had passed since I'd interacted with another person and I worried I wasn't doing it right. As the woman folded and stuck pins in my shirt I felt vaguely chastened by the disapproval I sensed from her.

"Having a good year so far?" she asked.

"Absolutely." I'd forgotten it was a new year.

"Getting lighter every day now, isn't it."

"I guess it is!" I said with too much excitement in my voice.

"I wonder if the snow has something to do with it."

"Mmm," I said, "all that reflected sun."

"What's that, honey?"

"Oh—the . . . glare."

"Beats me," the woman said; she must have misheard me. She asked for my name and phone number and I gave them. "Two-one-two, where's that from?"

"New York!" I again exclaimed where I should have simply said.

"New York *City*?"

"New York City," I said maybe too quietly, overcompensating.

"My granddaughter went to college in New York City. I always wanted to make it out there. Somehow never did!" I wondered why she spoke as if her life were over. She laughed and asked if I'd like to pay now or later.

"Now's good," I said, and reached into my pocket, but my wallet wasn't there. I checked my other pants pockets, then my coat, patting myself down with mounting concern. I must have looked distraught because the woman behind the counter said, "It's okay, sweetie!"

"No no no—"

"Pay when you come back! We trust you."

A big emotion welled up in me, something like gratitude laced with embarrassment—gratitude for the woman's motherly concern, embarrassment that I should be its object—and I had a fleeting urge to bury myself beneath her Cyclones cardigan. "Let me just go check my car," I said, recovering.

After a minute of frantic searching I found my wallet in the glove compartment. I tried to remember putting it there, couldn't. Was I losing my mind? I laughed at the question. "Am I losing my mind?" was something people said in movies—bad movies—or TV shows. Then I thought, in Ashwini's voice, "Maybe I have early-onset Alzheimer's," which was what she used to say whenever she lost or couldn't remember something. "Oh my god," I always felt obliged to say. "You just said that a minute ago."

I reentered the dry cleaners and the woman behind the counter was several decades younger and wearing an oversize white button-down and black cardigan and seemed to know tricks involving hair clips and bangs. She sat hunched over a thick black hardcover, reading with a look of concentration so intense I found myself unable to interrupt her. I stood there, waiting. The room was silent. I considered leaving; I could pay when I returned. Behind the counter, freshly dry-cleaned clothes hung from an electronic revolving hanger that curved through the room in an elegant "S."

"Find your wallet?"

"Excuse me?"

"Gimme all your money!" Her voice was a muted shout. A part of me didn't understand she was joking, and, a little scared, I tossed my wallet onto the counter. She laughed, and I laughed, parroting her. I told her she could use any card she wanted; she took one. She swiped it a few times before it took. As she waited for the information to go through she said, "So my grandma tells me you used to live in New York."

"That's true," I said, aware I should say more.

"What did you do there?"—a complicated question.

I confessed that I had written a book. It was the easiest answer, but also the most dangerous; I segued into "Your grandma says you went to college there?"

"That's right." I could tell she wanted to ask about my book.

"NYU or Columbia?"

"NYU."

"Political science?"

"Close: art history and religion."

She slid me my receipt and I signed it and we talked for a while about neighborhoods and trains and real estate. She exuded a sort of "New York is so over" attitude in which was concealed, or so it seemed to me, an affection or even love for the city. I accused her of this and she smiled in a way that neither confirmed nor refuted my suspicion but seemed to acknowledge me as a potential ally. I got the sense she hadn't been smiling much lately, and I felt a rush of sympathy. I asked her what she was doing in Des Moines. She'd just graduated a few weeks ago, she said—a little sheepishly, I thought—and was spending a few months with her parents, saving money, reading, going for walks. She had no idea what she'd do next, nor where she'd "end up." I told her it was nice to meet another transient, and she smiled again. I was about to leave when I noticed four numerals stamped on the spine of her book in metallic red: *2*, *6*, *6*, and *6*. "Good book?" I asked. I hadn't read it but I'd read enough about it to know it was Bolaño's masterpiece, the first great novel of the twenty-first century, a towering achievement, unimpeachable.

"No. It's not a good book. It's bad. It's a bad, boring, stupid book. I've never read anything so tedious in my life. On December twentieth, a woman got raped and murdered. On January fourth, a woman got raped and murdered. On March fourteenth, a woman got raped and murdered. Okay, we got it, Bolaño, thanks. And you can tell he sort of loves it, too. He gets off on all those corpses in the desert, there's something almost funny or cute about it to him. He's enamored with his own bleak vision of the world. When actually it's just more fashionable gloom, that hip apocalypticism. And we let him get away with it because he's a man and because death seems cool and romantic when it's in Mexico. If an American woman wrote this book and it were set in like, I don't know, Des Moines—forget it, no one cares. But Bolaño—what a genius! Such bullshit."

"Why are you reading it?"

"I started it. If I start a book I have to finish it."

"I'm the same."

"It's a curse."

"It's terrible."

The woman smiled and extended a braceleted hand across the counter. Did she notice the moment of hesitation during which I struggled to recall the custom? We shook hands and traded names: hers was Jeff.

"Jeff?"

"Jess. With two esses. Ssss."

On my way back to my mother's friend's house, I considered what Jess had said about *2666*. As she was speaking, I'd felt myself agreeing with her, which didn't make sense, since I hadn't read the book. Her take on it had struck me as brave, iconoclastic, indicative of an appealing independence of thought. Now, though, in the car's clarifying solitude, I saw it as affected and immature. What did Jess know about murder or drugs or literature or Latin America? She might feel a little gloomy, too, if she'd had to flee a military dictatorship. Her little speech had been nothing but a pose. What easier way to promote your own discernment than to attack something generally acknowledged as great? (Now that I've actually read *2666,* I have to confess I agree with her assessment.) I turned on the radio, which was tuned to the classical station, a piano sonata by Schubert or -mann, or possibly a lesser-known Beethoven. On Thirtieth, I held steady at 35 mph. As I waited at the stoplight at the Lower Beaver/Douglas intersection, a cello sonata by Bach came on. There was something big and remote in the music, and also small and intimate, and I thought of aerial time lapses of cities, wives outliving husbands, war, collapsing empires, migrating birds, global warming, cold fronts, planets, orbits, Kubrick, galaxies moving always away; and beneath or within all that a solitary rower, me but also not quite me, rowing a boat against a creek or stream's gentle current on a moonlit night, and then I felt a familiar presence beside me, apparently come to keep me company on my journey. I waited for the presence to speak or disappear. The light changed and as I drove past my elementary school I realized I was listening to the sonata that had triggered an argument with Laura several years earlier, on a spring-break road trip from Minnesota to Mississippi near the end of our relationship. Laura, who had played cello since she was three, criticized what she took to be the anachronistic Romanticism in the cellist's undeniably virtuosic performances. I lacked classical training but knew enough to argue that we had no way of knowing Bach's exact intentions, and that each performer should be allowed to interpret his scores as he or she saw fit, and that in any case the cellist's expressive playing, if that was the right way to characterize it, sounded good to me. Laura, probably correctly, interpreted my stance as a hostile provocation, and we fought about that and other things for some time before falling silent. The bare branches of the trees alongside the interstate had gradually given way, starting somewhere in Missouri, to a haze of yellow and pale green buds, then to leaves in their familiar fullness, then to a seethe of big, thick, waxy, greedy leaves shooting forth from trees from another planet. It felt like we'd driven from winter to spring. In retrospect we both knew our romance was doomed, and the whole trip had something of the feeling of an afterlife. As we walked through the sad winding garden behind a mansion on the banks of the Mississippi—pecan trees, magnolias, moss-heavy live oaks; derelict neoclassical statues; the scent of camellias, azaleas, and roses heavy in the air—we both felt out of place. Why had we come here? Two Yankees who had wandered off course. On our endless tours of antebellum houses, no one else looked younger than seventy-five. All the guides said the real tragedy of the war was that it caused the South to "lose its way of life." One unhappy night we actually stayed up late watching a documentary about neo-Nazis. On the way back to Minnesota, sick of each other and silent, we passed through Des Moines on I-35, and because we were only passing through I experienced it, maybe for the first time in my life, as one place among many, a drop in the pool of the universe, an agglomeration of people so unlikely as to seem essentially arbitrary, rather than as the warm center of the world it had been for me till then.

As soon as I got back to my mother's friend's house I called

Laura. I knew she'd be patient enough to indulge my nostalgia for what had been for both of us an unhappy time. But the more we reminisced about our trip, the less unhappy it became, and I found myself wondering if I'd miscast it all these years in light of subsequent sadnesses. Remember that high school talent show we went to? Remember the bike ride down the Natchez Trace? Remember when we "accidentally" broke into that houseboat and spent the afternoon drinking bourbon on deck? Such memories, which should have heightened my nostalgia, instead threatened to dissolve it—I didn't *want* this memory to be unsettled; what if I had gotten it all wrong?—and maybe it was my dawning awareness of this that Laura detected when she asked if I had a cold; I told her I didn't think so, no. She said my voice sounded strange, a little off.

I changed the subject: "How's your yoga-class boyfriend?"

Laura sighed and said with heartfelt sadness she'd just discovered he was a coder.

"Oh no," I said. She had a thing about coders.

"I know. So—back to the drawing board I guess."

"Any prospects?"

"I don't know. I think I need to make some changes. I think my new haircut makes me look like a lesbian; suddenly I have to be careful about my outfits. And I'm going gray."

When I tried to picture Laura with short gray hair, all I could see was her mother: I almost laughed.

"Listen," said Laura, "I have some advice. Actually it's from my sister but I've found it super helpful. It's four things to do when you're feeling down."

"Sounds like an article for *Real Simple.*"

"And they really work. They're like scientifically proven.

Your brain lights up, serotonin or whatever. You don't have to do all four, necessarily, but the more you do the better you'll feel. Ready?"

"But I'm not feeling down," I lied.

"In case you ever do, then. Ready?"

One was go for a run. Two was masturbate. Three was take a shower. Four was drink a cup of coffee. Dark chocolate would also work in a pinch. And that was it. Four things. Easy, right? It was best if you did them in the order she'd listed. And she added a fifth item to the list, a sort of bonus, which she liked to do after all the others, though this one was strictly unofficial: listen to the Alec Baldwin interview podcast.

I hoped I conveyed the skepticism I felt when I said I'd keep her list in mind.

"I really think it could help, my dear."

"I've always thought gray hair was sexy," I said.

Half an hour later I was on the living-room floor, listening to the Alec Baldwin podcast. I'd considered running but hadn't run for months and convinced myself the icy sidewalks were unsafe. I wasn't in the mood to masturbate. I rarely drank coffee in the afternoon. And so, after a few minutes of disingenuous internal debate, I'd walked to the Kum & Go and bought a chocolate chocolate chip muffin, which I was eating as Alec Baldwin interviewed, in his husky seductive almost-whisper, a film director I'd never heard of. "Loss is my great theme," the director was saying. "If you watch my movies carefully, you'll see that, at heart, what they're all about is loss." No shit, I thought. Every movie is about loss. Every work of art ever made is about loss. Loss of innocence, loss of illusions, loss of identity, loss of loved ones. Laura had been right after all, I decided: the performer's role should be simply to set Bach's music into motion, as though turning over an hourglass or pulling back and releasing a pendulum, and not to urge it forward with extraneous feeling.

The podcast ended and I found myself standing by the windows I was drawn to all winter long. Sometimes as I stood there I saw signs of human life—dog walkers dressed in defiantly bright outerwear; salt-stained cars spinning tires in the snow; garage doors opening and closing like mouths; Amy Sampson emerging from the house across the street and, instead of stopping at her car in the driveway, continuing toward my driveway, my front door, as I so often imagined her doing when I was a teenager before she moved with her family to California, never to return until now, unchanged, fifteen or sixteen years old, quick gait, tight jeans, long blond shoulder-length curls, small breasts, narrow shoulders, thin lips, soft lips—but more often the world outside seemed deserted. The houses across the street seemed to welcome the snow that blanketed their roofs and hedges. They seemed to want to recede into the whiteness. Ghost robins hopped and pecked in their white yards. Ghost families lived behind their walls. Above them hovered clouds of impossible vagueness, emanations without edge or contour—*winter* clouds, breaths, abstractions of abstractions; or they gathered into a single gray solidity, dark roof; or it snowed, white disappearing into white; or the sky was clear but suffused with gold, sourceless light glowing within the blue; or the sun set the snow-covered world to flame, yellow-white dazzling my eyes.

If you concentrate hard enough on a UPS truck, you can will it to stop in front of your house. The question of who might be sending me something, among the few people who knew I was there, flickered at the edge of my mind, dimly, as I watched the truck lumber down the street to a faint accompaniment of a Bach keyboard invention. As it drew closer it seemed to slow down and my hope became edged with desperation, almost panic, and I closed my eyes. When I opened them the truck was out of sight. I feigned disappointment (to whom?) but was relieved. Then I heard the insistent beeps that meant the truck was backing up, and as in a dream it reappeared behind the windows, moving as if in super-slow-motion rewind, and I watched as it stopped in front of the house and ejected a woman dressed in the same chocolate brown as the paint that covered the truck's surface. The woman walk-ran up the driveway toward the door, and then she was too close to the house for me to see. Her three knocks shouldn't have startled me, did, and I retreated on tiptoe into the family room, where the Bach was playing from my open laptop. I stood with one hand on the couch, my mind a blank, until I heard the sound of the truck starting up, and—after an interminable pause—retreating up the street. Then I went to the front door, pulled it open, and jumped back slightly when a large yellow envelope fell across the metal threshold. It must be something for my mother's friend, I thought, as I picked it up and saw it was for me, from Maria.

I sat down on the living-room floor and tore open the envelope and pulled out a book, a biography of John Berryman. The package I'd sent hadn't made it to Maria. No, it was a different Berryman biography. The photo on the cover was almost identical to the photo on the cover of the one I'd read: here, a young Berryman sat with crossed legs on what looked like a low stone wall or pile of sacks, holding a cigarette between forefinger and thumb, the collar of his jacket flipped raffishly up. As on the other cover his expression was ambiguous and his lips were slightly parted as if to speak, but now he looked out from beneath a short-brimmed hat and his defiance was softened by what appeared to be knowing amusement. The author of the biography was Stephen Crane, which was impossible, and then I saw that Crane wasn't author but subject, the handsome man looking out from the cover who so resembled Berryman, who was the author. I opened the book and something slid out, three sheets of paper covered on both sides with small, neat handwriting in bright green ink. I scanned the letter for I had no idea what, a thesis statement, a place to hide, a sentence that laid a hand on my shoulder. I went to the family room and turned off the Bach and returned to my position on the living-room floor. Then I read the letter from the beginning.

Maria started by thanking me for sending her the biography, as if I hadn't taken it from her in the first place; Berryman was one of her favorite poets and she was glad for the excuse to return to him. She understood the pity I felt toward him but didn't understand the anger, she wrote. It seemed to her Berryman did the best he could under very difficult circumstances. Could you imagine if your father shot himself when you were eleven? And your mother remarried a few months later? And you took the name of your mother's new husband so that your father's suicide got mixed up in your identity in such a way that you'd never be able to ignore it, much less "get over it"? (Was she quoting me?) Maria couldn't imagine, she wrote, but she knew it wouldn't make life any easier. That Berryman was able, in spite of this tragedy, to not only lead a long and meaningful life but to convert it into infinitely tender and funny and sad and challenging works of art in which others might find or create meaning for themselves: this was truly extraordinary, and spoke to a courage and generosity of spirit beyond the normal human range.

In our culture, Maria went on, when someone kills himself we are all quick to call him a coward. It was a way of congratulating ourselves—wasn't it?—for continuing to eat and breathe and sleep. But suicide could be a courageous act, or just a necessary one. Of course it's sad. It's beyond sad. But everyone's life was sad in a million different ways, no matter how it happened to end. All Maria knew was that Berryman's poems—the Dream Songs especially but also *Bradstreet* and parts of *Love & Fame,* not to mention a handful of short stories and one or two critical essays, plus the letters—had given her a lot of pleasure and companionship and solace over the years. They'd *given her back to herself,* she wrote, they'd *returned her to life.* How could you feel anything but gratitude toward someone who'd done that?

Our anger should be directed not at Berryman but at his awful biographer, Maria continued. She hadn't remembered how bad he was, how incompetent, how disingenuous. Most literary biographies were bad, of course, but this one was even worse than most. It was all *He was undoubtedly feeling* and *He must have sensed* and *We can easily imagine.* Maybe we can, but should we? Is it right to? Does it actually reveal something interesting about the subject? Or does it reveal that old urge to *master,* that eagerness to patch together our lives out of scraps of other people's (those of the voiceless, if at all possible, those of the dispossessed)? Not to mention the writing was abominable. *Even if his heart made life hell for him, Berryman knew, he could not live without it.* Can you imagine writing that sentence and letting it stand? Or: *The act of evaluating one's world responsibly was damned hard, Berryman knew, but there was no way of avoiding that responsibility if civilization was to survive.* Huh? That insane pretension to omniscience, that sham authority—it was just so reductive and presumptuous and invasive. It was like a combination of a Dan Brown novel and a History Channel voice-over. Every other sentence started with *After all.* I hate *after all,* Maria wrote. There is no *after all.* And not once did the biographer have the grace to point out how little he was actually working from, how Berryman's life was in fact much larger than the letters and drafts and notebooks and journals he'd pillaged in the name of *research.* Not once did he acknowledge the gaping void on the other side of the historical record, all the parts of a person's life that aren't recorded anywhere, by anyone, ever, all the thoughts, half thoughts, feelings, dreams, everything said but not written down, everything written down but thrown away, every sensation and memory. Even when the biographer quoted Berryman himself, he failed to note the provisional and contingent nature of whatever passage he quoted, Maria wrote, as if a single sentence from a journal entry, for example, could be an uncomplicated revelation of a person's most authentic longings and fears. Biography! The genre was rotten to the core (a good example of the sort of cliché that characterizes it, she wrote). It reduced once-living beings to the level of facts, to the level of information. Life is experience, Maria grandly asserted, and experience is the opposite of information. You felt this disparity in literary biographies more strongly than in any other kind, because the richness and ambiguity of literature—of the subject's poems or novels or whatever, the literary output that presumably made this person worthy of a biography in the first place—contrasted so starkly with the unimaginativeness of even the best biographies, scummed as they almost couldn't help but be by strained elisions, knee-jerk generalizations, and dubious-at-best causality. Why were biographers so clueless and smug? Couldn't I just imagine Berryman's biographer hanging out with his biographer buddies, chomping cigars and drinking port and complaining about their wives? Portly men drinking port. Hunting fox. *Berryman's world was even more interior than Wallace Stevens's.* What does that even mean? Or this: *Meantime the larger world outside went on.* Meantime the larger world outside went on!

As for Berryman's relationship with fame, Maria continued, it was surely more complicated than I'd pretended in my note. Berryman writes all about it in the Crane biography, which, she wrote, you'll see if you read it (*no pressure*). No doubt things got confusing for Berryman. No doubt a part of him just wanted to be loved. (Maria: *Who doesn't want to be loved?*) And, as you allude to in your note, he came of age along with TV and advertising and PR and all that stuff. We can imagine that it must have been getting harder and harder to distinguish fame from celebrity. But that only makes Berryman's grappling with fame all the more necessary and poignant for us, living as everyone readily admits we do in an age in which image and spectacle and role-playing overwhelm reality at every turn. Berryman was way ahead of his time, Maria wrote. In fact, she considered him a sort of prophet.

The letter—unexpected, expansive, proud, challenging, righteous, mildly chastising, vulnerable—pulsed through me the rest of the afternoon and evening: as I backed my mother's friend's car down the driveway (very slowly) and onto Cortez Drive; as I passed the Kum & Go, Lawnwood Elementary, the Muslim Cultural Center, the veterans' hospital; as I drove down and up the Thirtieth Street ravine; as I parked and took a deep breath and entered the dry cleaners and Jess greeted me like a long lost friend (it had only been a few days since we met), and we talked for a while about things I don't remember before she admitted to having Googled me and discovered who, to the world, I was; as Jess's grandmother appeared from behind a curtain, caught sight of me, smiled, retreated behind the curtain; as Jess suggested we meet up sometime soon and asked for my number and typed it into her phone and texted me, *Let's hang out. Up for anything;* as I drove back through the streets of Des Moines with my newly altered shirt. I was moved by Maria's defense of Berryman, and I was persuaded so fully by her case against his biographer that it seemed as though I had made it myself, the vague objections I'd felt as I read the biography expanding in memory into full-throated rebellion.

Back home, if home is what it was, I remembered an essay by Virginia Woolf that I had read several years ago, a review of a biography of Elizabeth Barrett Browning that when I discovered a PDF of it on the Internet turned out to be a review of a biography of Christina Rossetti: "Here is the past and all its inhabitants," writes Woolf,

> miraculously sealed as in a magic tank; all we have to do is to look and to listen and to listen and to look and soon the little figures—for they are rather under life size—will begin to move and to speak, and as they move we shall arrange them in all sorts of patterns of which they were ignorant, for they thought when they were alive that they could go where they liked; and as they speak we shall read into their sayings all kinds of meanings which never struck them, for they believed when they were alive that they said

straight off whatever came into their heads. But once you are in a biography all is different.

I made a note to send the passage to Maria.

That night the mansion was full of drama. Emotions were running high. It started on the group date, in a pool on the rooftop of an L.A. hotel, where the Bachelor wasn't paying enough attention to Michelle. All she wanted was to feel special on her thirtieth birthday, and here she was on a date with fourteen other girls! Your thirtieth birthday is supposed to *mean* something. Not to mention Keltie was wearing the worst outfit *ever.* But the Bachelor's the type of guy where if there's a problem, he's going to address it, so a few nights later he gave Michelle the first rose. That sent a signal to the rest of the girls that you *have* to put yourself out there if you want to fall in love. Not in the way Melissa put herself out there, though. Melissa just popped up out of nowhere and was like, "I'm so, like, dadadadada, and I'm not normally like this," and it's like, "Well what *are* you normally like?" "Basically I'm very spontaneous," explained Melissa. Raichel definitely felt like Melissa should go home. And here's why. Because she wasn't being authentic and she wasn't being real. She was nothing like Raichel and she never would be. As if Melissa wanted to be anything like Raichel! From the day they got there, Raichel had been literally pulling the positive energy out of Melissa. But that was only because Melissa was like a toxic disease to Raichel on this journey. "It absolutely breaks my heart to see any woman cry," said the Bachelor. All the girls agreed: he was smokin' hot. "He's perfect. I love his suit. His face," said Raichel. He was a brand-new man from the last time he was the Bachelor. "I never thought I'd fall so quickly for someone," said Other Ashley, who'd been chosen for one of the one-on-one dates. She and the Bachelor spent the whole night just laughing, connecting, being themselves, just letting go and having fun and living in the moment. Other Ashley made it easy for the Bachelor to open up: *her* father hadn't been around much either, and it definitely didn't hurt that she looked *amazing.* She *felt* amazing. She felt like a princess. It was a perfect night. A few nights later the Bachelor went on a date with Jackie. "I feel like a princess," she said. She looked amazing. But the Bachelor worried she might not ever really let someone in. "Because at the end of the day this is very real," he said. "I know," said Jackie. "I'm here and I see it." And she knew she had trouble making herself vulnerable. That was part of what made Jackie Jackie, unfortunately. The Bachelor wondered if she'd ever be able to throw caution to the wind. Still, they had the time of their lives. Jackie seriously was living in a dream. She was on cloud nine. It was a perfect night.

The bachelorettes were bringing it, and the Bachelor was well on his way to finding a wife. Whoever it would be, though, it wouldn't be Keltie, who walked away from the Rose Ceremony empty-handed. If they gave out an Oscar for Worst Dater Ever, it would go to Keltie. "I'm just so awkward," she told America. "Honestly, I don't know if love is in the cards for me. I think I'm maybe meant to be alone. This was kind of"—wiping tears from her eyes—"kind of my last-ditch effort." She laughed and cried. "'Cause I've done, like, the regular dating. I've done the dating people at work—that never works out well. And I've done the being set up by people I don't know. And then I did the online dating. So I've kind of exhausted all the avenues." I wanted to put an arm around her, tell her everything would be okay, but how could I know if everything would be okay, plus we were separated by a TV screen. I didn't have a new favorite bachelorette yet, but it was only the third episode and anything could happen. Emily, a poised blond coal miner's daughter from West Virginia, seemed in good position. "I feel like an idiot when I talk to you," the Bachelor told her. "You make me lose words."

4

JOSEPH RIDDICK HENDRICK III, WHO ALL HIS LIFE HAS gone by Rick, came into this world on July 12, 1949, on his family's tobacco farm in southern Virginia, according to my research. Rick's father, Papa Joe, was good with his hands, and Rick used to follow him around the farm, watching as he made repairs and tinkered with equipment. Saturday nights Papa Joe would take Rick to car races in nearby towns—Hillsborough, Charlottesville, Martinsville, Richmond. When Rick was fourteen he fixed up a '31 Chevy and set speed records with it at the local drag strip. Two years later he won the Virginia division of the Chrysler-Plymouth Troubleshooting Contest. He wanted to take a shot at professional racing, but his mother wouldn't allow it—too dangerous—so instead he went into the used car business, where he proved to have a talent for selling cars even greater than his talent for racing them. He climbed the ranks to general sales manager, and then risked selling his assets to buy a franchise, becoming the youngest Chevrolet dealer in the country. It was 1976 and business boomed. He opened more dealerships across the South, then all across the country. As I write these words, the Hendrick Automotive Group, headquartered in Charlotte and chaired by Rick Hendrick, employs over ten thousand people at more than one hundred franchises in fourteen states.

Hendrick's extraordinary success as an automobile dealer allowed him to invest in his first love, racing. In the late seventies he founded a drag-boat racing team that would go on to win three consecutive national championships. His boat *Nitro Fever* set a world speed record of 222 mph. In 1982, at a race in Litchfield, Illinois, Jimmy Wright slammed one of Hendrick's boats into a bank. Wright, a close friend of Hendrick's, died on impact. Hendrick lost his passion for the sport that day. He gave up his boats and started a NASCAR team. He had five employees and a boat shed for a garage and didn't think the team had much of a chance to make it. But in 1984, its first year, the team won three races. It started attracting major sponsors. It won more races. Today, Hendrick Motorsports has won more than two hundred races; it's one of the largest and most successful teams in the history of stock car racing. Hendrick served as a technical adviser for the 1990 movie *Days of Thunder* starring Tom Cruise, and it's Cruise who narrates the 2009 documentary *Together: The Hendrick Motorsports Story.* "The Hendrick Motorsports story is about victory," intones Cruise—"and loss."

Rick and Linda Hendrick's only son, Joseph Riddick Hendrick IV—they called him Ricky—was born in Charlotte in 1980. He inherited from his father a strong work ethic, faith in God, and a passion for moving at unnatural speeds along the surface of Earth. At first Rick and Linda discouraged Ricky from racing, but when he decided that's what he wanted to do with his life, they gave him their full support. By the time he was eighteen he was driving for his father's team. An interviewer asked him: "With your dad so renowned both in NASCAR and corporate America, is it hard to find your own identity?" "No," answered Ricky, "not really. I'm a lot like my father and I'm nothing like my father. The way he grew up—on a farm—he made his own identity when he was young in his love for cars. Well, I grew up in the city, and was this punk kid that snowboarded and all this stuff, so I made my own identity but I also love cars a lot. So we don't dress alike, nothing like that. It's different, his identity and mine. That's a really good question, because I've never really thought about it like that. I feel like I just kind of formed it on my own. I'm kind of the new generation, Next, X, whatever it is."

Ricky was laid-back and sweet, with a quiet intensity. He called his elders "sir" and said "I love you" at the ends of conversations with family members. His sleepy brown eyes shone out of a soft face; his chin was round, his hair was blond and floppy. In 2001 he had nineteen top-ten finishes, with one win, in the NASCAR Craftsman Truck Series, and was runner-up for Rookie of the Year. In 2002 he switched from trucks to cars. Later that year, at the Las Vegas Motor Speedway, driving somewhere close to 200 mph, he lost control of his Chevy Impala and crashed into a wall. He walked away with a separated shoulder. He was alive, but when he returned to the track two months later, he wasn't the same driver. Every turn, he pictured his car hurtling into the wall, the shredded metal, the flames. He worried he'd mess up his shoulder again or worse. So, with his parents' support, which was unwavering, he opened a motorcycle dealership and became a partial owner of Hendrick Motorsports. Now that he wasn't racing anymore he could think more seriously about women. He fell in love with a beautiful young blonde and soon they were engaged.

This is where the loss part of the story starts.

In 1996, Rick Hendrick III had been diagnosed with chronic myelogenous leukemia. The year after that he pled guilty to fraud, having for years given houses and BMWs to Honda execs in exchange for more Hondas to sell at his dealerships. He paid a $250,000 fine, served three years of probation, and started the Hendrick Marrow Program, a nonprofit that helps find bone marrow matches for patients and gives money to uninsured marrow transplant recipients.

Not long after that, his father died. Papa Joe was eighty-four. He was born in the era of the Model T. He was a gunner for the air force in World War II. He grew up on a tobacco farm and died a rich man, thanks to the acumen and generosity of his son. When Rick's time came, Ricky would take over his empire; adjacent offices for father and son were in the works at the company's headquarters.

On a Sunday morning in October 2004, just fourteen weeks after Papa Joe's death, Rick went out for brunch with his wife at one of their favorite restaurants in Charlotte, then headed across town to see his mother, who was still mourning the loss of her husband. Earlier that morning, at nearby Concord Regional Airport, Ricky had boarded a small plane, a Beechcraft Super King Air 200 twin propeller, to fly to a race in Martinsville. Rick was driving when his cellphone rang. It was Ken Howes, Hendrick Motorsports' director of competition. He told Rick to pull over right away. The plane was missing, Ken told him—that was all they knew. Later all the bodies were recovered.

The plane had crashed, in heavy fog, into the side of Bull Mountain in the Appalachians. Nine people besides Ricky were dead: John Hendrick, Rick's brother; Kimberly and Jennifer

Hendrick, John's twenty-two-year-old twin daughters; Jeff Turner, general manager of Hendrick Motorsports; Randy Dorton, the teams' chief engine builder; Scott Lathram, a pilot for NASCAR driver Tony Stewart; Joe Jackson, a DuPont executive; and pilots Richard Tracy and Elizabeth Morrison. Saint Paul, 2 Timothy 4:6–7: "For I am now ready to be offered, and the time of my departure is at hand. I have fought the good fight, I have finished my course, I have kept the faith." Linda Hendrick, Ricky's mother: "It's not natural for a child you carry in your body to leave you. When am I going to stop hurting so much? I thought you were supposed to go before your children."

The morning of the day Ricky died, his fiancée, Emily, wasn't feeling well. Normally she traveled everywhere with him, but today he suggested she stay home and rest. Probably she had the flu. "I absolutely wished more than anything that I was on that plane, too," she'd say later. "I didn't want to live without him. I didn't. It was the worst time in my whole life." This is an important part of Emily's story: she includes it each of the three times she tells it on *The Bachelor*—to an interviewer in episode one, to a group of sympathetic bachelorettes in episode three, and to the Bachelor later that same episode, at a crucial point in their one-on-one date, just when he was starting to wonder if she'd ever open up. They were having dinner in a repurposed barn at Cambria Winery and Vineyards in Santa Maria. Candles in glass vases sat on haystacks behind them. Emily must have intuitively understood that by emphasizing the extent of her despair she'd heighten the dramatic impact of what came next: "That Friday afterwards, I learned that I was pregnant with our daughter, and I could not have been happier. I knew there was a reason I wasn't on the plane that day. Right then I knew: I wasn't supposed to be, because we have this perfect daughter that makes me the happiest person in the world." Rick Hendrick, too, saw a higher intelligence at work: "At the lowest time of our life, it was like a miracle that happened for us, because we got a chance to have a piece of Ricky left. It was like God had given us back something. We had lost so much."

Two years after Ricky died, Rick and Linda Hendrick donated $3 million to Charlotte's Levine Children's Hospital, which put the money toward the Ricky Hendrick Centers for Intensive Care, where Emily was able to find work as an event planner. People had always told her everything happened for a reason; now she saw that this was true. Josephine Riddick "Ricki" Hendrick, proof of God's divine plan, has her mother's bright blond hair and big brown eyes, her father's soft face and shy, crooked smile.

"Trust me when I say this," said the Bachelor with impossible earnestness after Emily had finally put herself out there for him: "every single thing you've told me makes me like you even more." I understood what he meant. I liked Emily, too. She came across as guileless and smart and a loving mother, qualities only heightened by being at odds with her Barbie-doll looks. Plus she'd waited longer to open up to the Bachelor than a lot of the other bachelorettes, which made her seem prudent and full of integrity. "What makes you you?" he'd asked, not for the first time. It was a good question. What makes you you?

On the face of it, it may seem like an awful idea to reveal deeply personal things about yourself on a TV show like *The Bachelor,* since to do so is to risk trivializing not only your own life but the lives of the people closest to you, to cede primary control of your identity to *People* and *Us Weekly* and the Internet comment monster. But if you want to make it past the first few episodes, sooner or later you're going to have to tell the saddest story you know about yourself. It will be about something terrible that's happened to someone you've loved, or about the terrible pain someone you've loved has inflicted on you. It will make you cry. As you wipe away the tears, the Bachelor will put his arm around you, maybe run his hand through your hair, maybe even kiss your forehead. You'll laugh and say, "I can't believe I'm crying." The Bachelor will tell you it's okay to cry. He'll be so grateful you finally made yourself vulnerable for him. He really will. He knows it's not easy for you to open up. Those tears will tell him you're here for the right reasons.

And if nothing terrible has ever happened to you, nor to someone you've loved? If your father didn't kill himself or abandon or abuse you? If all of your grandparents, even, are still alive? If you grew up on a quiet, dead-end street in a city renowned for the decency of its residents and the quality of its public school system? If accident of birth has protected you from hunger and displacement and prejudice and violence? If the most traumatic event of your life so far has been the death of a childhood cat? Can a self be carved out of minor disappointments, periods of boredom, and occasional low-level suffering? Intermittently, I felt significant. Could I love? What made me me?

"At times," I read, "he regarded the wounded soldiers in an envious way. He conceived persons with torn bodies to be peculiarly happy. He wished that he, too, had a wound, a red badge of courage." Somehow I had made it almost three decades without picking up Stephen Crane's great Civil War novel, with its relentless piercing irony and the bracing compression and lucid-ity and loveliness of its sentences, and now I was reading it in conjunction with *Stephen Crane: A Critical Biography,* by John Berryman. What immediately struck me about this biography, in contrast to the one I'd just read *about* Berryman, was the extent to which the author seemed to have given himself permission to let his personality come through the writing. Berryman's tone was one of swashbuckling authority, the tone of a young man forming opinions. His criticism of Crane's work was magisterial and sharp, full of fine and helpful distinctions; his narration of Crane's life was close, bold, verging at times on novelistic: "He held dead cigarettes and listened. He was the author of a book; he was waiting. Privation gained." Berryman presumed as much about Crane as Berryman's biographer did about Berryman, but Berryman's presumptuousness felt not only permissible but, mysteriously, almost just: maybe because he seemed almost aware that his true subject wasn't Stephen Crane but John Berryman.

I remembered reading that Berryman had felt a deep identification with Crane—he even experienced, as he was finishing Crane's biography, a brief, hallucinatory sensation of total merging—and now I encountered several passages in which Berryman might as well have been writing about himself. "After all," Berryman quoted Crane (though of course there is no *after all,* I thought), "I cannot help vanishing and disappearing and dissolving. It is my foremost trait." Berryman's, too. Meanwhile, his lively discussion of Crane's poems drew attention to their inscrutable, "dreamlike" quality, as though the young biographer-poet were discovering or highlighting the qualities he wanted his own work to exhibit.

The biography's final, fevered section, moreover, was full of Freudian overreaching that only made sense, if it made sense at all, as oblique, semiconscious self-analysis. Crane's father, like Berryman's, died when he was a boy, and Berryman interprets all of Crane's many romances in light of the theories he'd recently encountered in the Manhattan offices of Dr. Shea. Every man is a father figure to be killed. Every woman is a mother surrogate to fuck. "She alone when home combed Stephen's fair hair and nursed him through recurrent colds." Clearly, Berryman is trying in these pages to make sense of his own traumatic past. But you get the sense that he has a second aim, equally important, equally submerged: to rescue Crane from the pain and confusion and suffering of actual life. In this respect, I thought, his biography served a function directly opposite to most. What's more, his writing had a tenderness, and an intimacy, and a deference that was missing from his own biographer's.

I gathered these thoughts, and a few scattered others, into an email to Maria—they seemed too urgent for a letter—and as a P.S. typed out Woolf's passage on biographies as magic tanks; and thus began the electronic correspondence that would soon become so important to me. At first we exchanged emails every one or two days. Words on screens weren't real, plus they gave me headaches, so from the start I printed out Maria's emails and read them with pen or pencil in hand. I have them here in front of me, stacked two inches tall, messages from another world. Who wrote these sad and hopeful confessions? What do they tell us? What do they mean? Their author-protagonists are strangers to me, and also strangely familiar. I knew them once.

In the beginning they talk almost exclusively about books, aware, at least intermittently, that talking about books is always more than just talking about books. They embark on a highly subjective, non-comprehensive study of the manifold connections between Berryman and Crane. They agree that *The Dream Songs* is *the* epic of our time, and Henry, its gentle, stricken protagonist, our age's exemplary antihero. They mock the term "confessional poetry"—as if a poem as deeply strange as *The Dream Songs* were any more or less confessional than, say, *Paradise Lost.* (He still hasn't read most of *The Dream Songs,* so he orders it from Powell's.) Maria is interested in everything and passionate about her preferences. Her taste, like his (who can tell them apart?), runs toward the smooth-surfaced dreamlike narrative that quietly crystallizes strange but familiar moments of consciousness or sensation. The best realism is also experimentalism, they agree. The best criticism acknowledges its own contingency. Books should not go down like warm milk. Literature is worthwhile precisely to the degree that it conditions you to live more fully, to see more. Their co-enthusiasm expresses itself most purely in quotation, which they turn to with ever-increasing frequency, a way of speaking in code. "All these things happen in one second and last forever." "The long, waning whiteness of the afternoon stained towards sunset." If they are showing off, or at least establishing their credentials, they are also building, and populating, a common world in which they might begin to feel at home.

The Dream Songs flew in from the Pacific Northwest and I sat down with it on the living-room floor. "Many opinions and errors in the Songs are to be referred not to the character Henry," I read, "still less to the author, but to the title of the work." John was John, Henry was Henry, the songs were dreams—what could be more clear? I turned the page. The first few songs passed through my mind without depositing much residual meaning, so I started over, this time reading aloud. I hadn't read anything aloud for a long time, maybe not since the early days with Ashwini, when we used to read aloud to each other in bed (why did we stop doing that?), and now the sound of my voice in the empty house was making me self-conscious. But then I reminded myself I was alone and soon settled into the poems' strange rhythms, splintered one moment, honeyed the next, and felt through these rhythms meaning starting to ease forth. Henry sulked, complained, lusted, lectured, raged, remembered, comforted, loved (*That is our 'pointed task. Love & die*), mourned the death of friends, his father's death, his own (celebrated, a little, his own death, too), came back to life, traveled, broke limbs, brooded, thrilled, pushed his daughter on a swing, walked at the funeral of tenderness, fell out of a tree, repeated himself, suffered, played tennis, sighed, *the whole implausible necessary thing*. There was another character in the poem: the World, sometimes called "God," sometimes "they," sometimes "mail"—a shape-shifting incomprehensible cruel figure who from time to time shows up at Henry's door with bad news. Henry hates him. *God's Henry's enemy. . . . The world is lunatic. . . . What the world to Henry did will not bear thought.* The sun went down, I skipped dinner, kept reading, and my voice was Henry's was Berryman's was everyone's, childlike and quavering and brave and in the dark. It rose through the floorboards of Maria's room.

I picked up Jess and we drove to Jordan Creek Mall to watch in 3D a Werner Herzog documentary about prehistoric art. When Jess offered to share her enormous box of Whoppers, I declined, affecting repulsion, for no reason. The lights dimmed to black and the eminent Bavarian descended into the unknown. We saw through our glasses woolly rhinos, cave bears, a horse whose eight legs suggested movement, a woman with grotesquely inflated sex organs, ibex, the former president of the Société Française des Parfumeurs, stalactite shadows edging across red handprints, white dots arrayed in a significant pattern (but what, exactly, was its significance?), an ex–professional unicycler whose dreams were filled with peaceable lions and other large cats, a fleshy man dressed in animal skins and playing a bird-bone flute. "These images are memories of long-forgotten dreams. Is this their heartbeat or ours?" Walls can talk. Men can become animals or trees, and vice versa. This was what the expert meant by *fluidity* and *permeability*. But which came first, love or beauty? Language or music? Love. Music. What was art for? Art was for communicating human truths across expanses of time and space.

Statues of Lincoln and Reagan flanked the exit: Jess took a selfie with them on her phone and posted it for semi-public viewing. Then we drove to Tasty Tacos, where we discussed the film over a plastic basket of their famous flour nachos.

"You found it pretentious and gratuitously gloomy," I accused the woman I barely knew.

"And you found it . . . profound?"

"Exactly."

In fact, Jess said, she'd almost liked it. The cave art itself, she admitted, was amazing, and she liked the albino alligators at the end. But Herzog was so proud of gaining access to the cave; half the movie was an advertisement of his own importance. And didn't I think there was a cruelty to his gaze? How he kept the camera trained on his subjects for such a long time after they'd finished speaking? It was like he just wanted to make people uncomfortable, she said. I disagreed, just to be contrary, maybe, and when Jess very reasonably countered my argument I reasserted it with a vehemence so ridiculous we both couldn't help but laugh. Her bangs hung exactly halfway down her eyes. All our fingers were drenched in cheese.

I don't remember which of us suggested we go to the Hessen Haus, a German bar just outside downtown, in keeping with the evening's theme—"Cavemen?" Jess said. "Paleoanthropology?"—nor do I remember what we talked about there, only the sweaty, crazy-eyed hordes drinking from big glass boots and yelling and pounding the long communal tables with their hairy cavemen fists. And I remember feeling that I was one of these people, that I was a member of the hordes, the *nameless hordes,* which allowed me, along with the two pints of beer, to speak to Jess as though I were another person, one for whom nights like this were all I needed to fend off life's bad and boring parts. As we danced the first of our three or four polkas I couldn't stop thinking, You look like a princess.

Then we were walking in hooded coats through the empty streets of downtown Des Moines. Downtown Des Moines is always empty, even at five o'clock on a weekday, or seven o'clock on a Saturday evening—the skywalk system allows pedestrians to traverse many blocks without stepping outside—but at this hour, maybe 1:30 A.M., it seemed even emptier than usual. A fine snow fell, almost invisible, and the air seemed almost warm. We walked through countless abandoned lots and barren corporate plazas, sobering up, past rows of brick buildings of mysterious purpose, through thc shadows of featureless, unreal skyscrapers, ridiculous in their modesty, their lack of grandeur, the Equitable Building and 501 Grand and the EMC Insurance Building. Des Moines, city built on ethanol and insurance! As we walked past the Ruan Center, Des Moines's second tallest skyscraper, I found myself telling Jess about the summer I worked as a temp in a cubicle on its thirty-second floor. My job—as mysterious to me now as it was then—was to type up birth certificates for children born out of wedlock. (Why were they separated from other birth certificates?) I was eighteen and had just graduated from high school and hadn't known time could pass so slowly. At the end of that summer, I told Jess, I promised myself two things: first, that I'd never work in an office again, and second, that once I left for college I'd never come back to Des Moines to live. She laughed, and after a longish silence said she'd once had a similar job. Temping, data entry. She'd just turned sixteen. It was the summer between her sophomore and junior years of high school. The job was at the national headquarters of the Church of the Open Bible, a Pentecostal denomination whose members could speak directly to God.

From eight in the morning to five in the afternoon, five days a week, for almost three months, she entered addresses and phone numbers into an online directory. It was work a first-grader could've done, Jess said—an unusually patient first-grader. And no one in the office so much as acknowledged her existence, which made her feel that the work she was doing had been assigned for the express purpose of occupying her time. She'd been granted two ten-minute breaks per day, one in the morning and one in the afternoon, and she used to stretch them into fifteen-minute breaks, twenty minutes, half an hour, just to see if anyone would notice, and of course no one did. Or if they did they didn't say anything. A lot of that time she spent reading the Bible, copies of which were everywhere in the office. She'd barely glanced at it before that summer, though of course she was vaguely familiar with a lot of the stories, and she remembered reading Jonah over and over, she told me, each time feeling she'd just missed its lesson.

The other big thing in her life that summer was that she was getting into music in a serious way. Before then she'd listened, without much enthusiasm, to whatever her friends happened to be listening to, but now she started seeking out music on her own, music that felt like hers and no one else's. This was a familiar rite of passage, of course, but what made her process especially exciting was that she was under the belief that her parents didn't allow music in the house. Which wasn't true! She couldn't explain now why she thought it was, except to say that not once in her life had she heard her parents listening to music by choice, whether at home or in the car. As unlikely as that sounds, she said, it was true. But it's not like they were at all conservative or strict; they weren't *against* music, they just didn't choose to listen to it.

"What kind of music were you listening to?" I asked.

"Alt-country?" Jess said, and we both broke out laughing. We'd reached the lawn of the capitol building, its golden façade and copper domes, modeled after the Hôtel des Invalides, lit by floodlights whose beams were given shape by the now more thickly falling snow. We admired the imitative magnificence for a moment, then headed back toward our car.

And so by day, Jess continued, I was entering data and reading the Bible, and by night I was listening to music in secret and reading about my favorite bands on the Internet. I went to a few shows in Des Moines, always alone—to have shared my passion with my friends would've killed it—and then I found out that my favorite band (she gave the name, but I didn't know it) was about to go on tour. But the closest they were coming to Des

Moines was St. Louis, five and a half hours away. I really, really wanted to go, Jess said, but A) I'd never driven that far, B) I'd have to leave work early to make it in time, and C) I had a midnight curfew. So I think I just decided it was impossible and told myself not to think about it.

So the day of the show arrives, and I'm typing away, just making sure all these people get their monthly Bible newsletter or whatever, and out of nowhere I think, I'm going. I'm going to that show. And I get up from my desk and very calmly and purposefully walk past my quote unquote colleagues and out of the building, knowing as I do so I'm never coming back, even though my job is supposed to last a few more weeks. I drive to St. Louis in my parents' car, feeling more free, more *adult,* I guess, than I've ever felt in my life, and at the same time—maybe this was part of that feeling—terrified a semi will swerve into me and crush me. How long would it take my parents to find out? Well, that doesn't happen, I get to the concert just as it's starting, and somehow I maneuver my way to the front. And I know I must be imagining it but ten or twelve times over the course of the show, often during super emotional moments, the lead singer looks right into my eyes, and holds his gaze, as if he's singing just for me. I don't know, I don't have words for what I felt. It was the most transcendent experience of my life.

Afterward I'm in a sort of trance. I'm dimly aware of my parents now, who are probably starting to get concerned, but I just think, I'll explain it all later. They'll understand. Nothing bad will happen. Nothing bad will happen anymore. I've seen the face of God, you know? And I'm heading toward the exit, full of love for the world, when I feel a hand grip my shoulder, hard. And I think: They've found me. They're taking me in. They're locking me up. It's all over. Fuck. And I turn around and this *man,* this security guard's looming over me. He's enormous, a giant, maybe six-ten. And the giant says in his giant voice, Something from the band, sweetheart. And he hands me a folded-up sheet of notebook paper, and I unfold it, and there's a very short note, two words, super scrawly, I can barely make them out. But I'm pretty sure they say, Stick around. *Stick around.*

Well, you can imagine the sorts of fantasies that sprung up in my sixteen-year-old mind at that moment. I'd be invited backstage, hang out in the dressing room, share a bottle of whiskey with the band, listen to records, we'd hit it off, and next thing I know I'm on tour with them, maybe playing tambourine or something, maybe singing backup. Drugs, sex, and scandal ensue. Maybe I'd write a book about it. I never saw that movie *Almost Famous,* but I imagine it's something like that, or no, in *Almost Famous,* it's a teenage boy, right? It doesn't matter. The point is I was beside myself. And *yeah,* it *was* like I was in a movie, and I was both on-screen and in the audience, waiting to see what would happen next.

Well what happens is the bass player reappears and invites me to hang out with the band backstage. And I'm thinking, It's just like I imagined. . . . A lot of what went down after that is lost to me. I remember bare lightbulbs, plastic red cups, the smell of cigarettes, acoustic guitars, yellow foam bulging out of a couch cushion, laughter, a purple hamster, harmonicas. There were probably about twenty-five people in the room, the five band members and a bunch of other randos—groupies or roadies or friends of the band, I couldn't figure out the nature of the relationships—but everyone seemed to know everyone else, except of course for me. I remember I got into a conversation about Sting with a woman wearing a rhinestone dress. Then at some point I'm talking to the bass player, who to me is just, you know, this *legend,* and he's asking me all sorts of questions about myself and all I'm thinking is God, your eyes. Your blue eyes. His eyes were that whitish, silverish blue that I've always associated with wolves. Beautiful eyes. And next thing I know we're in a smaller room, alone, at first just talking but then making out, and I remember he asked me to go down on him but I don't remember if I did.

"Jesus. This guy's what, twice your age?" Suddenly I felt twice Jess's age.

"Probably not quite but almost. Yeah."

We'd reached the parking lot. We got in the car. "So did you make it home by midnight?" I asked after I'd turned onto the street.

"Ha. I woke up in a hotel room with like six other people at like four or five A.M., and then I caught a cab back to the performance venue and got some coffee and drove home. I got back maybe around eleven-thirty, noon. Apparently at some point in the night I'd texted my parents, so they were angry but they weren't, like, overly concerned." After a pause, Jess said, "The crazy thing? I got paid for another month of work. No one in the office even noticed I was gone."

Streetlamps spread their light across the road, gleaming from filled potholes and tire tracks worn into the macadam. I sensed Jess was looking out the passenger-side window, and I stole a quick glance in her direction. Dim houses slid past her half-turned face, which was full and alive with remembered intensities.

I hadn't realized there was more to her story. "The bass player—his name was Brett—texted me the day after the show, thanking me: *Thanks for a lovely night.* I still have it. And I texted back, *No, thank you!* But the more I thought about it over the next few days, the more disturbed I became about what happened. I didn't use words like *consent* or *minor* in my mind, but I suspected I'd been taken advantage of. And yet a part of me was also reveling in it. I mean, the bass player for my favorite band! I think that's what kept me from telling anyone what happened. Anyway, maybe a few weeks later, I text Brett and ask for his email address, and he sends it and I write him this long, meandering email, trying to explain what I've been thinking and feeling, not really expecting him to write back, I don't think, just trying to get some closure, something. But a few days later he *does* write back, and he says, you know, God, I'm so sorry, you're right, I did an awful thing, I'm a monster. I'm so sorry. And then he goes into this whole long story about how his dad left his mom when he was two, he never had a father figure in his life, he never knew how men were supposed to act, all this really deep stuff about his childhood, so that by the time I finished the email I felt genuinely bad for the guy. It was almost as if *I* were the one who'd done *him* wrong. All his life, he wrote, his only sources of solace had been music, alcohol, drugs, and women, and now when I listened to his music, his band's music, all the songs seemed to be about him."

Another block passed before Jess said, "I wrote him back, expressing sympathy, you know, 'I didn't mean to call you a monster. You're not a monster. You seem very sweet,' or whatever. And he writes me back saying basically I'm the only one who's ever understood him. Which, you know, makes me feel very good. So we develop this correspondence, and we keep it up my last two years of high school, and we really start to get to know each other, or at least that's what it feels like. I mean, I'll be honest: I felt closer to Brett than I'd ever felt to anyone in my life. And it was partly *because* we were so far apart and only communicating long-distance, I think."

We'd arrived at her parents' house and were idling in the driveway. No lights were on inside, nor in any of the neighboring houses. Warm air brushed against our faces.

"Did you see him again?" I asked.

"Not while I was in high school. His band didn't tour for a couple years, and he split his time between Nashville and Athens, Georgia. But then I went off to NYU, and we started talking about meeting up in New York, since he traveled there occasionally for one reason or another. So toward the end of my freshman year we made a plan to meet."

"You must have been so nervous."

"I was, but by this point I felt I knew him really well. I didn't really see how things could go wrong."

"Oh no."

"No, actually, it was great. We hit it off. We went out for ramen and walked around Manhattan for hours, just talking, or just sitting and watching people. And the next day we went to the Cloisters together, and again walked around Manhattan for hours, and by the time he flew back to Nashville the next day we were more or less a couple."

"What?"

"We dated my last few years of college. He moved to New York. We just broke up a month ago. And it's strange, but it's only in the past few weeks that I've started to realize what an asshole he was. Like, he really was the monster he said he was in that first email he ever wrote me! Of course, the moment I say that out loud I start to think, No, he wasn't so bad."

I assured Jess that he was very, very bad. She smiled and leaned across the gearshift toward my shoulder to hug me.

Then she abruptly broke off the embrace, thanked me, said good night, and left.

As I drove home through the vacated streets, I turned Jess's story over in my mind, trying to draw some lesson from it, if only one that clarified, even a little, the nature of our relationship. Was this the saddest story she knew about herself? That she'd worked a shitty job and read the Bible and discovered music and under the spell of her discovery convinced herself she was in love with a man who may—or may not—have taken advantage of her or worse? What did it mean? And why did she trust me with it? Should I have leaned in, after she finished talking, and pulled her close and kissed her (she was "up for anything")? It had crossed my mind, of course, but I was so much older than her, and I liked her, it was nice to have a friend. Also, of course, Ashwini (she was still in India). Also, I was a little intimidated by Brett. A part of me had always wanted to be a rock star, to be onstage, to have fans. To go on tour and night after night abandon myself to the living moment, not caring about physical or emotional or any sort of consequences. What did Brett know about life, I wondered, that I hadn't allowed myself to learn? And yet: Brett was a monster, maybe. I was pretty sure I wasn't. That's why Jess had trusted me with her story, I thought, because I wasn't Brett. And it felt good to have Jess's trust, it made me feel solid and real. If I could be the anti-Brett she needed, I would play that role.

5

BY THE FIFTH EPISODE OF *THE BACHELOR* THERE HAD BEEN enough one-on-one dates that most of the remaining bachelorettes were starting to feel emotions they couldn't describe. They tried to describe them, but the words they knew weren't equal to what they felt. They said "amazing" and "magical" and "perfect" and "I'm in heaven." "I'm the luckiest girl in the world," they said. "I haven't felt like this about somebody for so long." And always, inevitably, bachelorette by bachelorette: "I didn't expect to feel this way." They were confused, visibly so; more: metaphysically disturbed. They'd come on the show knowing just what to say (they'd been fans of *The Bachelor* for nearly a decade): that they were here to fall in love, they were ready for a husband, they wanted to take that leap of faith, they believed in fairy tales. No one believes in fairy tales. They were here to have fun, to taste fame, to *have an experience.* At best they half-believed the words they mouthed. They weren't stupid. They knew the Bachelor almost never ends up, in real life, with the woman he chooses on the show. But now those distinctions—the show, real life—were starting to break down. You could see it in the women's faces, and it was unsettling, thrilling. They'd been living with each other in the mansion for weeks now, contractually deprived of the usual diversions—computers, phones, TV, magazines—and their poignant fantasies of romance and leisure and wealth and luxury and escape, which they'd been so used to ignoring beneath the crush of their lived realities, were drawn out and made solid by everything around them. The show had become their only reality (as it had been for the Bachelor from the start): not in the way a novel becomes our reality while we're reading it, but in the way a novel might become our reality if we were able to step through the pages and share the world its characters inhabit—not just what the author's chosen to record in words, but everything, their whole lives, all the unconsidered and in-between stuff, everything too multiform or fleeting for words. Emotions were seriously running high.

I'd just gone for a run and now I was in bed, propped up against what I think is called a husband pillow, long underwear and shorts scrunched down around my ankles, open laptop beside me on a folded blanket against which lay a bottle of fragrance-free hand lotion. I'd tried and failed to perform the second item on Laura's list; I couldn't stop thinking of Ashwini, and that made me too sad to continue.

The date card was addressed to Chantal, an executive assistant from Seattle who was emerging, along with Emily, the Ashleys, and Michelle, as a serious contender: "How deep is your love?" read the handwritten note. All the girls wondered, What could that mean? Chantal went upstairs and put on tight jeans, a tight gray T-shirt, a black leather jacket, dark makeup, and silver hoop earrings, then came back down to wait for the Bachelor in the living room, a yellow-gold and glacial white and royal blue den full of enormous candles and vases. Densely floral-patterned fringed curtains hung from doorways and windows. Beneath them the bachelorettes waited on couches, sizing each other up in their morning clothes. The Bachelor arrived smiling in a leather jacket to match his lucky date's. He sat with the bachelorettes for a while, making them laugh with everything he said. Just a good-looking dude hanging out with his girlfriends, waiting for the helicopter to arrive. When it arrived, the women shrieked and brought their hands to their mouths and clutched each other's forearms and said, "Oh. My god," and "Shut. Up." They scampered in their yoga pants and ponytails to the Italianate front patio, with its palm trees and rose bushes and cascading fountain, and watched the helicopter's descent with touching excitement, gaping to expose their perfect teeth. Michelle didn't like thinking about Chantal and the Bachelor going off together in a helicopter, enjoying a magical romantic night that ends with some sort of make-out. Ashley wanted to tear Michelle's head off. Other Ashley just looked sad and worried. Then the Bachelor and Chantal were in the sky, his hand on her knee, her hand on his hand, looking out over green hills dotted with mansions.

I muted the fibromyalgia drug commercial and closed my eyes and waited. I'd already watched this episode once, so when the commercial ended I wasn't surprised to see the helicopter land on Catalina Island, then the Bachelor and Chantal walking arm in arm down a pier surrounded by bobbing yachts, condos glowing pastel behind them, to an accompaniment of breezy acoustic guitar music they couldn't hear, and then the Bachelor's disembodied voice: "I have something in store for Chantal and I that will make us feel like we're completely out of the real world." They boarded a red motorboat. The music stopped. The Bachelor took Chantal by the arm and said, "Can I tell you now?" She nodded. "We are going to walk *on the ocean floor.*" Wide eyes. Ominous string music. "Shut. Up." "Swear to god." Wet suits. Men in flip-flops. Astronaut helmets with handles like tusks. Being in the ocean was one of Chantal's biggest fears. "When I'm in deep water I feel absolute anxiety and terror," she said, a feeling I could relate to—the blue-black light, the obliterating sense of infinite space, the water's surprising viscosity and weight, the slow-motion movement through a prehuman world, the strange creatures we never see but are always there, lurking, indifferent to us. Chantal really, really didn't want to get into that water. But if she just gave up and didn't face her fear, that would show the Bachelor she wasn't willing to take chances for him. She knew that if you put yourself out there, a whole new world could open up to you. "So I have to do it."

She stepped onto a ladder, took a breath, began the slow climb down. She laughed and whimpered and brushed her hair behind her ears, giving a glimpse of her blood-red nails. One of the men in flip-flops put a helmet over her head. What if she went down there and didn't come back up? Sheer cliffs shot up from the distant shore. She couldn't tell if she was shaking from cold or fear. Then she was underwater, holding hands with the Bachelor, the air they breathed out bubbling to the surface. They brought the transparent face shields of their helmets together in a joke of a simulated kiss, and the show went to commercial (cholesterol drug) and I closed my eyes and waited and a doorbell rang. On the show? It rang again. I pulled up my long underwear and shorts and tossed the bottle of lotion into the bathroom and walk-ran down the hallway and stairs to the door. I opened it.

"Oh!" my mother's friend said as I said, "You're early!" It was nice of her to have rung the doorbell.

"Am I?"

"Maybe I misread—it doesn't matter. Welcome!" I think I wanted to acknowledge in my overenthusiasm the weird inversion of our roles.

"Thank you! What a lovely home you have."

"Isn't it?" I worried my face was flushed. "I'm going for minimal. Is it too much?"

"Oh, *no,*" she said. She set down her suitcase. "I'm a big fan of the *furniture-free* look. It has a certain purity."

She looked younger than I'd imagined by ten or twenty years; certainly she was younger than my mother, who was sixty-three. She wore a slate-colored stylish-seeming knee-length wool coat, tall black leather boots, a bright red scarf. Her long, curly hair was black and graying slightly; it blinded me as we hugged.

She stepped back and looked me in the eyes for a long moment. "God, it's so great to finally *see* you. I've heard a lot about you, you know."

"Likewise." In fact my mother had told me very little about Sadie before putting us in touch a couple months ago. They got coffee together sometimes, she'd said. They exchanged gardening tips. Apparently they hadn't been close enough for me to know she existed when I was a kid. Now that I was face-to-face with her, she didn't seem like the kind of person my mother would be friends with, but I wouldn't have been able to say quite why. "Thanks for letting me stay in your house," I said.

"Oh"—she made a gesture that said, *No need to thank me.* "How has everything been *going*? Have you had any problems? Is there anything you need that I can *get* you?"

I shook my head and said everything had been great.

"You've found enough to do?"

"I'm good at amusing myself."

"That's important. A very important skill. The older you get the more important it becomes." Her voice had a distinctive clarity and poise that struck my ears as almost British.

I half-laughed. I think I was sweating sort of a lot.

"Well!" she said. "That was the longest flight of my *life.*"

"Oh man, I'm sorry I didn't—"

"Don't be silly."

"Can I take your suitcase upstairs?" I offered.

"Gentleman," Sadie said, and followed me to her room.

"Sorry about the—I was going to change the sheets," I said.

"Please, *please,* don't worry about it." She slipped off her boots, removed her coat, and threw it on the floor and herself onto the unmade bed. Then she nestled her head into the pillows, sighed, seemed to remember I was standing there, sat up, and said, "I hate to be such a rude houseguest, but would you mind if I slept off the tail end of an Ambien?"

"Not at all."

"When I wake up maybe we could go for a walk."

The wind was in our faces and the cold thrilled through us. Wind chimes were its audible expression. Dusk was approaching and the overcast sky and fallen snow were the same grayish mauve. Almost all the Christmas lights and lawn ornaments were gone. Smoke raced horizontally and somehow comically—as when steam shoots out from a cartoon character's ears, I later realized—from small cylindrical metal chimneys. As we walked down the street we both used to live on, the space between Sadie and me seemed fogged by politeness or uncertainty or reserve, or maybe the cold. Then Sadie attacked the silence with questions. Was it good to be back? What was happening here? Had I liked growing up in Des Moines?

Good? Happening? Liked? It hurt to speak—to contort my tongue and lips. But there was something at once warm and disarming in Sadie's manner that made me want to answer honestly, and I found myself talking (which question was I answering?) about my unending dream of a childhood, a succession of parks and backyards and playgrounds and friends' bedrooms and basements and TV and video games—scenes floating through my mind like clips from a movie, as if my childhood were something that had happened to someone other than me. It was one long summer vacation, I said. I rode my bike everywhere, or walked. I did as I pleased. I knew nothing bad would ever happen to me, and I was right, it didn't.

"Nothing?" Sadie said.

"No. I mean my cat died. Everyone's cat dies. We got another cat."

"Mittens? I love Mittens."

"Mittens was two cats after Fritz. First there was Tom, but he died of cancer. So—two cats died. I had a happy childhood. Protected. Sheltered, I guess you could say. And insofar as it's impossible for me to separate growing up from growing up in Des Moines—"

"*Growing up* is such a weird phrase, isn't it? I still feel like I'm growing up."

"I know. I mean, I don't know but I know. Anyway, yeah, I liked growing up. By which I mean—this is what I was trying to say—growing up in Des Moines. But what's funny is that for the longest time I went around telling people I hated Des Moines. I guess I'd come to think of it as a sort of no place, the same mess of strip malls and fast food restaurants and big box stores you see everywhere else."

"I mean," Sadie said as we turned right onto Lower Beaver; I wasn't sure which of us had chosen that direction.

"And yeah," I said, "it sort of is that, but it's also more than that. Or maybe its blankness is part of what I like about it: you can make it whatever you want to. I don't know—you didn't like living here?"

A steady stream of cars went past: men and women I imagined as versions of my parents, returning from their jobs in agribusiness or state government or insurance. Well, Sadie began, this neighborhood—it wasn't a *community.* Not really. No one *walked* in Des Moines—she waved an arm at the empty sidewalks—and there were no *squares,* no *stoops,* not even *porches,* and even though everyone had these big front yards, people only ever hung out in their big *back*yards, on *patios,* everyone had to have a big backyard *patio,* the houses were turned inward, toward themselves, away from the street, away from the *world.* No one gardened. Or they did but they grew only the showiest flowers, all non-native of course. Except for the stray tomato plant, no one grew vegetables. When she told people she'd started growing vegetables they looked at her like she was from another country, like she couldn't afford to buy food from Hy-Vee. Instead of these big vacant lots—she pointed one out—there should be community gardens. *Community.* That's what was missing from Des Moines, she said. Probably that was why no one here had anything resembling a political conscience, except of course when the caucuses came to town—but even then, *even then* what people cared about wasn't policy, wasn't *issues,* the real, pressing issues of our society, not really, it was glamour and fame and the spotlight, it was *attention,* election years were the only times the rest of the world paid any *attention* to Iowa, then and whenever a new farm bill was on the table and suddenly all of Washington cared passionately about corn. Corn and soybeans. Vast deserts of corn and soybeans. And pigs and cows hopped up on growth hormones. Did I realize, Sadie asked, that Iowa was directly responsible for what was happening in Egypt and Tunisia? I told her I hadn't really been paying attention to the news. "Well what's happening is that people in the Middle East are starving, and they're starving because they can't afford food, and they can't afford food because our government's giving money to farmers *right here in Iowa* to grow corn not to *eat* but to feed pigs or cows, or else to turn into gasoline. And no one here"—she nodded at the houses—"cares, or even knows what's going on. I mean, they just reelected *Branstad.*"

Terry Branstad was the avuncular mustachioed monster who'd governed Iowa for almost my entire childhood. But he'd retired. Now he was back? What else had I missed? "I should really start reading the *Register,*" I said pathetically.

"Sorry, I didn't mean to rant. There really was a lot I liked about living here. Good schools, surprising diversity, low crime rate. Not a lot of extreme poverty or ostentatious wealth. The Art Center's nice, the sculpture garden. And people here take their time. I like that. That's what happens when your ancestors are pioneers, I suppose."

I doubted the causality but made an affirming noise. "Why did you decide to move to New York?"

"It's where I'm from."

"You wanted to be closer to family," I suggested.

I thought I heard her stifle a laugh. "They're all gone."

"I'm sorry to hear—"

"No, it's nothing," she said with a finality that made it clear it was not nothing. Who was this woman, this friend of my mother's? She was out of place in this city, clearly, too avid and voluble and opinionated. That's why her friendship with my mild-mannered mother—mild-mannered in the Des Moines, Midwestern way—was unlikely, I saw now. The question was not why she'd moved back to New York, but why she'd moved to Des Moines in the first place. And why was everyone always moving? Why couldn't we just stay put? What was wrong with us? Did I know this neighborhood was farmland till the sixties? Sadie was asking. I hadn't known. That house right there—she pointed to the only all-brick house in the neighborhood—that was the original farmhouse. I'd made dim note of the house's difference from its neighbors on hundreds, possibly thousands of occasions; to discover the difference's source released a pleasure that shot through my body and back to my childhood. "Wow!" I said, then felt very silly. Sadie looked at me and smiled with her eyes, brown.

We came to an intersection with a paved foot- or bike path I couldn't remember ever seeing. "This way?" Already Sadie was turning onto it, and I was, and then we were walking through thin deciduous forest that rose on our right to a row of houses and fell on our left to a frozen river, the Des Moines? I tried to call up a mental map, but its shapes kept shifting and dissolving in my mind. We'd only been walking for twenty minutes, couldn't have been more than a mile from Sadie's house, a little less than that from my childhood house, and yet this was foreign territory to me. I wondered if these woods connected up with the woods at the end of Cortez Drive. I regretted never going in those woods as a child. Then again, there was still time.

The sun had set and the world had dimmed to a thousand

browns and grays. The woods on our left gave way to a view of the frozen expanse of water. Sadie stopped. This was a great place to see bald eagles, she said, and she fished a pair of binoculars from a pocket and pointed them at the tops of trees on the opposite bank. I scanned the dark branches for bird shapes, movement, suddenly needing to see an eagle. Sadie handed me the binoculars—"Wanna try?"—and I aimed them at everything, forgetting the cold, yearning (why?) for birds. The frozen river creaked and groaned. It was Sadie who finally ushered us onward. I was crushed. I needed eagles. I hadn't known. As we walked between marshland and open field, fallen now into near-total darkness, Sadie told me she used to walk here with my mother. There was always so much to see back here—not only eagles but osprey, hawks, foxes, otters, all sorts of little mammals. "Once we saw a bobcat!" she practically shrieked, as if she'd just spotted it again. "Everyone we told refused to believe it, though," she said, "so eventually we just stopped telling people."

I hadn't realized until that walk that I'd been missing my mother terribly. For the past decade or so I'd seen my parents an average of two or three times a year, but my last year in New York, and my months in Halifax, my mother had been a near-constant companion: the novel I'd been working on, I told whoever asked, was a disfigurement of her father's memoirs. A few years ago he sent five long sections to my mother, whom he hadn't spoken to or seen in many years, and she photocopied them for my siblings and me, "in case you want to understand what I've had to deal with my whole life." Beneath or within its parody of self-aggrandizing political memoirs, which itself belied my grandfather's actual self-aggrandizement, it's a story of missed chances, disillusion, frustration, resentment, and latent violence. He spent most of his life in the air force, drifting from base to base. If he'd been born two years earlier he would have flown in World War II, maybe dropped bombs on Japanese islands, maybe gotten shot down. He would've been a member of "the Greatest Generation," would've been called a hero, which would've masked the fact that he was a standard-issue American narcissist and boor. "We all have a secret, private life that we try to conceal from world view," he writes redundantly. "Our culture dictates a system of moral values that is in conflict with our true nature. We are all hypocrites, steeped in dissimulation, fackery [*sic*] and pretense. Autobiographies are usually attempts to justify our peccadilloes and illuminate our magnanimous nobility." It takes a man of my grandfather's moral courage, implies my grandfather—who the only time I saw him, when I was six or seven, I watched throw a waffle at his fourth wife's face—to puncture our culture's false ideas of itself.

Beyond the anger I felt toward my grandfather on my mother's behalf, I felt almost no connection to him the first time I read his memoirs. He may as well have been someone else's grandfather. Then the anger faded and I began to read them as if he were a character invented and controlled by a novelist, a narrator whose unreliability was exposed through the steady accrual of dubious information; shoddy writing; and crude, self-serving forgeries. I marked up the text with little notes, then started making edits to heighten by any available means the irony generated by the distance between my grandfather and my imagined novelist. I conflated women and invented new ones to make his love life more complexly patterned, and elaborated anecdotes into fuller and stranger stories. The working title of my novel was *My Grandfather's Memoirs,* but I saved it on my computer as "Grandpa."

I explained my project in an email to Maria around the time of Sadie's visit, using the present tense instead of the past—she'd asked if I could say anything about the novel I was working on—so that my lie seemed less a lie than an inconsequential matter of grammar. The content of our emails, though still largely literary, was moving toward the more expressly personal. I'd written her about my recent one-on-one, lightly caricaturing Jess, it seems to me now, as a self-involved youth who lacked (*unlike Maria*) the aesthetic sensitivity necessary to appreciate foreign documentaries. Recounting the events of that evening, I discovered—the movie, the nachos, the German beer house, the walk through downtown Des Moines, Jess's story—gave them a solidity and texture they'd lacked both as they unfolded and immediately afterward, as if the whole night hadn't actually happened until I wrote about it to Maria. Similarly, telling her about my novel made me feel as though I hadn't abandoned it, as though I still believed I could count on myself to tell the truth through fiction.

Maria, too, had begun to open up, relating funny anecdotes, anxieties, the texture of her days. Tensions between housemates (Maria not excluded) smoldered, then flamed up or petered out, a constant source of drama, intrigue, annoyance, anger, and amusement. Lately, Maria wrote, her upstairs neighbors, an on-again, off-again couple, Sam and Jo, had begun waking up at five A.M. to argue about what to make for dinner. "I feel like we've had a lot of basmati recently." "Fine, we'll use whatever rice *you* want to use." "Baby, I didn't mean it like that." "Mean it like what? We'll use a different rice. What do I care what rice we use?" "No no no you *should* care." Etc. They went on and on, these fights, somehow encapsulating everything Maria disliked—a larger category than she had been willing to admit, at first—about her "intentional community."

Nevertheless: the time, the time. Maria bathed in it, luxuriated in it. She walked, she lay on the floor, she read. Could days and weeks be filled in this way? They could. I was beginning to learn that filling days and weeks required far less than we typically imagined. Still, a part of me wanted to ask her the bad question: *What are you doing with yourself?*

Well, for one thing she'd started to do some translations from the Finnish. She'd been teaching herself the language off and on, she told me, for the past year and a half. She liked to imagine, as she studied and translated, Finland's snow-caked pine and spruce forests, its frost-coated ferns, its frozen earth, its bears and wolves and foxes and elk, the low afternoon sun laying streaks of gold on fields of blue and purple ice. What was her connection to Finland? None. She'd never been there and had no plans to go. Sometimes she wondered if her fantasy of the place was the source of whatever vitality her amateur translations might possess. (She was proud, she wrote, to be an *amateur*—from the French and Latin for *lover*. Amateurs did what they did out of love. They didn't *instrumentalize.* They lacked ulterior motives.) There was a Finnish word for homesickness felt for a place one has never been: *kaukokaipuu.* That's what she felt for Finland: *kaukokaipuu.* "Will you send me a draft of your novel when you're done?" she wrote, and I promised her I would.

We had crossed (we both felt it, I was sure) some critical threshold—of what? Intimacy. What is intimacy? A feeling, a register, a hum, little touches on the shoulder as you do the dishes. Maria referred to our correspondence more than once as a "collaboration." We were, from a certain perspective, ridiculous people, alone in our houses in the heart of the part of the country no one cared about. We needed each other; I understand that now. When I imagined Maria I saw her sitting, legs crossed, on her bedroom floor, leaning in toward a book or screen, her shifting eyes skeptical, demanding, intent, concentrating so hard she almost vibrated. When I imagined her imagining me, I saw myself working on the novel I'd abandoned, which made me feel as though her correspondent wasn't me but a version of myself from the recent past, a version who not only still wrote novels but who also was still in love with Ashwini, and this lent an undercurrent of illicitness to our innocent-seeming emails. But the flashes of guilt I felt from time to time only fed a larger excitement. I was a little suspicious of this feeling, but more than that I was interested to see what would happen.

The evening of our walk through the wilds of Des Moines, Sadie attended the Art Center fundraiser that was the reason she'd flown in. Next day she went on a series of "friend dates," and I felt much more strongly than usual like an intruder in someone else's house. I sat for a long time on the living-room floor, reading and rereading a single paragraph from Berryman's posthumous novel *Recovery,* force-feeding meaning to the starving sentences, trying to leave myself behind, if just for a moment. But the walls pressed in on me, the carpet itched, shadowy forms peered in from the windows, and finally I closed the book and went to watch late-afternoon ESPN. There was a new episode of *The Bachelor* that evening, and I was hoping Sadie wouldn't return till it was over.

Eight o'clock came and she was still out, and, relieved, I changed the channel to ABC. The show had barely started when I heard the moan of the garage door. I waited a few seconds, debating what to do, then clicked to the beginning of the Bulls-Magic game I'd been planning to watch during commercial breaks. But this was the week of the *dreaded two-on-one date,* and the scene was about to shift to Las Vegas (a city full of wedding chapels, noted Alli, an Ohio apparel merchant), and the bachelorettes were staying in *the most beautiful hotel ever;* how could I abandon them now? The host was right: it was time to go big or go home. I pressed the PRE CH button. "We are in Las Vegas," announced the Bachelor. "They're happy. I'm happy. Fresh beginnings. Viva Las Vegas."

"This show still exists?" Sadie asked, walking into the room.

"It does!" I said superfluously, and she sat down in her sleeveless, dark purple dress on the opposite end of the couch from me, her dark-lipsticked mouth a little parted, her eyes fastened—the cliché felt true—to the TV screen. The Bachelor was delivering a date card to the bachelorettes in their high-ceilinged enormous-windowed suite in a Vegas skyscraper. Marissa: "The second the date card hits the table, it's very real." I watched through Sadie's eyes as the date card hit the table. She couldn't have known to be surprised that the date went to Shawntel, a mortician from Chico, California. Shawntel had no idea what the Bachelor had planned. The Bachelor couldn't wait to tell her. They were going on a SHOPPING SPREE. Delirium. Tears. And not at like the Chico mall or whatever: at one of *the* nicest malls in the world. The other girls were literally *dying* of envy. It was every woman's dream to go from store to store and pick out every single thing she wanted. But Shawntel was the only one who got to live that dream.

The date was amazing. Shawntel cleaned house. And she and the Bachelor felt so *natural* together. "This is a *real* feeling, this is *real* love," she said. When she got back she passed around a $5,000 handbag for the rest of the girls to look at and touch. Shawntel was *so* living every girl's dream. Michelle pretended to hang herself with her scarf. "It's like the perfect *Pretty Woman* moment that every girl dreams about," said Ashley.

"Why do they keep saying that!" Sadie said as the show went to commercial. "It is *not* this girl's dream to go *shopping* in Las *Vegas.* Actually that sounds like a nightmare." I nodded. "This show is awful, awful, awful," she said. "It's pernicious. It's really evil. How can you watch this?"

It was upsetting to hear such a vicious appraisal of something I had grown to love. "I guess I just really want to know who wins," I said, but that sounded unconvincing even to me (though it wasn't false), and immediately I added, "It *is* awful. Of course it's awful. It commodifies love and demeans women—"

"It demeans *everyone.*"

"It demeans everyone, you're right. I mean—of course. And it's cynical and trashy—"

"And heteronormative."

"And heteronormative and exploitative and of course, of course. But"—I wasn't sure what my counterpoint would be—"the thing about it is these are *real* people, they're not actors, and I really think they start to develop—some of them—actual emotions toward the Bachelor, and vice versa. And yeah, those emotions get confused with the emotions that come from being on TV and living in this world full of pools and helicopters, but I actually think that some of the women might be falling in love. I really do. In some actually meaningful sense of the word *love.* And whatever you think of these people, how they talk and act and their jobs and clothes and priorities or whatever—I don't know! It's hard not to feel some empathy for them. Because all they want is to be happy, right? And everyone deserves to be happy, don't they? The pressures they're feeling to find a romantic partner—aren't those only magnified versions of the pressures we all feel?"

"You're telling me it's not all scripted."

"Only in the sense that all these people are repeating things they've heard on previous seasons of the show. I mean, I assume—this is the first season I've watched. Also things they've heard on TV and in movies or whatever. But I'm ninety percent sure the producers aren't feeding them lines. Maybe once in a while, but usually not, I think."

"I just find it hard to believe that anyone believes they'll find love on a reality TV show."

"They *don't* at first! That's part of what's so compelling! They're all as skeptical as we are until they start feeling these real feelings!" I was all worked up. This was the first time I'd been asked to articulate my interest in *The Bachelor,* and I hadn't realized I felt quite so strongly about it. Maybe I didn't until this moment. I could tell from Sadie's face that I hadn't convinced her of anything, but when the show returned from commercial she didn't leave the room, and after a few minutes she half-reclined on the couch and covered her bare legs with a blanket.

On the second part of Shawntel's one-on-one, she and the Bachelor sat down to dinner on the roof of the mall they'd just finished eviscerating. Shawntel wore a gray sleeveless dress from her shopping spree. She looked incredible. She felt like a princess. The Chardonnay became champagne. It was a perfect night.

"She's going to win," Sadie said. "She's hot, and she's not

stupid, and they have a physical connection." A wave of relief passed through me: Sadie was *in*.

"Maybe." I hadn't been thinking of Shawntel as one of the favorites, but I had to admit she had a pretty solid date. "Let's see what happens the rest of this episode."

If the one-on-one enacted every girl's dream, the group date enacted every guy's: to drive a NASCAR race car on an actual NASCAR track. "Oh no," I involuntarily said as soon as the date's premise was announced.

"What?" said Sadie, and I told her Emily's story—Ricky, the engagement, the plane crash, little Ricki. "Oh my god," said Sadie, "how can they *do* this to her? It's so cruel."

Apparently Emily hadn't told the Bachelor yet that Ricky had been a race car driver—I'd thought she had, but maybe she only told the TV audience—so when the Bachelor saw her on the verge of tears he didn't understand what was wrong. He asked the other women if they'd mind if he took Emily aside for a moment. On the one hand, yes, they definitely did mind, but on the other hand this was yet more evidence of his sensitivity and kindness and compassion and real husband potential. They watched as he and Emily sat down on the infield lawn, the grass glowing weirdly bright in the spotlights. It was windy and Emily kept brushing strands of her bright blond hair behind her ear. ("She's actually very pretty," Sadie said.) When she told him Ricky had been a race car driver, the Bachelor didn't know what to say. He looked away. Emily picked at the grass. Finally he said, "I feel like a jerk." She didn't want him to feel like a jerk. "Em, I *care* for you," he said, jaw clenched. ("He's so earnest!" Sadie said.) "A lot. And I want you to know that." (Sadie: "He's insane. I think he's insane.")

The way he reacted to her revelation made Emily think of

him in an even better light: he was *there* for her, she saw that now. He made her feel really good about herself. (Sadie: "They're *enthralled* by him. They really *do* love him.") She knew she didn't have to but she climbed into the race car. She cried a little. The first few laps were for Joseph Riddick IV and the last lap was for herself.

During the commercial break, Sadie poured us each a glass of wine. "Who *is* this guy anyway?" she asked as she handed me mine.

I told her what I knew, that he was from Austin, that this was his second appearance on *The Bachelor,* that his father hadn't been there for him when he was a kid and that that's what made it hard for the Bachelor to open up.

"And this show is supposed to make that *easier*?"

"This show is all about opening up."

"Has he considered therapy? SSRIs?"

"I don't know about the drugs but he's seeing a therapist. Thomas Parker. He appears on the show once in a while."

"How *modern,*" Sadie said.

The commercial break ended and the pool party began. The Bachelor and Emily continued their conversation, sitting on chaises longues at the edge of the pool. The Bachelor looked newly troubled; he was quiet. He didn't know what to say, he said. "What are you feeling?" Emily asked. His hard eyes bored a hole through the silence. His brow had assumed its characteristic furrow. (Sadic: "He looks like a leader of a cult.") "Em," he finally said, "I'm feeling like I like you a lot. It's really tough for me to sit here and have feelings beginning to develop if, ah—ooh, I need to be careful of what I say." "No you don't. *I'm* not." (Sadie laughed.) Okay then, he needed to say something about Ricky: "That's a hard, hard, hard space for any man to fill."

Emily looked down, nodded, bit her lip. "In that moment," she'd say later, "I just felt like: Great. Another one runnin' for the hills." She'd seen it unfold a million times before. Guys pulling away after they learn about her past. Feeling like it's just too much to handle. (Sadie: "God, that's really sad.") She told the Bachelor she was ready for her past to stop mattering, for it not to be an issue in her life anymore.

"That's really sad," Sadie repeated during the next commercial break. "It's like—I don't know, it feels almost tragic. Like Sophocles-level tragic."

"I know!"

"It's really a *dark* show."

"It really is."

"I think there's something dark at the heart of that man. He's got this almost monomaniacal look."

"He takes his role very seriously," I said.

Then Sadie asked a question that had never occurred to me: "What's his job?"

"I mean—he's the Bachelor." She took it as a joke.

After the two-on-one date had concluded—Other Ashley beat out Ashley, who wept and regretted not opening up sooner—Sadie turned to me and said, "That was the most extraordinary thing I've ever seen." Her mascara was smudged; I hadn't noticed it before, but I also hadn't looked her in the eye till now. She asked a few more questions about the show and I answered them to the best of my knowledge. Then she said in a serious voice: "They should make a *Bachelor* with people like us." What kind of people were we?

Next morning I drove her to Des Moines International. When we got to the terminal she thanked me for taking care of her house—nothing there really needed taking care of—and told me not to worry about the rent anymore. "You're an artist," she said, to which I strenuously objected. "Fine," she said, "then you're a friend," which I was surprised to find felt true. As we hugged goodbye she said, "See you in a couple weeks." I hadn't realized she'd be returning so soon. She headed with her suitcase toward the revolving door. "We'll watch *The Bachelor* again!" she called over her shoulder.

6

AS THE WEEKS PROGRESS AND THEIR COMPETITION thins, the bachelorettes start to feel enormous pressure to say, "I'm falling in love with you." It signals to the Bachelor that they're here for the right reasons, plus it's one of the easiest ways available to them of ratcheting up the intensity of their connection. It's never "I love you," always "I'm falling in love with you," a little less definitive. *I'm not there yet, but I'm getting there.* Falling. *It's a journey.*

And what's crazy is that saying the words seems to make it happen, you can see it on the bachelorettes' faces, in the moment, the words seem attached to the feelings they name, pulling them up and into existence, changing everything: the words make the feelings real. Chantal, Shawntel, Emily, Other Ashley—I watched each start to fall in turn. And what does the Bachelor think about all these women professing their burgeoning love? Does he believe them? Yes. His gaze goes deep; it touches the souls of bachelorettes. He doesn't doubt the truth of their words for a second. But he also knows something they don't. By this point he's spent a significant portion of the middle of his adult life on *The Bachelor.* And he's seen what it does to people. He's felt it in himself. He knows how the show can make you feel what in the world outside you never would. He knows that cameras make things more real. He knows *The Bachelor* is a laboratory for synthesizing love from its two most basic elements, bodies and words. He believes the bachelorettes are falling in love, but he wonders if their love will survive the conditions—unreplicable, unrepeatable—of its birth. And it makes him sad to have to wonder this. It would make anyone sad.

So when Sadie said she saw a darkness at the heart of the Bachelor, I had no trouble understanding what she meant. I saw it next episode in the Bachelor's eyes, as he stood solemnly gazing this time not at a SoCal vista but at or through a waterfall somewhere deep in the rain forest (the action had shifted to Costa Rica), his purple-blue polo all the way unbuttoned, veins faintly visible on his forearms and neck, and I saw it especially as his gaze shifted downward, first to the waterfall's churning basin, then to the reddish, muddy ground, finally down to his shoes, his chest, the beating heart within. I heard the darkness, too, in his strangely flat voice, when, for example, later in the episode, he said to Chantal on a treetop platform at the end of the longest zip line in the world, "Can I tell you something? I have so much fun with you" (clearly he was having no fun at all). And it was there in his mute nod, on the dismal group date, in response to Emily's inexplicable confession that she tended to "sabotage" her relationships. Well then.

But where Sadie saw "monomania," I saw sadness and fatigue and frustration, signs of a struggle to hold himself together, as if beneath his otherworldly physique throbbed an inchoate violence. The Bachelor had come on the show with pure intentions—to fall in love, to *find somebody.* No one who had watched the entire season could doubt that he was here for the rightest reasons. But his conviction that he *would* fall in love, I sensed, had always been tied to the felt imperative that he *must,* that he *couldn't afford not to* fall in love. He couldn't allow a repeat of his first season's failure: it would spoil this season's redemption story line, not to mention leaving him just as alone as when the show began. And that was the Bachelor's greatest fear: *ending up alone.*

Six weeks in, there were eight women left. That he preferred some over others was obvious. But—because this was how the show worked, because ABC needed twelve two-hour episodes—he had to go through the motions of weighing the virtues of all these women he didn't care about. He had to fake it. And faking it was exactly what he'd come on the show determined more than anything *not* to do, hyperaware as he must have been of the general suspicion that the *entire show* was fake, maybe even occasionally suspecting it himself. It would blacken anyone's mood to be forced to spend a day exploring a cave with someone you've mentally dumped, then listen to her gush about you over a moonlit chicken dinner before you were allowed to dismiss her from your life. You might start to experience the show you were starring in less as an opportunity than as a trap. You might remember similar feelings from your previous season on the show. You might start to wonder, in the predawn light, why you signed up for it all again.

I sat, I read, I looked out windows, I ran through the streets of the city of my youth, I watched my Bulls, I watched my Bachelor, I wrote Maria and she wrote me. I started eating balanced meals. I shoveled my neighbors' driveways and sidewalks. Now that I was reading the *Register* every day, I felt a renewed connection with my hometown. I slept well. When I dreamt it was often dreams of flight. (In the only dream from that winter I remember in any detail, because I wrote it down right after I woke up, I was walking through what seemed to be Lawnwood Park—though it was much larger than Lawnwood Park, it expanded beyond the horizon in all directions—when a big bird flew over me and dropped something and I caught it. When I awoke, I didn't remember what it was—maybe I hadn't known in my dream—only that catching it was the most important thing that had ever happened or would ever happen to me.) A fissure had opened up in my life, but now I felt myself starting to regain a feeling of—not quite continuity, but unseveredness. I was returning to myself, or leaving myself behind. I think I was starting to feel at home.

For me, the opposite, Maria wrote. She didn't know how much longer she could stay in her house. Sam and Jo were getting worse. This morning they'd woken her up at five-fifteen, yelling at each other about root vegetables. Maria put in earplugs—she had finally bought earplugs—but she couldn't sleep with them in, so she read. She'd recently started a memoir about a man's obsession with a pair of peregrine falcons. At the time the book was written—the 1960s—it seemed likely that peregrines would go extinct, largely due to massive-scale DDT poisoning and other effects of the agrochemical revolution; and the book, Maria wrote, had something of the feel of a fierce and ecstatic elegy. The author was a mysterious figure. He apparently lived his entire life in the same small town. He married, but had no children. Did he have friends? He worked either as a librarian or as a manager for the Automobile Association—or possibly for a fruit juice manufacturer, no one was sure—and spent his spare time cycling through the countryside and translating it into crystalline prose. No one knew when he died, or how, Maria wrote.

She read for several hours, took a shower, and walked to the Institute of Arts, something she often did late mornings, to look at, along with a few other works, Diego Rivera's Detroit Industry Murals. She'd always been strangely comforted by the murals—their clean lines and symmetry and their mysterious integration of human and cosmic scales—but now their depiction of autoworkers on an assembly line, which had always struck her as joyful and ennobling, a celebration of human ingenuity and accomplishment, took on a disturbing, sinister aspect, becoming a prophecy of the city's imminent decline, which stood in for civilization's. What she found especially haunting, she wrote, was the downturned gazes of the autoworkers, each intent on his own assigned task, unaware of the gleaming machines that towered menacingly on all sides—that and the giant fetus encased in the bulb of a sprouting plant, which instead of symbolizing fertility and life seemed to be cowering from it.

As she made her way to another room, she heard someone calling her name, and turned around, and standing there was her first boyfriend, Roger. She'd dated him for two years in high school and hadn't seen him in a decade. He looked exactly the same, she wrote. He was almost thirty but looked eighteen. They hugged, and she asked him how long he'd lived in Detroit, and he said he didn't live in Detroit, he lived with his "beautiful wife" in New York City, if she could believe it, he was only visiting for a few days, to attend a conference on aquafarming. He was looking to get into aquafarming, he said, did she know what aquafarming was? So we talked for a while about aquafarming, Maria wrote, and made plans to meet up for dinner that evening, which ended up being at the same sushi restaurant I took you to when you were in town.

Well, she continued, I felt very, very weird. I was sleep-deprived and still unsettled by the murals and sitting there with this person who for two years of my life had been closer to me than anyone else in the world and now was a total stranger. And at first it was interesting, it was sort of exciting, to talk with this apparition. We gave versions of the stories of our adult lives, but I could tell he wasn't really listening to mine, he was way more interested in telling his. So I listened as he told me how after college—he'd majored in political science at Princeton—he enrolled in the Peace Corps in Tanzania, which is where he met his wife, an Australian, one of those perennial Australian tourists. He'd always enjoyed telling me, when we were dating, that he wanted to dedicate his life to helping "the less fortunate," but his wife convinced him the best way he could do that was to go to business school, where he discovered he had a talent for algorithms or bullshitting or whatever, and before he knew it he was working for Lehman Brothers and living on Park Avenue. And from this point forward, Maria wrote, it was like he was reading from a script: the job, at first exciting, became soul crushing; likewise the money; the marriage became a functional arrangement at best; and the past two years he'd spent in secret torment, daydreaming of ways to start over. The undercurrent running beneath it all was that *he* wasn't to blame for his unhappiness: his wife was. He was a casualty, a victim. His wife didn't even know he was in Detroit, she thought he was at a meeting in Amsterdam, because he knew if he told her about his plans they would immediately seem ridiculous. And so they are, Maria thought as she nodded in fake empathy and polished off her second California roll.

He was obviously hoping I'd invite him to my house, but I ordered him a cab and practically pushed him inside (he was pretty drunk) and walked back home feeling as though I were moving through a nightmare, Maria continued. And the first thing I see when I get back is a note—a letter really—on the kitchen whiteboard, signed Jo, concerning waste separation. Our house adheres to a byzantine system of trash, recycling, and compost, Maria explained, and apparently (so Jo alleged in her note) *someone* had gotten lazy: plastic bags did *not* go where crunchy plastic went, and crunchy plastic did *not* go where carton plastic went, *none* of which, it went without saying, went where glass or cardboard went. Plastic *caps* were acceptable if attached to their containers. Metal caps went with the rest of the metal. Next to her note Jo had thumbtacked several incorrectly sorted specimens, labeled with sticky notes.

It's hard to explain what happened next, Maria wrote. I felt a sort of outrage that was also a performance of outrage, which was actually pretty enjoyable. And before I knew quite what was happening, what I was doing, I was carrying the compost and trash receptacles upstairs, then dumping their contents on the stairway that led to the bedroom shared by Sam and Jo. I'd never done anything like that in my life! Of course Sam and Jo were furious, but I felt sort of great. In fact fantastic. The only thing is that now it's generally agreed that I need to leave this house. Any ideas for a place to live, even if only short-term?

I went for a run to see if when I came back Maria's email seemed less like an invitation for me to invite her to live with me in Des Moines. In spite of the intensification of our correspondence, the idea disturbed me a little: that she would want to live with me didn't fit with my conception of her as defiantly independent. At least as strong as this concern, though, was excitement at the prospect of living with her, which by the time I got back from my run I was certain she had suggested. Then again, did I want to live with anyone? I was coming to enjoy my solitude, my space; I wasn't sure this era of my life, the post–Ashwini Era, had run its course. (The couple of times Ashwini and I had talked, we'd managed to avoid discussing our status, but our relative silence for a month and a half said more than either of us could on the phone.) More than this, I didn't trust my desire, was maybe a little afraid of it. No doubt a part of me didn't want to risk the pain I would feel if things didn't work out.

I rewatched episode six of *The Bachelor,* walked the route I had just run, showered, made and ate an enormous salad, wrote an email to my parents ("Things are good . . ."), read a few articles from the day's *Register*—"SUV plows through house, kills woman," "Tree-killing gypsy moth spreads at rapid pace," "Iowa soldier loses portion of leg," "Meatless days bedevil producers." The commodity price spike appeared to be general. A tank full of anhydrous ammonia was leaking. Detroit was nine hours from Des Moines by car, an hour and a half by plane. I had two options. One, I could invite Maria to Des Moines. Two, I could not invite Maria to Des Moines. But within those options were innumerable sub-options. I could invite her with disarming boldness ("Why don't you come live with me in Des Moines for a while?"), maybe even phrasing my invitation as a demand ("Come to Des Moines," or even "Come here"); I could invite her in an ambiguously jokey way ("They say Des Moines is the next Detroit!"); I could hint at an invitation without actually inviting her; I could prod: "Are you inviting yourself to Des Moines?" No option felt right, or each did then didn't.

An unexpected text presented a solution. It was from Jess, inviting me to a concert the following evening in Ames. She had an extra ticket, she said, and it would be great to finally see me again. We'd texted a bit since our evening out, but I'd ignored her Facebook friend request and the few times she'd suggested we meet up again I'd always claimed I had prior commitments. If I was a little afraid of falling for Maria, I think I was also a little afraid of Jess coming between me and her. I'd never dated more than one woman at a time and doubted my emotional capacity for it. Plus, ever since I'd told Maria about Jess, whom I hadn't told about Maria, Jess had come to seem less and less like a person than a minor character in our story. Now, though, I devised a plan that would require Jess's presence, her reality: I would go with her to the concert; we would dance; afterward, if the night had gone well, we would kiss (*up for anything*), maybe more; and if after that I still felt an urge to invite Maria to Des Moines, I'd do it; if not, I wouldn't mention the possibility and we'd continue pretending our correspondence wasn't a courtship. It was not a well-thought-out plan, but it was a plan, and it felt good to have one.

P.S., Maria wrote, Sam and Jo are engaged. Don't know when that happened. No one told me!

Next day, insane with optimism or lust, I decided to set forth and apply for jobs. I drove to Jordan Creek Mall and walked around for two hours collecting applications, and then, to congratulate myself on the effort, bought an M&M cookie from

Panera. I sat and ate it near a big gas fireplace, listening to adult contemporary music blend with echoey conversation, and everything looked airbrushed and glazed in honey and I felt an incipient dizziness behind my eyes, and I shoved the rest of the cookie into my mouth and tossed the applications in a wastebasket by the entrance and fled past the two great Republican heroes and drove down the interstate back to the city. On impulse, I followed signs for the Botanical Center, a geodesic dome on the east bank of the Des Moines River filled with tropical plants and birds.

As a kid, I'd loved coming here, a world within a world, immersive, the air redolent with strange vegetation and so thick you felt you were underwater; and now, on a February morning in my young adulthood, I found myself, amazed, back in that world, which, as if for my sole benefit, had been perfectly preserved. I don't know how long I wandered among the cacti and palms, the banana and olive and coffee and fig trees, the waterfalls and ponds stocked with ornamental fish, pausing once in a while to look up at tessellated triangles of cloud and sky, but I do remember lingering for a long time in the bonsai room, staring at those stunted trees (cedar, elm, sycamore, pine) until they became not stunted but distant—normal-sized trees viewed from high above—and I saw myself sitting reclined against their trunks, looking up at their sun-shot, translucent leaves, so that when, later that afternoon, as I walked down the path along the river behind my house, I had the sensation of watching myself move through a miniaturized, enclosed, and enchanted world. Thin snow fell like sprinkles of light. Snow tufts shooting up from the ground became birds. The hawk perched in the tree across the river became an eagle, then a peregrine, then a plane. The forest I'd avoided all my life, out of a combination of ignorance and fear, was in fact a sanctuary for all that entered—protecting not only space but time—whose center was me as I moved through it. It contained all the scenes of my past and future, and I knew that when I died those scenes would still be there, giving form to the river, the trees, the shrubs, and the animals they sheltered. The thought of a squirrel became a squirrel. I was the creator of all I saw, step by step, view by view. From outside the dome I sized myself up: I looked *good,* resplendent with anonymity and readiness, and perhaps also love.

That evening, I watched from the living-room windows as Jess pulled her grandmother's station wagon into the driveway. As I walked toward it I was a little crushed to see two other women inside—friends of Jess's, I was told as I climbed in: Stephanie and Amanda. "Here he is!" the one in the passenger seat said. "Here I am!" I said, trying to mask my disappointment as Jess pulled out of the driveway at alarming speed. They were all wearing dresses or skirts; their makeup was prominent; I realized I didn't know what kind of concert we were going to and I worried I was underdressed in my jeans and button-down, my old mittens and plaid wool scarf.

The half-hour drive up I-35 was mostly taken up by Jess and her friends recounting—not for the first time, I gathered—the details of Amanda's recent breakup. She kept saying she was worried she would never find anyone else, what she needed from a guy was too specific, too strange, and somewhere in my impatience with that sentiment was the thought *I am the oldest person in the car.* Still, a part of me enjoyed the conversation, which was full of coded phrases and intonations indicating the warmth that comes from a shared history. After listening for some time in silence, I chimed in: "Amanda. I know we met like ten minutes ago, but it's obvious to me already that you deserve way, way better than this chump." Everyone laughed, and after that, the three friends made more of an effort to include me.

The concert was in a hockey arena on the Iowa State campus. By the time we entered, it had already begun: three or four thousand standing fans packed tight toward the flashing, hazy stage on which two men paced deliberately, rhythmically, to an accompaniment of a heavy, programmed hip-hop beat. Jess and her friends discovered or created openings I hadn't seen and led me through the crowd till we were halfway to the front. By that time the two men had started rapping, but the words were drowned out by the crowd noise and the beat, whose bass I could feel in different parts of my body, sometimes in my collarbone, sometimes in my stomach, once in a while in the region of my heart, as though my internal rhythms had been hijacked by the music or else were in control of it.

Everyone around me was bouncing or bobbing; most people held one hand in the air. Through the forest of arms I watched the two men half-walk, half-dance back and forth across the stage. One of them was much, much smaller than the other, but I couldn't tell if that was because he was small or because his partner was extraordinarily large. The big one was the main one, I soon understood: he did all the rapping, or almost all, while the little one chimed in only once in a while, either to give emphasis to a word or phrase or to help enact a brief call-and-response. The men were dressed almost identically in old-school Lakers jerseys—Magic for the big one, Worthy for the small—black sweatpants, dark sunglasses, thick gold chains, and knee-high neon green boots or slippers that looked like they were made from mammoth fur. Most of the time they seemed to be doing more or less their own thing—in addition to the slow-mo rhythmic walk-dancing, lots of bouncing, pointing and fist pumping, punctuated by occasional crouching, rocking, spinning, swaying, air-smoothing, and pulsating—but every minute or two their movements synced up for a few seconds in such a way that it seemed coincidental, though it couldn't have been, and often in these moments the beat would change or drop out, and everyone would cheer, including me, because it was amazing. Jess and her friends had started bobbing the moment we arrived, and at some point I realized my body was bobbing, too. "Throw your hands in the air," the men called out, but everyone already had their hands in the air; we were testifying to their amazingness; we were volunteering to be taken with them.

Other people in the crowd were continually brushing against me, so it took a moment before I realized someone was nudging me in the ribs: Amanda, not so much offering me a pipe as placing it in my unraised hand. I hadn't smoked pot for over a year: half the time it made me pleasantly sleepy, the other half like my heart would explode through every vein and artery in my body. But by this point I wasn't really myself, I'd been absorbed into the music and mass of bodies, so when I took three long, deep tokes from the pipe it felt like an action outside my control. The high was almost immediate, and so intense; it threw me back onto myself. I didn't like it. The music had receded into the background, as if it were coming from another room. The rest of the audience had disappeared. My eyes searched frantically for something to attach to. The last thing I remember seeing before I lost my vision was two big men in black T-shirts onstage, standing behind or in front of the rappers, arms folded, glaring directly at me. Then my legs stopped working and I was down. That felt nice. I could relax on the floor for a while. The music became audible again down here: so *that's* where it had gone. Then it occurred to me that it wasn't right that I could hear and think when I couldn't see or move, and in the same moment I heard voices near me saying, "Oh shit oh shit," and "He fell asleep!" "Don't worry," I said, "it's okay, I feel fine," but no one answered so maybe I hadn't said it. Then I felt me being lifted by the arms, which were attached to my torso by rubber bands, and those arms being draped around two sets of shoulders, and I couldn't really feel myself being dragged out of the arena but I could hear male voices saying, "Oh shit oh shit," and female voices saying, "He's fine. He's going to be fine." Then the music had receded again and sometime later a change in temperature or air pressure told me we'd made it outside the building.

I was sitting on the ground, propped up against a wall. Someone was rubbing my arm and shoulder saying, "You're going to be all right," in Jess's voice. "I *am* all right," I tried to say. Somewhere nearby a group of voices were debating whether to take me to the hospital. This went on for a few minutes or hours. Then I heard myself moaning or laughing, and everything came back at once—vision, mobility, speech, volition—and I said, "I'm ready to go back inside now." Everyone laughed, so I did. "Jesus Christ, man, you scared us." Who was *this* dude? "Go fuck yourself," I said, and everyone laughed more.

Back inside, the concert was still going. We stood in the back where there was more space, more air. It felt wrong to just bob or bounce back here, so we started dancing and wow! Wow. I'd forgotten what a fantastic dancer I was. Everyone was smiling and laughing in circles. Fragments broke off from the main crowd to join us, until the room was centered on me. I took turns dancing with my new friends, then with strangers, until all the strangers had become my friends. The concert ended; everyone cheered; the rappers disappeared; we kept cheering, we refused to stop; the rappers returned and the concert began again.

They launched into a cover of "Sexual Healing" and everyone went nuts. Jess started dancing with me or vice versa and as we danced we couldn't stop smiling and laughing. Our bodies drew closer of their own accord. I leaned in to kiss her and she laughed and shook her head and said something I couldn't hear. I laughed. We danced together for the rest of the song before dissolving back into a larger group. The duo did a few more songs, we cheered, and the concert ended again, this time for good.

The car moved south on I-35, holding its shape against the limitless night. The imagined cold of invisible farmland made the car warmer, or made its warmth closer. I felt charged. It was a perfect night. There were five of us now: some guy with glasses had joined us; he was sitting up front with Jess, while I sat in back with Stephanie and Amanda. I was in a state—new to me—in which there was more pleasure in wanting than there ever could have been in having. I *had wanting.* Amanda sat next to me, in the middle seat, lovely. She'd find someone new to fall in love with soon. Meantime she had the consolation of riding in cars with beautiful friends. In my mind I wished the man with glasses and Jess a happy life together. "He's a writer," I heard her telling him, and he turned to me and asked what I was working on. As I heard myself summarizing my grandfather's memoirs—his five wives, his many reputed mistresses, his mistreatment of and eventual estrangement from my mother, his just missing out on World War II, his aimless drifting around the world—I found myself, to my surprise, feeling almost sorry for him. I talked about his childhood and adolescence, the beginning of his obsession with flight. The Great War, which ended a few years before his birth, had made pilots the heroes of his generation. He read the pulp magazine *G-8 and His Battle Aces,* about an American fighter pilot flying missions in France. The newspapers told of the intercontinental adventures of Charles Lindbergh, Amelia Earhart, Howard Hughes, Billy Mitchell; my grandfather built wooden models of their planes. Saturday mornings, he and a group of friends would pack food and fill their Boy Scout canteens and ride their bikes through the St. Paul suburbs to the airport, where they lay on their backs on a grassy hill and watched navy biplanes landing and taking off, passing so close, if the wind was right, they could see streaks of grease and oil on the cowlings, flames shooting out from the exhaust. The day he turned fifteen he joined the Civil Air Patrol cadet program. His first flight was on a gray day in fall. As he sat behind his instructor in a high-wing Aeronca, the noise of the engine coming to life seemed to engulf him physically, mingling with smells of hot oil, leather, hydraulic fluid, rubber, and burnt plastic. Then the plane was rattling down the runway. He was sure it would fall apart. The moment of its losing contact with land was impossible to isolate.

The *bodilessness* of flight—he was a breath, or a shout, an exultation issuing from the earth itself. It was a feeling he knew only from reading and dreams. Contracting patterns of brown, gray, and gold spread themselves out beneath the plane. The world is enormous. He'd never seen it before. Horizon opening onto horizon. The cities he'd mistaken for the center of the universe proved to be transient and fortuitous settlements, temporary deformations of the landscape. Everywhere the artificial blurred into the natural. Everything is connected to everything else. The instructor made a series of gentle turns, and my grandfather leaned away from them, trying to keep his torso vertical to the ground. Then he relaxed and let his body move with the plane, the horizon tipping up and settling back, tipping up and settling back. The plane was setting the world in motion: the plane was flying the world.

The sky is dark and hazy now, and lights flick on in houses and farms, and shadows creep like a flood over the earth, which slowly expands as the light leaves it, a second sky. The plane, though, flies on in sunlight, as if it's absorbed the fallen sun's rays to release them now in a gentle phosphorescence, visible, he imagines, from a long way off.

7

JESS DROPPED ME OFF IN THE EARLY-MORNING DARK, and after she and her friends drove away I lingered for a moment in the yard. The sky was clear. The night was alive with signs and stars. I went inside and heard music playing, a memory of the concert, I thought at first, but it turned out to be coming from my laptop—New Order—must have been playing the entire time I was gone. In another world, beauty's existence doesn't depend on its apprehension. Tears in my eyes, I turned up the music and wrote an email to Maria in which I recounted the evening and invited her to stay with me and told her I was falling in love with her. Then I ordered *Contemporary Finnish Poetry* and accepted Jess's Facebook request and looked at photos of her and her friends—Amanda seemed really into horses and shots—then photos of friends and exes and acquaintances, and their friends and partners and children and pets, maybe I should get a dog, and I spent a long time scrolling through photos on petfinder.com, started filling out an application for Mason, a border collie / Lab mix puppy, ostensibly, but no, before I could get a dog I needed a home, or at least a job.

Dawn came, I went for a run, showered, ate breakfast, and went to bed. But I couldn't sleep, my body craved movement, so I went for a drive at very low speed through the hushed streets of northwest Des Moines. No one was out. On the radio a man with a slight southern accent was telling a story about basketball. It was 1994 and he was playing in a Houston church league. He drove the lane and went up for a layup and heard not just through his ears but his whole body a sound like a drawer slamming shut. Bam! Everything went black. Time stopped. And he thought, *Hmm, that's a weird, funny sound.* And then the pain. It felt like something had snapped behind his kneecap. He couldn't walk. He had to shuffle around backwards on one leg, dragging his lame leg along the ground.

Next day he went to an orthopedic surgeon. "You tore your patellar tendon," said the doctor. "It's not good." The man didn't need some doctor to tell him that! "You need to have surgery right away," said the doctor. And the man said, "Gee, Doctor, I appreciate your opinion, but I've got this very important trip next week, and I won it in a raffle and it's all expenses paid, South Carolina," and hem and haw and this and that, and "Doctor, can't I go on this trip and *then* come back and have the surgery?" And the doctor said, "No, you can't. I'm sorry. You need to have surgery as soon as possible. If you wait, the tendon will shrivel up and I won't be able to put it back together." That's what he said. And I said, "Doctor, is this gonna hurt?" And the doctor said, "You bet!"

And it did. It hurt like hell. But you know what? I was a *wounded man.* And I needed surgery so that I could be healed. Tear your patellar tendon, thing don't heal on its own! Gotta get somebody in there, tie it back together! Because fact is, if I'd gone ahead and left for South Carolina, I'd be walking backwards to this day.

I turned from Fortieth onto Madison and headed back toward Lower Beaver. Cars pulled out of driveways here and there. Black treetops pierced the yellow-blue sky. Now what I want to talk about today, said the man on the radio, is men who have experienced wounds. But he wasn't talking about physical wounds. No. He was talking about deeper wounds. Heart wounds. From childhood. Those real early, deep-down wounds. He was talking about Wounded Warriors.

A Wounded Warrior was a man who was wounded as a boy and carried that wound around with him as an adult. Maybe you're a Wounded Warrior. Maybe your best friend is. Your brother. Your cousin. Maybe you know how hard it is. Maybe you want to do the right thing for yourself. But it's not easy to be a Wounded Warrior who mans up and does the things he needs to do to heal those wounds of so many years ago, those deep-seated issues, those heart wounds.

Fortunately, there is good news. There is good news for the Wounded Warrior. And the news is that the Lord wants to help you heal that wound. Because the scripture says, "He heals the brokenhearted." Because he is Jehovah Rapha, the God who heals, the God who binds up wounds.

When a boy gets his heart hurt, and doesn't deal with it, as a man he's still kind of stuck in boyhood. He's in a man's body, but his heart is a boy's heart. And it might cause him to feel insecure. And it might cause him to feel inadequate. He can have problems with anger. With confusion. With understanding what a man really is. Because he's stuck. He's stuck hanging out with the guys and "Let's play video games," and not assuming responsibility. And he can become an irresponsible person. He might have a wife, might have kids, two cars, but it's just like he is stuck. He's stuck. Let me tell you: the Lord wants to bring healing to that. He wants to help these Wounded Warriors.

There is a wound that so many men suffer. Women, too, but so many men. This wound—let me tell you what this wound is. This wound is the Absent Father Wound. The dad who wasn't there when you were a kid. Maybe he wasn't physically there, or maybe he was there but he wasn't. He was absent. And he inflicted on you an Absent Father Wound.

Dad is destiny! Mark it down. Who determines whether you're going to be happy? Dad. Who determines whether you're going to be successful? Dad. Who determines whether you're going to be responsible and courageous and provide for your wife and children? Dad. Love him or loathe him, Dad is destiny.

Colossians, chapter 3, verse 21: "Fathers, do not provoke or irritate or fret your children. Do not be hard on them or harass them, lest they become discouraged and sullen and morose and feel inferior or frustrated. Do not break their spirit."

A father can break his son's spirit. The son might not even know it's happening. The wound might remain hidden for many years. But you grow up and you discover you're wary of love, wary of relationships, and you don't know why. You don't know why you're unhappy in your marriage. Or you're not married and you don't know why you can't find a wife, that one woman in all the universe who completes you and is your soul mate. You have an Absent Father Wound. And there's pain. And confusion. And anger. And you don't know what to do with those feelings. You don't know how to heal that wound.

So what do you do? You turn to alcohol. Drugs. You turn to sexual immorality and perversion. Because why? Because you're trying to dull the pain of this wound at the heart of your very being. You're the kid who tore his patellar tendon, and you never went to the doctor to get it fixed.

Or you went to the doctor, and he told you to get surgery, and instead you flew off to South Carolina.

And you've been walking backwards since that day.

I was in Sadie's garage now, the engine off, reclining in the driver's seat, on the verge of sleep. John, chapter five, tells an interesting story. I think you'll find it very interesting. Jesus was wandering around the desert, when one day he ran into a man who was crippled. Crippled for thirty-eight years, is what John tells us. Thirty-eight years is a long time. And Jesus asked him a very simple question—a very simple question, but not the one you might expect. Do you know what he asked him? I'll tell you. He asked him, "Do you want to get well?" Do you want to get well? That's a pretty good question. Do you want. To get well.

Do you?

Hey there, Wounded Warrior, I've got a question for you: Do you want to get well?

I did. I wanted to get well. I had started feeling unwell only in the past half hour or so, but now I felt overwhelmed by a mix of extreme fatigue and shame. I was ashamed because my plan had been stupid and self-serving, because I had sort of blacked out in a crowd of strangers, because I'd told that guy to go fuck himself, because I was a terrible dancer and underdressed and old and I'd tried to kiss Jess—Jess who was seven years younger than me and recovering from a bad relationship—and also because I had gone on and on about my abandoned novel, and because I wasn't religious or a war hero or a Wounded Warrior. I didn't have an Absent Father Wound, and yet I still suffered from insecurity, inadequacy, and confusion. Who to blame? As I shuffled upstairs and fell into bed, I resolved to call my parents more often, taking comfort in the resolution, doubting I would keep it.

I felt vague pride that I made it three days before concluding that Maria would never respond to my invitation. On the fourth day I read through our emails, the whole stack, searching for something solid and unequivocal, peering behind and between our words, tapping the sentences for cracks or dead spots. "I'm very excited about our correspondence!" she'd written. I doubted I'd find a definitive sign of her love, but I thought I might find one of my delusion. In the end my investigation clarified nothing. If it was easy to convince myself Maria hadn't been so much as flirting (she was restless and bored and estranged from her housemates, our emails provided nothing more than comfort and release, so we happened to like some of the same books—who cared?), it was almost as easy to convince myself she wanted to spend her life with me. "For me, just leaving off with a book is as painful as—I don't know, seriously a missed romantic opportunity." We'd mentioned so often how much we loved our correspondence; wasn't that a small step from loving each other? You could fall asleep in one state and wake up in the next. Roll over in the middle of the night without knowing it. Or you could pretend none of it ever happened, we never met, never reunited, never went out for sushi or shared a bed, you never sent me John Berryman's biography of Stephen Crane.

I drafted two emails to Maria. In the first, I apologized for my previous email, which I'd written in a moment when I wasn't quite myself, and asked if she'd consider renewing our correspondence on the terms we'd established over the previous weeks: as co-enthusiasts and collaborators, as confidants and friends. In the second, I doubled down on my declaration, refusing to apologize or take it back, challenging Maria in no uncertain terms to admit that she, too, was falling in love, and re-extending my invitation to Des Moines, where we could start a life together. Both emails languished in my "Drafts" folder, where they remain to this day. The truth was I didn't know if what bound me to Maria could accurately be characterized as "love." Either we loved each other or we didn't, but somehow I lacked access to the salient information. Maybe it was blocked by fear or confusion. Maybe Ashwini stood in its way. The best I could do under the circumstances, it seemed, was to remain open to both possibilities, to wait, to see if Maria would respond.

Objectively, I told myself, little had changed: Maria hadn't been there before, and she wasn't there now. I was alone. The largely abstract nature of our relationship made it easy to imagine it wasn't real, and I stuffed the stack of printed-out emails in a box in the basement with Sadie's son's old school assignments, along with the small library I'd amassed since arriving, which seemed part and parcel of our correspondence.

A new beginning. Thrown back into solitude and silence, I recommitted myself to ambivalence, anonymity, and openness to whatever might come. I was re-resetting my life. I went back to sitting, back to staring. And I felt . . . I felt fine, for a nonentity. Wind chimes chimed at the limit of hearing. Falling snow reveals the secret form of wind. The shadows of the mullions wavered if you watched them, but the windows never moved: they framed bare branches which framed the sky which framed the soft winter world which framed me. My mother emailed: When would Ashwini visit? Would I mind if she and Dad came down when she did (not for the whole time, of course:))? How was the old street, the old city? Was I bored yet? "Sadie said the two of you had a nice time together." She did? Dress socks worn too long with slippers become reptilian second skins. House sparrows spoke to each other somewhere close. My arm fell asleep then off in my mind. Laura had a new boyfriend.

"I do not."

"You do the things boyfriends and girlfriends do with each other."

"I didn't know there was a checklist."

"There is. Walk, watch things, eat, kiss. Those are the four things boyfriends and girlfriends do." I was pleased with the elegance of the formulation.

"Dan is *not* my boyfriend. I think I'd know."

"That's where you're wrong. Sometimes you don't know. Sometimes it happens when you aren't looking, and then bam! Marriage, children, death."

"Right. Hopefully in that order, I guess."

"It's like that Talking Heads song . . . how does it go?"

" 'Burnin' down the house'?"

"Exactly. Apt, isn't it?"

"Very. Dan is *not* my boyfriend."

Laura had met her boyfriend on Match.com. Apparently she'd been a member for two years but Dan was the first guy she'd gone on a date with. She'd rarely even visited the website, she said, so anxious was she about her photo, her profile, whether she'd chosen the most important qualities and accomplishments and enthusiasms to highlight. Plus she'd have to read through a million notes of interest from men who couldn't punctuate or spell. Among the many things she'd noted in her profile were that she liked to play tennis and didn't smoke, and for some reason the Match.com algorithm had determined that these were her two most essential characteristics: every man who contacted her put strange emphasis on the fact that he was a nonsmoking tennis player. "But in their profile photos they're wearing, like, Vikings jerseys or they have their hair slicked back or whatever. I mean, I shouldn't—I'm sure they're really nice guys. I'm sure I could, like, get a drink with them and it'd be fine." In any case she had no problem meeting men in real life, went on occasional dates without the help of the Internet, and had been with a handful of serious boyfriends in the years since we'd broken up. She believed, it seemed to me as we spoke, what all sensible romantics believed: that dating sites destroy the adventure of love by minimizing its elements of contingency and risk. She'd joined Match.com to appease her mother, and because she was curious, she said. "You should do it."

I wasn't sure if she was serious. "I'm okay, thanks."

"No, I mean it. When's the last time you went out with another person?"

I told Laura about my outings with Jess, feeling they stood in for my emails with Maria, which I hadn't mentioned to Laura or anyone else. They felt too personal, too dangerous, too dear. I didn't tell Laura about the quasi-blackout, nor the failed kiss attempt, nor that I'd resolved not to see Jess again, not that Jess would want to see me.

"Match dot-com could help you find women your own age," Laura said.

"Love knows no bounds."

"I disagree. Love knows bounds."

"No bounds."

"Some. One or two bounds, at least."

"Will Dan be your date at your sister's wedding?" The wedding was taking place in about a month and a half, in Grinnell, an hour from Des Moines. (Iowa was the only state in the Midwest in which her sister could marry legally.)

She did the laugh I love that's basically her saying, "Ha," then said she didn't plan on bringing a date.

"Why not?"

"Because if I brought a date I'd pretty much be telling my mother this was the man I planned to marry."

"You don't plan to marry Dan?"

"I met him three weeks ago."

"It's about time, then. You and your sister could do a dual wedding. Two birds."

"He doesn't read. He's not a reader."

"What about speech? Can he talk? Does he know the alphabet?"

"He seems to. Could be faking, though."

"Bipedal?"

"Most of the time."

"Whoa. Let's not go there. Does he make you laugh?"

"We've gotten drunk every time we've been together. You know what happens when I'm drunk."

She can't stop laughing. "Is he *comely*?" I don't remember when or how that became one of our words.

"Very. In a cyclist, skinny-frame, thick-thighs kind of way."

"Thick thighs, knows the alphabet, gets you drunk enough to laugh—marry this man, I say!"

She said she'd think about it.

I picked Sadie up from Des Moines International, and after her nap we set off walking on the same route we'd walked before, two weeks earlier, though this time it was slightly warmer, the clouds thin, the light both brighter and softer. In the woods by the river she pointed out invasives—garlic mustard, black locust, tree of heaven—and a little farther on we stopped to look for eagles, once again unsuccessfully. I hadn't walked this path since the afternoon before the concert, and everything was different now. Emptied of anticipations, I no longer occupied the center of the world. The scenery was pretty or not pretty in turn, but it was no longer *mine.* It was only scenery.

As we walked through marshland filled with dead reeds and foxtails that reflected silver-gold in the sun, Sadie, interrupting the thread of our conversation, asked if everything was okay.

"Excuse me?"

"You seem a little down."

I feigned surprise at her show of concern but actually I was grateful: I'd been hoping, almost expecting, I realized now, she'd give me a chance to open up to her. Instead of talking about Maria, though, whom I'd been unable to banish from my thoughts, or about Jess and our ill-fated night, I found myself talking about Ashwini. I told her about our sort-of-breakup and then, prompted by Sadie's questions, went back to the beginning. I talked about how for a long time I'd been too afraid of Ashwini to speak to her. Whenever I saw her at friends' apartments she'd come across as cynical, knowing, a little mean. I didn't want to be the object of her judgment. I worried that if she got to know me, sooner or later she'd sort me into a category of young New York writer to be mocked and dismissed (which I'm sure, I told Sadie, says a lot about my state of mind at the time).

Finally, though, we found ourselves sitting next to each other on a couch at a phone bank for Obama. After we'd done enough winning hearts and minds of voters in battleground states, we got to talking. At first she didn't deviate from my conception of her. She talked about how she expected Obama to win and for his presidency to be a disappointment, a slightly more palatable continuation of Bush-era policies and political realities. Nothing would fundamentally change, she said. In some ways, things would probably get worse. (Not that she had to worry too much about it: she could move back to Canada whenever she wanted.) But then something happened that changed her for me. The host of the gathering had made apple pie, and when Ashwini took a bite her face transformed completely. I don't think I've ever seen someone experience pleasure so fully, I told Sadie. She gave a little moan and after she'd finished chewing raved about the pie to our friend, gesticulating wildly. It was the first time I'd seen her excited—and she was more than excited, she was passionately absorbed—and the contrast between this side of her and the side of her I'd seen until that moment drew me in, made me want to get to know her.

After we started dating, I told Sadie, I saw this side of her all the time. Almost anything could bring it out, it seemed—a song, a person, a quality of light, a subway line, a smell, a commercial. I loved these moments when she lost herself in a sensation or enthusiasm. But I also grew to love the other side of her, the serious, critical side. She seemed unhappy but she also made it seem like unhappiness was the only sane response to the world, and anyway if life contained these, what, *treasures,* wasn't that enough?

"Why wasn't it?" Sadie asked.

"I'm getting there."

"I'm listening."

For a year or so things were great, I said. We moved in together after a few months of dating. During the day she walked dogs for money; most evenings I waited tables. When we were both home we often worked at our respective novels at tiny desks in opposite corners of our tiny bedroom. I'd never dated a writer before and it felt exciting, romantic. We were a *literary couple.* More than one friend told me it never worked out for writers to be in a relationship, and I took special pride—we both did—in proving those people wrong. That summer my novel was accepted to be published, and Ashwini won a big story prize, and we felt like we were on our way to something.

Then, the following spring—last May—my novel was published and Ashwini got a prestigious teaching job in Halifax. It would begin that fall. In retrospect, I told Sadie, that was when things started to sour. Ashwini asked me if I wanted to come with her to Halifax, and at first I hesitated, I had it in my mind that I should stay in the U.S. in the months following the release of my novel. Then the response to my novel seemed over, and I said I would follow her, but now *she* seemed hesitant, what would I do for work, what would I do when the six months I was allowed to be in Canada expired? Eventually we agreed we'd try to make it work.

"That's never a good sign—when you're 'trying to make it work.'"

"No. That's when you know it won't work, isn't it."

I summarized our time in Halifax in much the same way I had to Laura on the phone a couple of months earlier: Ashwini's withdrawal from me, her frustration, culminating in the thrown chair, the broken lamp; arguments that lasted deep into the night and left me with no energy to write. One night, exhausted and only half serious, I tried out the idea that maybe we should just be friends. "As if we'd be friends if we weren't dating," Ashwini said, and in the moment I thought she was right, we wouldn't be.

"How so?"

"We were different people. We didn't like the same things. I remember one night, we were walking around her campus and I was telling her about a walk I'd taken that morning. It was in this beautiful park at the tip of a peninsula—I actually fantasized about proposing to her there—and I remember wanting to tell her about some little thing I'd noticed, I don't remember what, and she said, 'The difference between you and me is that I like walking on busy streets and you like walking in parks.' She said it sort of playfully, flirtatiously even, but I think that's when I knew it was over, you know? And it wasn't even true! I do like walking in parks, yes, but I also like walking on busy streets!"

"What about totally empty streets? With your mom's friend?"

"That too!"

Up until now I had found myself unable to tell the full story of me and Ashwini—surely one of the crucial stories of my life—but walking through my childhood neighborhood with Sadie, it had come easily, prompted by her frequent questions, which felt at once brazen and circumspect, at once tender and vaguely rude.

"You said you fantasized about proposing to her," she said as we neared the end of the path. "Did you actually want to get married?"

"I did!"

"Why?"

It took me a few moments to formulate a response: I wanted to answer as honestly as I could. "I wanted to make Ashwini happy," I finally said. "I thought making her happy would make me happy." Ashwini wanted to get married—at some point—because her parents wanted her to. She wasn't romantic about it, but she cared. She wanted to make her parents happy. And her parents cared deeply that their only daughter, a first-generation Canadian, should display as many outward signs of success as possible. And this made sense to Ashwini. How else would her parents know if they had made the right decision to leave their home? How could you know? In any case, Ashwini had already rebelled against her parents by choosing writing over the more reliably remunerative professions, and her desire to marry may have been in part a desire to abide by at least *some* of her parents' wishes.

As for me, I told Sadie, I'd renounced marriage a long time ago. Of course as a kid I'd assumed I'd get married: my parents stayed together and I had no reason not to believe that marriage was something you ascended to by natural law. It wasn't until I was a teenager that it even occurred to me to question it, and when I did I rejected it wholesale. It was an empty convention, I decided, an insidious cultural expectation whose purpose was to reduce autonomous human beings to reproducers, to *providers,* whose loyalty to the family unit was a cover for the ultimate egotism. It was a lie. And it was an excuse for a couple to stop trying, since what was there to try for if you'd made it, if you'd arrived?

Only after being with Ashwini for a while did my hard stance on marriage begin to erode, and the moment that getting married became a possibility for me was impossible to locate, I told Sadie. What seemed to me to have happened now, though I wouldn't have put it like this at the time, was that marriage came to seem less and less like a lie, and more and more like a fiction. It wasn't real. And because it wasn't real you could make it whatever you wanted, you could write its story. It would provide a template for the story, but that template was there for the couple to alter in any way it saw fit, or to dismiss. And even in dismissing the template you were using it; it was serving a function. In this way the unreality of marriage became an opportunity to create a new reality, or perhaps to give form to a reality that already existed. Marriage, I came slowly to believe, was a sort of transformational vessel. Or at least benign.

"You circled back around," said Sadie.

"I circled back around."

After seeming to consider my account for a moment, Sadie said that the progress of my attitude toward marriage—from unthinking approval to fierce rejection to more considered and qualified approval—reminded her of the progress of my attitude toward Des Moines as I'd explained it two weeks earlier. Her reference to our previous walk sent a small but potent thrill through me. She was creating a continuity, which felt good to be a part of, as she surely understood. "That's one measure of growing up," she said, "isn't it? Coming to see that the things you thought were terrible may not actually be so bad."

"How would you know?" I accused. "You don't feel grown up." Now I, too, had done my part in establishing the continuity, and I was glad to see Sadie acknowledging my contribution with a smile. "Anyway," I concluded after a moment, "I never felt a pressing need to get married, but I also didn't feel a duty not to. And since Ashwini wanted to so much, I thought sure, why not? Thank god I didn't. Even just a few months after leaving her, it's clear to me that she and I couldn't be less suited for each other."

"'To think that I wasted years of my life on a woman who wasn't my type!'" Sadie quoted.

"I'm not interested in types," I said. "I'm interested in connections."

"Wise man."

"I stole that from *The Bachelor,*" I confessed.

"Another wise man. Speaking of: I can't wait until tonight!"

"Me neither." I'd forgotten *The Bachelor* was on that night, and I was grateful to have something to look forward to.

We'd transitioned from the path back onto sidewalks and were climbing up Madison Avenue, Sadie setting a pace so brisk I almost had trouble keeping up.

"The difference between the people on *The Bachelor* and us," she proposed halfway up the hill, "is that they never went through that essential phase of rebellion against the givens of their childhood, like marriage. They're gullible. They're not grown up. They lack imagination. They can't believe in a world beyond the world they were born into."

I said yes, that was one difference, at least.

"What are some others?"

"I don't know. On the ABC website they all list their favorite book as *The Notebook.* Sorry if that's your favorite book."

"Well . . ."

"I mean, I haven't read it, so."

"No, I haven't read it either. Actually I can't read fiction at all anymore. No offense."

"None taken. I can't write it anymore." The moment I said it I felt physically lighter, and I realized this was the first time I'd told anyone, and that now I'd told Sadie, in one afternoon, two things I hadn't told anyone else.

She shot me a look that said, *Oh, come on*.

"I mean I don't care to," I tried to explain. "I've decided I'm not going to. I'm giving up. I've retired."

"Retired. You're what, thirty-three?"

"Twenty-nine." The four-year difference seemed infinite.

"Child," she said with a faint, warm smile. She didn't ask why I'd "retired" from fiction writing, and I was grateful for her tact, if that's what it was. We'd crested the hill, to my relief, and the sun was sinking behind trees and houses.

"So what do you read instead of fiction?" I asked.

"Memoirs mostly."

"So fiction."

She laughed. "Women's memoirs about their fucked-up parents. The more fucked up the better."

"What fun."

"Maybe you could try your hand at one, now that you're not writing fiction."

"I'd love to. Unfortunately, I'm not a woman and my parents aren't fucked up."

"All parents are fucked up," Sadie said after a moment. "Even yours. Because all people are fucked up. We can't help it. Even if we do everything right—and what seems right is constantly changing from one day, one moment, to the next—we can't prevent the stream of loss that will come to define our children's lives. Sorry to be dour, but that's just how things are. Life is loss. And lately it's seemed to me that our most important task as parents is simply to be honest about that fact. Sometimes it seems to me I was lucky my father died when I was a girl: I learned very early what life was about, and I think it's made things easier for me."

She fell silent after this little discourse, and, as we headed home on Lower Beaver, I turned over her words in my mind. The casual reference to the story of her father's death implied that she thought she'd told it to me, which made me hesitate to respond, either with sympathy or surprise, even though I was almost certain she hadn't. That life was loss could not be denied, but I didn't see how that made all parents "fucked up," least of all mine. It was a label that was impossible for me to accept—partly, I realized, smiling inwardly, because it's a term they would never use: I had never heard either of them curse, except once, when my mother was reading to me from a Michael Crichton book and couldn't avoid saying "shit," which had thrilled me.

Suddenly Sadie stopped, turned fully toward me, took firm hold of one of my shoulders, and, looking so intently into my eyes I had to fight an urge to turn away, said, "Speaking of loss, I'm so sorry for yours. I'm not sure I properly conveyed that. You must be hurting, and I'm sorry."

I told her I was actually fine, thanks, but not before wondering for the briefest of moments how she'd found out about Maria.

A little later we were on the couch, Sadie fresh from a shower in silk pajamas and smelling of aloe vera shampoo, holding glasses that held the last of a Côtes du Rhône and waiting for *The Bachelor* to begin.

"I've been thinking about this a lot," she said. "It's embarrassing."

"You'll get over that."

"Remind me what happened last week?"

I recapped the Costa Rica episode, the longest zip line in the world, group-date rappelling, spelunking with Alli, everyone falling in love.

"And how many women are left?"

Six: Chantal, Shawntel, Other Ashley, Michelle, Britt, and Emily.

"Britt?"

A food writer from Woodinville, Washington, who hadn't been getting much screen time lately; probably she'd be eliminated this episode—which was starting as I spoke.

"Oh my god, there he is! That voice! That jaw!"

For the next two hours we lived in a world of salt breezes and yachts and coastal villas—Anguilla! With its white sand, green palms, pink flowers and drinks, the turquoise and ultramarine of the sea, the oranges of sunsets and candlelight and midnight bonfires on the beach, clear skies; a world circumscribed and governed by simple rules, in which everyone spoke the same little language and love was the only thing that mattered.

This was the biggest week of the Bachelor's life. He and Emily stepped into a helicopter. "I want it to go to a whole other level. Someplace we haven't been before."

Their own private island in the Caribbean.

If things went well here, next week the Bachelor would fly to Charlotte, where finally Emily would introduce him to Ricki. Emily's ambivalence about such a meeting—"I don't want to confuse her in any way"—was enough to convince Sadie to switch her allegiance, at least for the moment, from Shawntel.

"Today was fun," Emily said. "Today was *perfect,*" the Bachelor corrected her.

The show went to commercial and Sadie said, "So wait, I have a question."

"Go for it."

"This has all already happened, right?"

It had.

"Like, how long ago?"

"I'm not sure exactly. A few months, maybe?"

"How come everyone doesn't know who wins?"

"They make the Bachelor and whoever he picks keep the whole thing a secret. They can't see each other till the season's over. Everyone signs something, I assume."

"So the Bachelor could be sitting somewhere *at this very moment* watching himself on TV?"

"Wouldn't you?"

He took Shawntel to the local farmers market, where they danced and jumped rope and drank coconut juice. "I like how I feel when I'm with you," he said. "I don't have to put on some act." "She's so pretty." "Whatever's happening between you and me, I like it." "I haven't felt like this in a long time." "They all say that." "I have a really tough time putting myself out there." "I'm scared." "Any man would be lucky to have her." "Albatross!" "What did I get myself into?" "I'm so nervous." "It's a little bit awkward for everyone involved." "Every moment is funny and meaningful and tragic and meaningless." "It's not real." "It's actually very real." "From here on out there's going to be a lot of heartbreak, a lot of devastation."

8

NEXT MORNING SADIE MADE US SCRAMBLED EGGS AND bacon and banana–chocolate chip pancakes and coffee, and we sat and chatted and read the *Des Moines Register,* passing finished sections to each other and quoting aloud from time to time. (*Said Warren County Emergency Management Director Mahala Cox,* read Sadie, *I'm not sure I have any idea of what the cause of the leak was or why the pipe broke, because that facility was just inspected by the Department of Agriculture and passed with flying colors.* "Well, how reassuring!") Then she announced that she was leaving to meet a friend for lunch. I said I didn't think I'd need another meal the rest of the week.

Almost as soon as she'd left the house my thoughts turned to Maria. It had been more than a week since my probably misjudged email, and I'd given up all hope of hearing back from her, almost all. When I thought of her now I detected stirrings of guilt—something to do with our night together in Detroit . . . no, I'd overlooked some element of our correspondence . . . no, I should have sent one of the emails I didn't send . . . no, it was connected to Sadie. Sadie? Maria had no idea who Sadie was, I hadn't mentioned her in a single email. Had I? Why would it have mattered if I had? I felt full. I'd been pacing back and forth between the kitchen and living room; now I lay down in a patch of sunlight on the late-morning-warmish living-room floor. I closed my eyes. I'd made some crucial oversight, I'd committed some irremediable crime. I dozed off. I was floating toward some long-neglected corner of my childhood where the answer to all my questions would be revealed when I was awoken by three sharp knocks on the door. Had Sadie locked herself out? I'd let her in. I went to the door and opened it and there was Jess, holding in one hand a plaid wool scarf, in the other a large padded envelope.

"Special delivery," she said, handing me both. "You left this in the car the other night. The package was leaning against your door."

I thanked her. "I'm always losing scarves."

"Aren't we all." The envelope had no return address, but my name and address were in familiar handwriting.

"Hey," I said, "it's nice to see you."

"Is it? You didn't return my calls." Jess had called twice over the past few days; I hadn't listened to her messages. I'd been waiting for my embarrassment about my behavior at the concert to dissipate; maybe it never would.

"It is!" It was! "Sorry I didn't call you. I've been busy." Ha.

"No, it's not a big deal. Anyway . . ." She turned slightly as if about to leave.

"No, hey—do you want to come in?" Except for Sadie I hadn't had any visitors in the house.

"Sure!" She seemed genuinely pleased. "Just for a second, though. I'm on my way to the dry cleaners."

We went inside and sat down at the kitchen table. I offered Jess a cup of coffee; she declined.

"Smells great in here."

"Big breakfast. Bacon."

"Bacon's the only kind of meat I can't give up. Whose house is this again?" she asked, looking around.

I explained who Sadie was, and Jess asked questions about her and my mother—it was cool that I was friends with a friend of my mom's, she said, and I agreed—but as I spoke she seemed distracted, as though she were only feigning interest, and the shame I'd felt the day after the concert began to rise up in me again.

"Hey, can I say something?" I asked, interrupting myself.

"Of course."

"I'm sorry about the other night."

She looked confused. "What do you mean?"

"The whole . . . fainting situation or whatever. I know that must have been annoying to deal with." I decided not to mention the attempted kiss; maybe she'd forgotten about it?

"What? No, it was scary for a second, but it happens. Don't worry about it. Seriously. And you were so funny after you came to. You seemed really happy."

A rush of gratitude overtook me. She was right: I *had* been happy. No one should be ashamed for being happy. I felt an absurd urge to kiss her, ignored it, thanked her for being so understanding.

"Don't worry about it. Seriously. We're all good. I wanted to ask—did you listen to my messages?"

"Oh, hey, I'm really sorry. I've just been so busy and—"

"No, it's fine, they were actually more messages from Amanda." Amanda? Heartbroken Amanda? "She was wondering if you might be up for drinks one of these nights."

No, no, no, no, no, no, no. Amanda seemed fine, but so young, younger than Jess—though actually they were probably around the same age—and anyway I couldn't handle someone new, suddenly my life felt improbably full, it was too much, the prospect of getting to know another woman, I didn't have it in me. I told Jess that Amanda seemed great, but she wasn't my type. Then I said something that scared me as I said it, the words just seemed to come out: "Actually, I was sort of wondering . . ."

"Oh! No, I'm flattered but—" She seemed to search for a reason, landing on, "I'm not interested in seeing anyone right now."

"Of course. No. I shouldn't have—"

"No, it's fine."

"Okay. Sorry."

"Stop apologizing. I'd better go. I'm covering for my grandma this afternoon."

"Tell her hello," a joke?

I walked her to the door, my face warm and pulsing. I couldn't account for my sudden proposal, it felt as though Jess had drawn it out of me, as if her physical presence across the table had summoned the words from my mouth.

"We should hang out," she said in the entryway. "There's no one else here to talk books with."

I couldn't imagine hanging out with Jess after today. "Steph and Amanda don't talk about books?"

"Not really."

"What about that guy we gave a ride from the concert?"

"Peter? Peter's a doofus. I mean he's sweet. Anyway—"

"Anyway," I echoed.

"Okay, well—" A car door opened, then slammed shut. "Who is that? Is someone here?"

"Yeah, so, I can't remember if—"

Sadie walked in with a loud, long sigh. "Well, that was about the—oh. Hello."

"Sadie, Jess. Jess, Sadie. Sadie's, ah, she's visiting for a few days."

"That's true. I also own the place."

"Oh yes," I said, "I didn't mean, I wasn't trying to . . ."

"Of course not. Well! Jess. Can I get you anything? Coffee? Juice?"

"No—thank you. I've heard a lot about you. I was just on my way out."

Sadie seemed to study my face, may have misread what she saw there, said, "I'll just go for a little walk."

"No!" I objected too strongly. "I mean—"

"Yes! I could use a little air." She looked at Jess. "So nice to meet you. Those boots are *amazing.*"

"Thank you! I love your coat."

They smiled at each other, my two new friends. Then Sadie left, then Jess, and I was alone.

I went to the living-room windows to clear my mind but immediately remembered the unopened package. I went back to the kitchen and tore it open and slid out an advance copy of Ashwini's novel. On the cover was a woman in a short turquoise skirt, feet too small for her black high heels, head and shoulders cropped out of the picture so that the reader could fill them in. I looked at the back cover: "magical . . . luminous . . . a dazzling mosaic of details and images . . . as heartbreaking as it is brilliant . . . a writer to watch." The novel told the story of a first-generation Indian Canadian family struggling through life's quiet challenges in suburban Toronto. "Written with humour, grace, and heartbreaking honesty, *Go Away* is Ashwini

Dasgupta's stunning debut novel about finding one's place in the world, and discovering the rare beauty of those one cannot live without." I flipped to the author photo: there she was, those eyes, that shy smile, looking as always like she wished she were elsewhere. The smell of her hair wafted up from the paper. I scanned the acknowledgments page for my name, not there, but a few mutual friends were "readers without whom," etc. On the cover page was an inscription: "Let's not. Love, Goose." A heaviness besieged me, as if the full weight of our separation were descending on me for the first time, and maybe it was. The book was dedicated to her parents and younger sister. I doubted I'd ever read it. Books are tombstones. I closed my eyes for a moment. I was so tired.

Sadie walked in the front door and I looked up. "Jess is gone," I said. "You didn't need to leave us alone here. We're just friends."

"I never suggested otherwise," a lie.

"I met her at the dry cleaners."

"She dresses very nicely." Sadie was hanging up her coat. "I'd love to talk but I've had a difficult afternoon."

I apologized, offered to leave the house for a while. "No, please don't. No need for that." She walked into the living room and sat down against a wall at a right angle to the one I was sitting against. Hadn't she just said she didn't want to talk? "You'd think after twenty years of living here I would've at least bought a *chair,*" she said. "Don't laugh at that. I'm exhausted. My heart is hurting."

She looked distraught, but I wasn't sure if I was supposed to ask what happened. I considered telling her more about Jess, the concert, imagined her telling my mother, said instead, "I'm reading an advance copy of my ex's novel," as if that might set her heart at ease.

"How is it?"

"You wouldn't like it: it's fiction. Sort of."

She smiled, then stopped smiling but continued to look at me, probing my eyes as if fathoming their depth, as if trying to decide if I was worthy of confiding in. She must have decided I was, because she said, "You're not the only one dealing with a breakup."

It took me a second to understand she was talking about divorce. My mind scrambled for condolences, oh god, when did it happen, I'm so sorry, are you okay? is your son okay?

Sadie's gaze was direct and even. "Ethan will be fine. He and Mike only met a few times." On my face, she had to have seen the confusion that it must have been her intent to sow. "Ryan and I are still together. I had a boyfriend. I don't have a boyfriend anymore."

"A boyfriend." What a ridiculous word.

"My marriage is open."

"You mean . . ." The meaning was clear.

"I'm *in an open marriage.* We see other people. It's done. It's something that people do. Try not to look so stunned."

I *was* stunned, and I was embarrassed to be stunned. How little I'd experienced of the world!

I told Sadie I was sorry about her breakup, fuck Mike, and she laughed and thanked me. The decision to end things had been set in motion the last night of her last visit, she said, but it wasn't finalized until this afternoon. "So now we can commiserate," she said.

I didn't feel especially like commiserating so I said, "Yeah, I mean, at least no one died, right?"

"Breakups are worse than death," she said. "The person who's causing all your grief is *still there.*"

I laughed and told her she had a point. She sighed. She was always sighing. Then she got up and headed upstairs to take a shower, turning before she reached the stairwell to half-shout, "Do you want to go to a retirement dinner this evening? Suddenly a spot has opened up."

The dinner was in a "modern American" restaurant in downtown Des Moines's recently christened East Village, a slowly but proudly gentrifying neighborhood wedged between the Des Moines River and the capitol. The restaurant hadn't existed when I was growing up, and I tried to take it as the sign of progress it so clearly wanted to be. The ceilings were high; the walls were exposed brick; one was lined with wine bottles whose curving necks all caught and reflected the dim track lighting at almost exactly the same spot, serially gleaming; they echoed the gleaming gold and silver balloons that were tied to chairs and tables here and there. The whole restaurant had been rented out for the evening. Near the entrance was a life-sized Superman cutout with the transposed head of a friendly-looking man—the retiree, I assumed and Sadie confirmed. On the ride over she'd called the man "a saint"; he'd been in charge of the Des Moines Art Center's educational programs since their inception more than thirty years ago. "And he's one of the ones who stayed friends with me after Ryan and I made our decision," she said. She and Ryan had never tried to hide their open marriage, she said. "That was always very important to us."

Seating was assigned; we searched for our table, stopping occasionally to exchange a few words with Sadie's friends and ex-friends and -colleagues, central Iowa's cultural elite. Sadie had an easy, frank way with everyone, which wasn't always reciprocated. Everyone asked about everyone else's children. I felt preposterous among the distinguished women with their makeup and pearls and brooches and heels, the men with their suits and goatees and rimless glasses. I wore a suit, too (my only one), but mine was a disguise. Sadie wore a tight iridescent knee-length dress that most often shone either green or gold. She introduced me as her friend. I felt drunk from the wine that lined the wall. "He's retired, too," she told one woman, and the three of us laughed conspiratorially.

We found the place cards for Sadie and "Sadie's Guest" and sat down, the first to arrive at our table. Underneath our chairs we each found a gift bag that contained a disposable camera, a dog treat, a curlicued straw, a pair of tickets to an Iowa Cubs game, and a packet of vegetable seeds. Each gift, Sadie explained, referenced an interest in the life of the retiree. Straws? "Milkshakes. Stephen loves milkshakes." We compared our seeds: she got kale, I got parsnips. She wanted to trade but I held firm. Almost before I realized I'd taken a sip, a waiter materialized to top off my wine.

"Excuse me!" Sadie grabbed the shoulder of the departing waiter. "Me too, please," and he poured more wine into her goblet, which I was pretty sure she hadn't drunk from yet. "Bottomless," Sadie said, and smiled. As she raised her glass and I raised mine to meet it, a man with a slight southern accent yelled, "Hold on now, let me get in on this!" He sat down next to Sadie and raised his glass and we all clinked to Stephen. "To Stephen!"

The man, broad-shouldered and totally bald, with a thick mustache, leaned in to kiss Sadie on the cheek. "Dave Corwyn," he said, extending a hand to meet mine. His head gleamed like the wine bottles and balloons. He had the build of a former football player, but maybe that occurred to me only after he'd started talking about the Super Bowl, which he'd attended the previous weekend on the invitation of NFL commissioner Roger Goodell. On his phone he showed us photos of himself with his two sons and the offensive line of the Pittsburgh Steelers.

"I thought you were in the Amazonian rain forest," said Sadie.

"That was in December. Now, that's some river. Ever been there?" He was looking at me; I'd never been! "If you ever decide to go, give me a call." His hand was on my wrist. I nodded gravely. "Let's just say I'm on good terms with some of the natives." He smiled and released my wrist, to my relief, then gave a winking sort of look to Sadie.

A waiter came by with salads and a stiffly rehearsed offer of "freshly ground pink peppercorns, freshly grated Parmigiano-Reggiano." Sadie accepted ungodly amounts of both; Dave seemed determined to accept even more. Feeling suddenly compelled to one-up them both I waited until the waiter stopped grating, then said, "More, please," and let him go a while longer as Sadie and Dave exchanged wide-eyed looks. I repeated the act with the pink peppercorns, nodding, suddenly feeling like a king. "Thank you."

"My man!" Dave said when the waiter left, and I gave a look like *Damn straight.*

Meanwhile another waiter had topped off our wine, and as we ate and drank, newly bonded by our tacit competition, Dave told the story of how he'd come to be invited to the Super Bowl by Roger Goodell. He'd recently had the good fortune, he explained, to attend a breast cancer awareness fundraiser and wine-tasting event at which Goodell was the featured speaker. *Everyone* was there—DiCaprio, Seal, Joe Montana, I mean *everyone.* This was in Sonoma, not far from his new house. Beautiful country. I mean—my god. You guys'll have to come out there sometime. He was sitting at a table with Sean Penn and Michael Dukakis, who was a good, upstanding, God-fearing man, whatever you thought of his dumb-ass politics. The three of them were drinking wine and having a grand old time. "Did you know Sean Penn fucked Cher? It's true. Don't know how they managed to avoid the tabloids, but there it is! Don't tell anyone I told you that. So anyway, me and Penn and Dukakis are getting good and drunk on Cabernet, just comparing war stories, shooting the shit, and one of them, can't remember if it was Penn or Dukakis, brings up the very important topic of which NFL team has the hottest cheerleaders. I knew you'd love that, Sadie. Ha! Now Penn, he's a California boy, he goes with the 49ers, okay, whatever, can't blame him for that, and Dukakis—Dukakis goes with some crazy wildcard, the St. Louis Rams or some shit, I can't remember, he's obviously not an expert on the subject. Now, you and I both know there's only one correct answer and that's the Dallas Cowboys. But Penn, he's not having it, Dukakis, not having it, so I say, Boys, boys, there's only one way to settle this. And right about now it's time for Goodell's Q and A, and wouldn't you know it I'm called upon to ask the commish a question. And I stand up from my table. Smooth my suit. Straighten my tie. Clear my throat—ahem!—and say, 'Um, yes, Commissioner. Sir. I wonder if you could settle a very important difference of opinion between myself and the other two gentlemen at the table.' 'I'll certainly do my best. What's on your mind?' 'Yes, uh, thank you, Commissioner, sir. Mr. Penn and Mr. Dukakis and I are having, shall we say, a *gentleman's disagreement.* You see, Mr. Penn is of the unfortunate opinion that the most, um, *attractive* cheerleaders in the league belong to the San Francisco 49ers.' Some tittering in the audience, right? 'And Mr. Dukakis, I'm sorry to say, is of the opinion that it's the St. Louis Rams.' The whole room trying not to laugh at this point. 'Whereas you and I both know, Mr. Commissioner, that the most attractive cheerleaders in the league, without question, are the Dallas Cowboys Cheerleaders. I'd just appreciate it if you could confirm that. Thank you. That's all. Sir.' And Goodell, he's real serious, he's playing it cool: 'You raise a very important question, Mr. Corwyn. I sure am glad you brought that to my attention,' and he goes on in his very official way about how all the cheerleaders are wonderful assets to the league, it's impossible to choose one squad over another, blah blah—but later that evening, after the Q and A, he comes over to me, leans in close, and says, 'Goddamn right it's the Cowboys Cheerleaders.' *Goddamn right!* What do you think of *that*? Well, hell," Dave concluded, "I knew right then we'd be friends, and by the end of the night he's offered me two seats in his box for Super Bowl Forty-five. I told him I already had tickets to the game, but he insisted on having me and my wife as guests."

Sadie and I expressed the requisite amazement, and a minute later Dave got up to go to the bathroom. I looked at Sadie in mock panic, and we laughed. "I'm sorry," she said. "I didn't know we'd have the good fortune of being seated with Dave."

"He seems nice."

"He's a boor, I mean obviously, but what's funny is that he's also actually one of the nicest guys you'll ever meet. If you can get past the . . . Texasness." He was an oil tycoon who spent money on art, buying it and donating to arts organizations. He had homes in Houston, Calgary, New York, and now apparently California, but his wife had grown up outside of Des Moines and he'd been involved with the Art Center for a long time. "He comes to events and actually *helps out*—hands out pamphlets, sets up chairs, whatever's needed. Everyone here loves him. He's sort of despicable, but he's also really kind."

Another couple had joined us at the table while Dave was talking; they were eating their salads and chatting in low voices. "Linda, hello!" Sadie said. Linda turned toward us and said evenly, "Hello." Sadie introduced me and I said I was pleased to meet them. "Yes," said Linda and turned back to her husband, who gave a little smile as if to apologize. Sadie nodded at the couple knowingly, then took a gulp of wine.

Dave returned and Sadie asked him about his new home, she hadn't known he'd been looking to buy in wine country. Oh yes, he'd been looking for a long, long time, it was just a matter of finding the right place. It was on top of a mountain between Napa and Suisun valleys. Floor-to-ceiling glass walls, two stories, octagonal, indoor-outdoor infinity pool cantilevered over a cliff. "It looks like a fucking spaceship landed smack on top of the mountain." It had a name: House Above the Morning Clouds. Every morning the fog rolled in from the Pacific and surrounded the house like a cotton-candy carpet. The property was seventeen hundred acres. "Nice piece of land," Dave kept saying, and every time it sounded like "Nice piece of ass." On clear days you could see the Golden Gate Bridge, and in the other direction the Sierra Nevadas. The house had been featured in a Lexus commercial, and also the new *Sports Illustrated* Swimsuit Issue, maybe we'd seen it.

"Not yet," Sadie said.

"Nice piece of land," Dave said. The waiter took our empty salad plates. "But I've just been going on about myself. What do you do, my man?"

Me? It was hard to say—I did a lot of—I spent a lot of time—

"He's a writer," Sadie said. "He wrote an amazing novel. And he's house-sitting for me. Multitalented."

"A writer! I admire that, I really do. I stand in awe of people who can write. Me, I can barely throw two sentences together. Put a gun to my head and maybe I'll get a—what's it called? A paragraph? I'm kidding. But let me tell you: I love to read. I've always been a reader."

"Oh? What have you been reading lately?" I asked. I don't know what I was expecting him to say.

"Euripides."

What language was he speaking? "I'm sorry?"

"I probably have the pronunciation wrong. Euripides?" It was the correct pronunciation. "Ancient Greek playwright. Heavy stuff. You read him?" I said it had been a while. "Heavy stuff. Really makes you think about things. The big questions, you know. What are we here for? What do we do?"

"And?" Sadie asked.

"Hell if I know. You'll be the first to know if I find out, I promise you that. I've always loved those little Loeb Classical editions. You know what I'm talking about? With the green covers? You ever read those things? I have a pretty good collection. Handsome books. My wife got me into them. English major. Hey, I got a thought." He looked at Sadie. "Is this gentleman a decent house-sitter?"

"The best."

"Doesn't steal? Doesn't throw too many parties?"

"I haven't heard a single complaint from the neighbors."

Dave turned back to me. "How'd you like to watch my new house for a spell? We want to make a few improvements before we move in and it sure would help to have someone there. Be a great place to write your next book. If Sadie doesn't mind my stealing you, of course."

The brief look that Sadie and I exchanged contained a conversation: "Do you want to?" "I'm not sure." "You can if you want." "I need someone to tell me what I want." "No, you need to figure it out on your own." "How?" "Search within yourself." "But . . ."

"Yeah," said Sadie, "it's fine with me."

"Fantastic! My wife'll be so pleased. I'm texting her right now. Her sister was looking after the place but she got scared, couldn't handle it. Gets a little lonely but you'll be fine. I'll make sure the Jeep arrives before you do. You're going to love driving that Jeep. 2012. Kevlar. Super tricked out. What's the soonest you can get out there? So I can tell my wife. The glass people are coming up on Friday."

"I'll be there by Friday, then," I heard myself saying.

"My man. The wife is going to be thrilled, you have no idea. All she can think about is someone breaking in, stealing all her books."

The entrée was served, "risotto ai funghi." Apparently modern America was in Italy. I said that and Dave and Sadie laughed. The speeches began as we took our first bites: "a pleasure to work with . . . will be missed . . . more than a colleague . . . everybody's friend . . . hard work and dedication . . . grace and generosity . . . heroic patience . . . respected within the community . . . life well spent . . . one door closes . . ." Each expectant pause was filled with obliging laughter. A few of the speakers couldn't keep from crying. Behind them, a slideshow of Stephen's life cycled continuously on the tall brick wall, and between these images and the speeches and the wine I began to feel as though he and I had known each other a long time.

Then there was dessert, and more wine, and dancing, and mostly I watched while Sadie danced with Dave and people I didn't know danced with people I didn't know and Stephen danced with everyone else in the restaurant, but when Dave gestured me toward him and said, "I'm exhausted, she's all yours," I danced with Sadie for a few songs, Motown everyone knew by heart. Dave came back to hug Sadie goodbye. He'd email me details about the house, he said, slapping me on the back. Sadie yelled over the music, "He's coming off a big breakup!" and Dave said, "Oh, well then, this'll be *perfect* for you. Napa's full of pretty girls. You can tell 'em the house belongs to you if you want." In no world would I ever do such a thing, I thought as I said, "That's exactly what I'll do." Then Dave left, and the crowd began to thin, and soon it seemed time to go.

On the way home, through abandoned streets, Sadie said she had an idea. "You can say no. But it would be nice for me. I could use a few days to process and heal before going back to being a mom and wife."

"Okay."

"You might not want to do this."

"But I might."

Her idea was that we drive to California together; when we got there she'd take a plane back to New York; she'd figure out a way to get her car back to Des Moines. The two of us could see the country, eat at diners. "I'd completely understand if you said no," she said. I was surprised, not by the idea itself, but that it should seem perfectly reasonable, a natural extension of our burgeoning friendship. Plus, if I was going to drive across half the country, it would be nice to have a companion. I said it sounded like a great idea.

Back home, I said good night to Sadie and made a couch-cushion bed on the floor of the family room. As I was setting a phone alarm I saw I had a voice message: Laura, saying she'd had a change of heart and wouldn't mind bringing a date to her sister's wedding after all, and, since I lived so close, would I consider going? In my addled state her question sounded to me practically like a proposal, as though she were inviting me to her own wedding, at which I would be the groom. Once, while watching *Dallas* together a couple of years after we'd broken up, we'd promised that if neither of us was married by forty, though neither of us cared about getting married, we'd marry each other. I don't think we were joking, exactly. But we still had a lot of years to go before forty, and I'd made Dave Corwyn a promise, too, and it was only Laura's sister's wedding, and I was looking forward to my road trip with Sadie. I'd call with my apologies from the road.

For a long time I lay awake in the dark, trying to imagine the glass house on top of the mountain, but all my meager mind's eye could conjure was an amalgam of the Botanical Center and Jordan Creek Mall. I felt no sadness in leaving Des Moines; I knew it would never stop returning to me. And yet I had the dim sense of fleeing something: my memories or desires, Maria, or Jess. Eventually I guess I fell asleep.

Next day Sadie and I bought granola bars and potato chips and oranges and kombucha and loaded the car and headed west on I-80. Better to start out with a short day, we decided, than to leave the day after and feel in a rush. We'd drive to some town in the middle of Nebraska, find a steakhouse, and have a relaxing evening. It was always a good idea to take Nebraska in two days if you had time for it, we agreed.

9

SADIE'S MATERNAL GRANDFATHER (SHE TOLD ME SOMEwhere near Lincoln, interrupting what until then had been a more or less linear chronology) was an English director and playwright of French ancestry whose grandmother was one of the famous beauties in the court of Napoléon III. He was friends with George Bernard Shaw and Leonard Woolf, exchanged letters (Sadie had read them) with Yeats and Proust, was considered one of the rising stars of English drama. Then he fell in love with Sadie's grandmother. He was married, with three kids, a nice home, money; she was the leading actress in a play he was directing. They ran away to America together, first to Hollywood, where Sadie's grandmother acted in silent movies, then to New York, where he produced plays. Sadie's mother had always claimed they came over on the final voyage of the *Lusitania,* whose sinking by a German U-boat they survived, but at some point Sadie realized this couldn't be true, since the *Lusitania* sank on a crossing from America to England—neither the last nor the most outlandish of Sadie's mother's lies.

Sadie spent the first part of her childhood in a large, ornately furnished apartment that looked out on Gramercy Park. Her mother spoiled her. She'd take Sadie and her sister out for ice cream for dinner, or she'd pull them out of school for a day and drive them down to Coney Island, or she'd buy them little fur coats from Macy's so that the three of them all matched. She was fun. She had a way of making everyone around her smile. When she walked into a room people turned to her instinctively; they wanted to conspire with her, or sleep with her, or help her. Sadie's father, an investment banker, often worked so late that Sadie was in bed by the time he got home—though many nights she lay awake, she told me, listening for his footsteps. Most of her memories of him were from Cape Cod, where they spent a month or so every summer in her grandmother's beachfront home. She built sandcastles with him, and collected shells, and climbed the hundred and sixteen steps of Provincetown's Pilgrim Monument, from which the curling strip of land that was the cape seemed to dissolve before her eyes into the ocean.

A steady stream of people passed through her grandmother's house, mostly other vacationing families. The adults drank cocktails and sat on the deck while the children ran around on the beach. One family in particular became close with Sadie's, another couple from New York with two boys the ages of her and her sister. One summer they started coming by every day, often arriving in time for lunch and staying late into the night. Same thing next summer. The parents liked to joke that Sadie and her sister would end up marrying the Thompson boys, thus making official the familial bond that everyone in any case already felt. Then, toward the end of the third summer, when Sadie was nine, her mother came to her one day and said,

"You're going to have two mommies and daddies now. And Ted and Philip will be your brothers. Isn't that wonderful?"

And it *was* wonderful, Sadie said, for the next couple of years. She split her time between her old apartment and a new, even bigger one on Park Avenue and Sixty-sixth. Her mother and Cam Thompson lived there now, while her father and Mary Thompson lived on Gramercy Park with the two Thompson boys. Weekends, the two families got together for brunch, followed by a trip to a museum and then, if the weather was good, a park. She'd rarely seen her father before anyway, so not living with him all the time didn't seem like much of a loss, plus Cam was always buying her things, which her father had rarely done. (Also, Sadie added, if it weren't for Cam she probably wouldn't have gotten into art: he was an art history professor and appraiser of antique furniture and seemed to take pleasure in explaining to her, in terms that made sense to a still-young girl, what made one thing beautiful, another not.) Sadie understood the arrangement was unusual, but her parents and the Thompsons projected a casual cheerfulness that filtered down to the children. A year into this reconfigured reality, the original couples divorced and the new ones remarried in a joint ceremony on the beach.

A year and a half later her mother and Cam divorced. Sadie hadn't sensed that anything was wrong; her mother had simply come to her and told her, in her easy, cheerful way. Sadie was twelve. Since they couldn't go back to the Gramercy Park apartment, Sadie, her sister, and her mother moved into a two-bedroom in the Village. It was much smaller than anywhere Sadie had ever lived, but her mother billed it as the next adventure. Sadie couldn't remember how long they'd been living there when she heard the news of her father's death. She also couldn't remember how she found out, though she sometimes had what she thought was a false memory of her mother coming to her one afternoon and saying, in her easy, cheerful way, "I'm afraid your father's fallen off a balcony!"

The next three years were a blur of new homes, new schools, new men who "loved" her mother, endless stretches of interstate, landmarks, vacations, vacations from vacations. Sadie moved with her sister and mother to Baltimore, Key West, Nashville, Tucson, Santa Cruz, Eugene, Bozeman. "Let's *see the country,*" her mother used to say. "Every American should see her country!" It was the seventies and lots of Americans were seeing their country, and Sadie's mother would attach herself to fellow explorers who she sensed could take her somewhere better than where she was—and then she'd find someone else, or a group of people, to help her break free and find the next place, the *next adventure,* always the next adventure. She either started regularly doing cocaine or stopped trying to conceal it from her daughters. She started dressing like a hippie. She smelled of sex. Shirtless men with dazed smiles roamed their homes. "Your mom's a real trip," one told Sadie; within three months they'd married and divorced. (Sadie still had the Eagles record he gave her for her birthday.)

It was around this time that Sadie began to notice her mother's compulsive lying. She lied about her age, where she was from, the reason she and her daughters were on the move (Sadie remembered her telling a new friend they were "fugitives from the law"), about topics consequential and inconsequential. "Their father's coming to join us in a few months" was a refrain. "He just has to close out the fiscal year," or, "He's tying up loose ends with the old apartment." She fabricated stories about her past: she and Sadie's father met at Oxford, her parents were Holocaust survivors, were Nazis. When she introduced Sadie and her sister to principals at schools, she invented special talents and accolades: "Sadie's state champion in the breaststroke for her age group." "Oh, no, Sadie can skip trigonometry. She's been learning that on her own." Since Sadie could never live up to her mother's version of her, this kind of lie filled her with fear. But mostly she accepted the lying as part of her life.

When her mother started stealing things, she wasn't surprised. Sometimes she volunteered to help. She loved the thrill of walking out of a store with a dress, a frying pan, a Thanksgiving turkey hidden beneath her coat. Her biggest score was a pair of speakers her mother had been coveting; she just picked them up and walked out of the store, counting on her twelve-year-old innocence to protect her. Sometimes when they were driving and they came upon a vista, her mother would stop the car, get out, spread her arms, and say, "Look around! Everything here is *ours.*" And a lot of the time that's what it felt like: everything they came in contact with belonged to Sadie and her mother and sister.

Then Sadie's mother was visited by pain—first in her stomach, then her back, then spreading through her entire body. Sadie didn't know what set it off, but over time she came to think it was psychosomatic. Her mother started taking Valium, Percodan, methadone, Demerol. Sometimes she asked Sadie to give her injections. She went days without leaving her bed; she barely spoke. Sadie had to take care of her sister: she made microwave dinners, walked her to and from school, took her to the doctor's when she got sick. When her mother felt well enough to move around a little, she was usually in a terrible mood, either morose or angry or both. One day she slapped Sadie in the face, hard, Sadie couldn't remember for what, and that evening Sadie began researching boarding schools. She found one in Vermont that would take her and her sister and bought plane tickets on her mother's credit card. When the day of the flight came she broke down and told her mother, but instead of scolding or punishing her, her mother just cried and told her to go, it sounded like too good an opportunity to pass up. "She seemed almost happy," Sadie told me as we drove, endless feedlots blurring by.

In Vermont she slept with everyone—classmates, teachers, everyone. It was her way of acting out. For a year she carried on a secret affair with a married sculptor slash goat farmer; they didn't break it off until he told Sadie he wanted to leave his wife for her. She was fifteen. When she was bored she took buses into New York, looked up old friends, hung out at bars. She called Cam, whom she'd been out of touch with since the divorce, and they went to the Met and then out to dinner. He hadn't gotten over her father's death, he told her. Five years ago, if he'd known this was how things would play out . . . Sadie nodded. After dinner she invited him to her hotel room, to test her powers. She thought she saw him hesitate for a moment before declining.

At school, she gravitated toward the artists, self-proclaimed, whose knowingness she identified with even as she saw through it (she knew more than they ever would). She started making art herself. Her draftsmanship was awful, it always was, she told me, but she had a decent sense of composition and lots of feelings to express. Her teachers singled out her work for praise, and she started to believe she might have a calling, or at least an aptitude that would take her places. In any case she didn't know how else to spend her life, so she applied to Rhode Island School of Design, got in, and went off to become an artist. Once there, she worked obsessively. Bored with sex, fed up with arty posturing, she locked herself in her studio and painted for two years. She hit upon a style she had the audacity to imagine she could one day, maybe, call her own. Many of her paintings, without her express consent, seemed to deal obscurely with her father's death, which she began to realize she had never really reckoned with in the whirlwind years of its immediate aftermath. "The biggest lie the world will ever tell you," she told me, "is that you can get over the death of a parent."

She graduated. She spent the summer and fall in New York, haunting galleries and museums and plotting her next move. Then she went to her grandmother's house to paint. It was winter, and she was alone, and her plan was to make fifty paintings by spring and go back to New York and sell them and be famous. Her paintings were abstract but with suggestions of figures, women mostly—mostly herself, though probably you wouldn't know it by looking. She had an idea that what she was doing was aligned with the feminism her mother had embraced and passed down to her: something about women being effaced by forces outside of their control, she guessed.

She set up her studio in the room she used to stay in when her family visited when she was a girl, the one with the balcony facing the harbor. She ordered paint, brushes, canvases, red pajamas from L.L.Bean. She installed a stereo system. She bought green tea. And then she stood in front of her easel for a week and didn't make a single painting. She felt oppressed by her grandmother's old furniture and smells, her pink carpets, the pantry that reeked of some unidentifiable herb; her grandmother's all-too-present absence seemed to stand in for the weight of art history. She felt trapped. She found herself wandering the dunes all day, as if she were in an Antonioni film. This was when she became interested in birds—seabirds, mostly, because that's what were there, and the occasional snowy owl, white lump against the beige. She thought, "I'll become an ornithologist!" having no idea what that would entail.

And then one day as she was walking along the beach she came across a man. A handsome man searching for seashells and taking photos. Normally she didn't see anyone on her walks—if the cold didn't keep people away, the wind did, and tourist season didn't start till May—so to see a young, attractive man, alone, especially without a dog, was an event. The sky was gray, the ocean was gray, the tide was coming in. He was on vacation, the young man told her, from Iowa, a place she'd never been, an unreal place. He liked going places off-season, he said, finding out what they were *really* like, and then a gale made them turn away from the ocean in unison, huddling against the damp, and they laughed. Plus he'd found a great deal in town, he added. Sadie invited him to dinner that night.

And that spring instead of moving back to New York, she moved to Des Moines, where Ryan worked in insurance. Within weeks Sadie had found work as assistant curator at the Art Center. Just being from New York could get you the job back then, she said. "So you see: I'm just like you. I gave up my art. I retired. And I don't regret it."

"Wow," I said idiotically. "That's a lot." We were sitting across from each other now, in a dimly lit faux-leather booth in the steakhouse across the parking lot from our motel just off of I-80 in North Platte, Nebraska. Sadie had parceled out her story in a few chapters over our drive and dinner, though some details I didn't find out till later.

A waiter who looked about twelve years old came by to take

our plates; Sadie ordered each of us a cup of coffee and a slice of cherry pie. When he left she said, "Well, if I ever want a biography of myself, I guess I know who to call." I smiled. "Do you want to hear something *really* crazy, though?" I told her I'd been waiting for the *really* crazy part.

"A couple years ago I suddenly got interested in my mother's parents, I can't remember why. My grandfather died before I was born, and my grandmother died when I was three or four. I barely remember her. But I started doing all this research. I became especially interested in my grandmother's acting; she was this child-prodigy stage actress in England before her career got cut short by the scandal of getting involved with my grandfather. And then it looked like she was going to have a career in Hollywood, but after starring in four films she got pregnant with my mother and as far as I can tell stopped acting. None of the films she was in has survived, but it wasn't hard to get their titles and dig up a little information about them. And here's what I found out: in one of them, two couples, each with children, swap spouses; they divorce and remarry and see each other regularly and everyone seems more or less happy with the setup, unconventional as it is, until one of the women starts to feel jealous and murders her ex-husband."

"Jesus."

Sadie nodded.

"You don't think your mother . . ."

"I doubt it, but who knows what she was capable of. In any case she couldn't have orchestrated not only her own life but the lives of three other self-willed adults to resemble the plot of a silent movie she probably didn't even know about. It's just strange. It's that kind of coincidence that probably happens more often than we imagine."

When the waiter returned with coffee and pie, Sadie had him take a photo of us with her disposable camera from the retirement party. "Make sure you get the buffalo head," she said as we posed with forkfuls of pie, our mugs aloft and about to touch. I'm looking at the photo now. The bottom two-thirds of the buffalo head is there. Sadie's looking at me and I'm looking at the camera and both of us appear to have reached that point where prolonged pretend smiles spill into laughter that, while often at least half put-on, comes through the camera as almost authentic.

We finished and paid and went for a walk through the desolate downtown in the late-winter darkness. Nothing was open; dirty snow clumped here and there; fathomless potholes pocked the streets. We circled back to our Holiday Inn Express, where Sadie FaceTimed with her son in our beige room while I sat in the beige lobby holding a book and thinking about the terrible things her loved ones had inflicted on her. No wonder she took a tragic view of life. No wonder she believed it was the duty of parents to model loss for their children. (Maybe, I thought, opening her marriage was, at least in part, a way of doing that.) I felt a bottomless sadness for her that was also a sadness for myself, almost as if the sad events she'd narrated had somehow also happened to me. And it was true—*wasn't it?* I asked myself, as a man in a cowboy hat sat down across from me and opened a thick jacketless hardcover book—that her story *involved* me in some crucial way. It had to. If it didn't, she wouldn't have told it to me, or I wouldn't have been affected by it, or maybe it would just seem incomprehensible, lacking interest and meaning. The man shifted in his chair and I tried to glimpse the title of his book, couldn't make it out. Sadie had confided in me, I smiled to think, she had opened up: and now her story was mine as well, and I felt proud and powerful and scared.

When I returned, the lights were off and she was asleep, the *Late Show* on mute. I brushed my teeth, peed, crawled into my bed, watched Letterman silently flirt with Susan Sarandon, turned off the TV, and went to sleep between one house and the next.

We were following a route I'd taken many times. Every two or three summers in my childhood (I told Sadie, as if to counterbalance her dark story with an almost unreal idyll), my family would load up the forest green minivan and—my father driving, my mother sitting shotgun, my brother in the two-person frontmost back seat and my sister and I sharing the three-person "way back"—head west on I-80 troubled by a small but persistent doubt: could the minivan, humble, elephantine, so adept at shuttling us to and from school, so at its bulky ease on the scruffy streets of Des Moines and western suburbs, its natural habitat, really convey us and our two weeks' provisions across other states, other landscapes? I remember the floaty feeling that came over me gradually as we drove down Cortez and Lower Beaver and Meredith and Merle Hay to the on-ramp, then the interstate, as if the leaving were making me lighter than air, my only anchor my father's irritation at our having left twenty minutes later than planned—that and my mother's attempts, ultimately successful, to assure him that everything would work out fine, we'd get there in plenty of time. My father used to make spreadsheets showing the distance between towns and the estimated times we'd pass through them on our trip, assuming an average speed of five miles above the speed limit and factoring in a fifteen-minute stop every two hours and a forty-five minute stop for lunch (fast food, usually McDonald's or Wendy's but sometimes the classier, more adult Arby's—never Hardees or Burger King, which we tacitly agreed failed to meet our standards). He'd print out five copies and distribute them among us, and although we made fun of him as we did it we secretly enjoyed comparing our actual progress against his model. For the first two hours or so of our journey we required no distractions, sustained on pure anticipation and the gum my mother had let us pick out the day before we left; only on entering Nebraska did we turn to books and music and games—the License Plate Game, the Alphabet Game, Car Bingo, Twenty Questions. Nebraska was the butt of jokes in my family; we used it to prop up Iowa, ourselves. Nebraska! Nothing was worse than Nebraska. It was a true no place, there was nothing there, just dirt, and more dirt, vast expanses of dirt stretching out under vast skies made of dirt. Nebraska. My father liked to threaten the family with the prospect of moving to Ogallala. "Your mother and I have been thinking," he'd start off, or, "I've been presented with an opportunity I'm afraid may be too good to pass up." Cue mock horror: Dad, no! Not Ogallala! Not Nebraska! Why did it feel so good to object to moving to a place we knew we'd never move to? Nebraska. I remember the excitement, only half-ironic, my family experienced the summer of the construction of the Great Platte River Road Archway outside Kearney. The arch, which turned out to be more of a bridge, would span the interstate in the middle of one of its straightest, most barren and never-ending stretches, a new landmark, something to look forward to. And the next summer we went west, there it was, the "arch," symbol of—surely a symbol of something, and inside, a museum where we learned it was built (by "a Walt Disney team," I later discovered) at the confluence of three historic trails, the Oregon, Mormon, and California. Trappers, traders, pioneers in covered wagons, the prairie, buffalo, Pawnee Indians, the gold rush, steam trains, the Pony Express—all dissolved in our interstate-addled minds into the swirling fog of History, so that by the time we left, with maybe a magnet or multicolored pen or packet of stickers from the gift shop, the arch had become just one more thing to mock about Nebraska. *Nebraska.*

I wonder now if the rest of my family's complaining was, like mine, mostly an act, if my mother and father and brother and sister actually took refuge, as I know I did, in the monotony and endlessness and emptiness of the state. (The emptier the landscape, I see now, the better for projecting vague desires onto it.) I remember wanting so badly to *get there,* and yet I remember this wanting much more vividly than any instance of actually getting there. Likewise, the forms that passed behind our windows mattered less than the fact of their passing us by, the perpetual recomposition of the view, in which I felt at home. Escape? No, arrival into motion, the pouring-away world of no attachment. The minivan became our home, with its attendant echoes of domestic rituals. We ate in it—Quaker Oats granola bars or, if we were lucky, Kudos bars, with their chocolate coating that in memory tastes of coffee and peanut butter. My mother and brother napped in their seats while I read book after book to my sister: *The Wide-Mouthed Frog, The Very Hungry Caterpillar,* Berenstain Bears books, *Are You My Mother?*, or, when she was a little older, *The Wind in the Willows, A Bear Called Pad-*

dington, James and the Giant Peach, books that my brother had read to me when I was my sister's age, he mine, and that my parents had read to him before I or my sister was born.

Dusk reminded us that time passed after all. A faint sadness that was also a happiness descended. Since we knew we wouldn't have to actually face it, we could take pleasure in our fear of the dark—of real dark, the absolute darkness of the prairie—maybe imagining we were pioneers on the Oregon or Mormon or California trail, and that pleasure mingled with the pleasure of anticipation for what we knew awaited us, as often as not in Ogallala, site of our collective fantasy: a motel. A motel! The airbrushed familiarity of our room, with its two queen beds and rollaway for my brother and thin carpet and sliding blinds and dark wood end tables, the coolness of the comforters tucked tightly in, the dusty clean smell of air-conditioning, water glasses topped with snug paper caps, everything neat and crisp and cool.

The moment we arrived I'd jump on a bed and turn the TV to ESPN, and since it was summer it was usually baseball, which I didn't care about enough to watch for long unless it was the Twins or Cardinals or Cubs, and if it wasn't I'd try WGN, if the motel had it, to see if the Cubs were playing there; and if not, or sometimes even if they were, I'd soon change into my swim trunks and go down to the pool (down, because in my memory we always stayed on one of the top floors of the motel) with my sister and mother and sometimes my brother; my father, probably exhausted from driving, almost never joined us; and after splashing around for a while we'd dry off and my mother would give us change (50 cents, then 60, later 75) for a vending machine candy bar or pop, which we'd eat or drink in the coolness of our room, into which we had brought the purifying smell of motel-swimming-pool chlorine. Then more TV until bedtime, restless sleep, mini-muffins and waffles and Froot Loops for breakfast, and, in the warmth of the morning sun, the return to the interstate, welcoming now, friendly, on this the second day of the trip.

"Where were you going?" Sadie asked. She and I had been back on the road for a few hours and had just passed into Colorado on I-76, a transition whose thrill had always been tempered for me by eastern Colorado's similarity to Nebraska. But I knew what was coming: an ascent so gradual you didn't notice it at first, sagebrush starting to dot the countryside, and then—signature moment of the journey—mountains appearing on the horizon, insubstantial as the clouds that shrouded them, so that whoever claimed to see them first opened herself to ridicule. *No, they're mountains! I swear!*

"I haven't said?"

"Maybe I missed it," Sadie said.

We were going to Sheep's Head Mountain Ranch, a rustic cabin-and-campground resort in the Rockies, two hours west of Denver, where for the next ten days I'd read and play miniature golf and wander through pine forests on the sprawling network of dirt roads and paths that had never not been familiar to me. Every two or three days we'd climb a mountain—starting with the easy Nine Mile Mountain and working our way to Sheep's Head itself, with its lovely maddening redundancy of peaks—and once or twice we'd go into town for dinner at the burger place or Italian restaurant (or maybe the burger place *was* the Italian restaurant, I can't remember). I loved the seclusion of the pine forest, its glowing darkness, its cozy density, so unlike anything I knew in Des Moines; I felt protected there, even as a part of me feared an encounter with a bear or mountain lion. I could never remember whether you were supposed to freeze or run or slowly back away, play dead or raise your arms above your head, shout at the top of your lungs or stay silent; whether when the bear or mountain lion attacked you were supposed to shield your head or fight back; whether the rules for one were the same rules for the other—and what about moose (they seemed so gentle), surely the rules were different for moose? Our first few visits we went horseback riding through the forest and fields of wildflowers, but when I was nine or ten I was thrown from my horse and had to get stitches on my tongue, unless that was my brother: whenever I see a horse I seem to remember falling, but I can also vividly picture the blood running from my brother's mouth.

"Sounds like a special place," said Sadie.

"It was, but something sort of terrible happened, which is that I went there to work at the front desk the summer after I graduated from college. I had a girlfriend at the time, Laura, who was living in Minneapolis. Our relationship was ending but we couldn't admit it to ourselves, so we had a lot of long, hard phone conversations. Then she came to visit for a week, and we just stayed inside the whole time, talking and crying. By the time she left we weren't together anymore, and the rest of my time there—a couple months, I guess—was clouded by her visit. What made it worse was that a big part of my job was greeting guests and I had to pretend to be cheerful. We had a script. 'Welcome to Sheep's Head Mountain Ranch, we want to make your experience great! How can I be of service to you and your family today?' It was awful. I spent most of my downtime in the library, reading Beckett. Just to depress myself further I guess. No, I shouldn't say that, it didn't depress me, it actually cheered me up. Anyway. Now when I think of Sheep's Head Mountain

Ranch all my childhood memories are absorbed into my memory of that summer. I can't be properly nostalgic about it. I sort of wish I hadn't gone back."

Sadie, who was driving, didn't speak for a while; she seemed intent on the self-replenishing road that was visibly gaining altitude now, bringing the horizon in close to us. I was thinking about Laura's invitation to her sister's wedding, which I'd forgotten to respond to; I'd text next time I had a moment.

"We have to go there," Sadie said finally.

"To Sheep's Head Mountain? It's not really—"

"No. We have to go there! Come on."

We couldn't go there, I said, it was out of our way, we'd never reach California by tomorrow, we should stick to the schedule we'd drawn up that morning, try to make it as far as we could into Nevada, but I knew as I spoke we'd end up going there. I let Sadie make her case: if I returned to Sheep's Head Mountain Ranch now, as an adult, I could create a new layer of memories to set on top of the memory of my bad summer there.

"What if our experience is even more awful than my last experience there?" I asked.

"I can't imagine having an awful experience with you."

"It won't make any sense to go there unless we spend the night."

Sadie appeared to consider this. "Well then."

The Rockies hazed forth from the horizon, we skirted Denver, then passed through the foothills and entered the mountains, rising through a valley of golden stone (I texted Laura: *So sorry but,* etc.), then the switchbacks of Berthoud Pass, ponderosa pines giving way to lodgepoles, the present flickering in and out of the past—and then the high, broad valley from my dreams.

But it wasn't the same as before, something was off. I don't know when I first noticed the discrepancy. At first I chalked it up to the inevitable distortions of memory and desire. Then I realized: snow. There wasn't much, but I'd never been here in the winter. That was it. Then I realized: No, that's not it. Or it was, but there was something else, something bigger: the countryside, though its contours were familiar, was barren; bald mounds stood in place of forested hills. I told Sadie and she said it was probably the pine beetle, she'd read about it in the *Times*, the past decade's outbreak was the biggest insect blight in the history of North America. She couldn't remember its geographical extent, but she wouldn't be surprised if it had hit this valley. In my mind I saw thunderclouds of beetles descend from the sky, alight on the vast pine forest that used to be there, and moments later swarm off in a deafening hum, leaving behind silence and the nothingness I saw on either side of the road. "It's a completely different place," I said.

In my disorientation we almost missed the turnoff into Sheep's Head Mountain Ranch, and as we drove down the long dirt entry road I couldn't suppress my astonishment. What in my childhood had been a magical tree tunnel now had the look of an abandoned lot. Mulch and scraps of lumber littered the snow. Stumps showed evidence of the former forest. Understory that was no longer stood exposed, embarrassed tangles of leafless shrubs. The handful of isolated pines still standing, some green but many the rust red of death, had the look of long, solitary strands of body hair, the kind that grow from moles. I'd remembered these trees as thick and full—an illusion born of their numbers, I saw now. Straight ahead, as if rising from the end of the road, Sheep's Head Mountain loomed in the middle distance; before, you only caught glimpses of it through windows in the pines. We had come here to rearrange my memories, but instead it was as if my memories had been erased.

We arrived at the main lodge and parked and Sadie asked me if I still wanted to stay here. I detected a note of concern in her voice and worried I looked sad or stunned. I told her I did if she still did, as much to show her I was okay as for any other reason. "Let's go get a cabin," Sadie said. It felt good to stretch our legs. The air was dry and smelled empty, clean. The lodge, at least, was as I remembered it: high ceilings, pine beams, large central stone fireplace, mounted heads of deer and elk and moose and buffalo and bear. "Welcome to Sheep's Head Mountain Ranch, we want to make your experience great! How can I be of service to you and your family today?" As Sadie inquired about availability with the front desk attendant who'd accosted us (*front desk attendant* had stained my résumé for the first few years of my post-college life), I tried to avoid eye contact with the other, who was checking in a mother and father and young daughter, and whom I was pretty sure I recognized. Just to be sure, I stole a glance, and in that moment he looked back for a split second, and though his eyes registered no recognition I had no doubt it was Jarry, the Polish marathoner. I'd only worked a few shifts with him, but we'd had a long conversation about his plans to return to Poland and go to business school and open his own athletic gear store, where he'd apply the lessons he'd learned in America—lessons about valuing *individuals* over ideology or groups of people, he explained—to selling shoes and spandex pants. He had a big, friendly smile and kind eyes. Sometimes I'd see him running up Nine Mile Mountain as I sidestepped my way down.

I looked away. Sadie was grilling the other attendant about the mountain pine beetle. It's actually a natural phenomenon, the attendant was saying, the pine beetle has been here for hundreds of years. Yes, Sadie countered, but never in such numbers; what we were seeing couldn't be *natural.* Oh no, it was natural, said the attendant, it's just that the forest was getting old, and mature trees had a tougher time fighting off the beetles. That may have been true, but didn't it also have something to do with warmer temperatures, with climate change? No, it was really about the forest getting old, it was a natural process, nothing to worry about. So it shouldn't concern us that the ranch looked totally different now than it did even ten, twelve years ago? Well, it was true some new views had opened up. New views? It looked like a hurricane had come through. Had the attendant been outside recently? It didn't look very natural to Sadie. And what was their plan with the remaining trees? Were they treating any with chemicals? Which ones? Carbaryl? Chitosan? Was it safe to drink the water? The attendant assured Sadie the water was perfectly safe. "It's a natural process, ma'am."

Sadie thanked her and turned from the desk, smiling at me and shaking her head. "Oh!" she said, turning back. "Do you happen to offer any ex-employee discounts? My friend used to work here a long time ago." The attendant, with a look of feigned solicitude that said, *Thanks for asking me a question I can answer,* said that they did in fact offer such discounts, and asked for my name, which I gave. After staring at the screen for a few seconds she asked me to spell it out; I did. "Hmm," she said, "you're not coming up." I assured her I really did work here for a summer. The longer she searched, the more I wanted to come up. For a second I considered appealing to Jarry, who was still occupied with the young family. "I'm sorry, you're not in the system," said the front desk attendant. Sadie started to protest, but I talked over her: It's okay, we appreciate your help, thanks for trying. . . . "If you're not in the system," the attendant said as Sadie and I walked away.

"You're not in the system," Sadie said as we got back in the car.

"If you're not in the system . . ."

"There's nothing we can do. So sorry!"

"I'm not in the system."

She started the car. "I got a yurt! Sorry I didn't consult you. The moment that stupid woman said the word I said, 'Yes! That's what we want.' "

I said a yurt was fine with me: there hadn't been yurts when my family used to come here and I was always up for something new. On the way to our yurt we talked about yurts. Had they even existed when I was growing up? Neither of us remembered yurts from the eighties or nineties, though Sadie said she had a dim sense of the seventies being a yurt-heavy decade. America was in the midst of a yurt revolution, we agreed. Yurtmania. Return of the Yurt.

Our yurt was one of seven that formed a yurt circle, maybe seventy yards in diameter, on the side of a south-facing hill from which the rest of the ranch, in the absence of pines, was almost completely visible. Words like *denuded, godforsaken,* and *moonscape* shuffled through my mind. Between the cabin area and the main campground rose an enormous structure that hadn't been there before; it looked vaguely like a ski jump. The yurt was appointed with woodstove, couch, kitchen table, toaster, a queen bed, and two bunk beds. We dropped off our stuff there and went for a walk through the denuded godforsaken moonscape.

It was late afternoon and no one else was out; was anyone else even staying here? The wind, angry the pines were gone, assaulted our unprotected faces, and I thought of our first walk together, through the freezing streets of northwest Des Moines, back when I used to live there, another time, when Sadie was *my mother's friend.* We walked toward and through the main campground, which was empty, to the base of the big new structure: not a ski jump, according to a banner attached to a fence, but a "Snowflex summer tubing slope," the third of its kind in North America and the first in Colorado; a "magic carpet" conveyed tubers to the top, and from there they slid down on a composite material whose surface mimicked certain qualities of packed snow. We'd have to come back in the summer, Sadie said, and I said yes, we definitely would.

From there we walked through the cabin area, where we saw a smattering of parked cars but no people. I recognized one of the cabins my family had stayed in from its name, Buckeye, carved into a block of wood that hung from two posts by the driveway. An informational placard at the area's entrance addressed the pine beetle damage: *Mountain pine beetles, a natural presence in pine forests. . . . As forest health is addressed on the Ranch, more great things are happening. New views have opened up, and though the scenery has changed . . .* "People are so stupid," Sadie said. "We just have no idea what we're doing on this planet." Soon, the placard said, the pines would be replaced by new growths of aspen and subalpine fir.

As we walked past the library Sadie asked, "So that's where you used to go to avoid thinking about—what was her name?"

"Laura."

"Laura. Your first love?"

How did she know?

"And you imagined you'd end up marrying her?"

"No. I didn't believe in marriage then."

"That's right. I forgot. Sorry. It's just that—well, when I met

Ryan, in spite of what I'd seen happen to my parents, I thought, 'Oh, how lovely! We'll buy a house and have kids and jobs and buy furniture and protect each other from the world. Well. I wish I could tell my twenty-two-year-old self what marriage was really like. Not that it's bad."

"I'm not sure your marriage is the normal model," I said.

"No marriage is the normal model. That's what you don't find out until you're married. Marriage is a negotiated common reality with another person." It sounded like she was reciting a definition from a dictionary. "It *is* about protection, I got that right at least. But what you're protecting is your spouse's solitude, his own unshareable experience. We love for selfish reasons. Everyone does. It's a way to get to another place. I'll be the first to admit I've used Ryan, and if you pestered him enough there's a chance he'd admit how much he's used me, too."

Pretending to reach for my phone, I said, "What's his number?" and Sadie smiled indulgently.

"How long were you and Laura together?" she asked.

"Three and a half years? Four years? I don't know. I guess it depends on how you count."

"And who hurt whom?"

I laughed at Sadie's brazenness, still not quite used to it. "I don't know. We hurt each other." Without looking at her I sensed she was dissatisfied with my answer. "I guess I probably hurt her more," I admitted. I thought of Ellen, the coworker I'd kissed—once, and chastely—a few weeks before Laura and I broke up.

"Is that typical for you? Are you the hurter?"

Again I laughed, almost embarrassed, then considered her question seriously. "I guess I've been on both sides. I've been hurt. And sometimes it hurts to be the hurter."

"Of course. But it can also feel good to hurt. It's a question of power. I'm sure you know what I'm talking about."

I said I did but I was trying very hard at the moment to renounce that kind of power. Its satisfactions, I said, were shallow.

"What an adult thing to say," Sadie said. I felt patronized but let it pass.

We walked down the dirt road to our yurt through wind that seemed to come from the top of Sheep's Head Mountain, carrying the alpine tundra with it. We bowed our heads and gritted our teeth and Sadie slipped her arm through mine. The sun dropped behind a western ridge.

We entered our yurt and fed the stove with complimentary wood and sat on the couch, thawing. Then Sadie changed into a dress and we drove into town for dinner. We wanted to eat at the Italian or burger place or both but found neither and ended up eating panini at a combination Mexican restaurant and crêperie. We were both tired but also reluctant to return to the darkness of the ranch, the spartan yurt, so we walked down the street to the nearest bar, where we each had two drinks and watched sad-looking men get rejected by slightly less sad-looking women. Everyone wore boots and cowboy hats, and we tried not to make ourselves conspicuous. Finally we left, everyone watching us, and drove back to the ranch. When we got to the yurt, which was no longer warm, Sadie changed into pajamas and we rushed into bed. She took a top bunk, I the bottom. I lay awake for a long time.

Day three of our trip began at dawn. Stopping at Sheep's Head Mountain Ranch meant we'd have to drive for fifteen hours, give or take, in order to get to House Above the Morning Clouds before the "glass people" arrived the next morning. We breakfasted on potato chips and gas station coffee, listening to *Morning Edition* until, some ways past Steamboat Springs, we entered the Land Without Radio (Sadie's moniker), a state we'd pass in and out of all day, and allowed ourselves to be absorbed by the scenery, which was flattening out but still looked vaguely "mountainy," we agreed. Soon, though, the mountains gave way to desert, and we took turns napping while the other drove, neither of us having slept well the night before. We listened to Top 40, oldies, country, until we reached that moment on all road trips when the music, instead of propelling you forward, starts to weigh you down. Then talk radio, if we could find it, silence if we couldn't. We picked up sandwiches in Salt Lake City, and ate them to guard against the encroaching emptiness of the salt flats just beyond.

Not long after we passed from Utah to Nevada, at a moment when it seemed impossible that we could cross this desert and another mountain range in half a month, much less half a day, I offered to read to Sadie out loud. She said that sounded lovely and I extracted from my backpack Berryman's *Collected Poems,* which I'd hastily packed the morning of our departure. Was poetry okay? I asked. Poetry was great.

"I've been interested in this poet John Berryman lately," I said, and probably I shouldn't have been surprised that Sadie knew all about Berryman, had read many of his Dream Songs years ago, and what's more felt a strong connection with him due to the sad coincidence of their both losing their fathers in tragic circumstances when they were children. *"There sat down, once, a thing on Henry's heart,"* she quoted. "I forget the rest of the poem." *"So heavy,"* I said. *"So heavy,"* she said—"that's right."

I started from the beginning of *Love & Fame,* the last of Berryman's books to be published during his lifetime. Written between and during stays in the hospital for alcoholism and related illnesses and injuries, it recounted the poet's sentimental and artistic education, paying special attention to his romantic triumphs and attendant losses. *I fell in love with a girl,* it begins. Next line: *O and a gash.* The next poem finds Berryman *feasting on Louise.* The next begins, *O lithest Shirley!* The one after that makes passing mention of *the great red joy a pecker ought to be / to pump a woman ragged.* From the next: *My love confused confused with after loves / not ever over time did I outgrow.* "No kidding," Sadie said when I read those lines. "He's fixated. He's obsessed with women." I told Sadie his attitude toward women had always been a little troubling to me, not only because of the more or less explicit Oedipal impulse behind it, but because he treated them—not all of the time, but often—as little more than conquests. "He was an old-fashioned womanizer," I said.

"He was a product of his time."

"He slept with his students."

"Everyone slept with their students back then."

I murmured a vague objection, and Sadie laughed in embarrassment or indulgence.

What happens when you read out loud to someone is that you are and are not yourself. You're Berryman and Berryman's myriad personas and the characters that populate his poems, his life, and you're your eight-year-old self reading to your sister, your four-year-old self being read to by your brother, and you're your parents, and your parents' parents; and the part of you that's aware of all this is what remains of yourself, and the part of you that's listening to him, to Berryman, to Berryman's personas, is Sadie.

We will all die, & the evidence
is: Nothing after that.
Honey, we don't rejoin.
The thing meanwhile, I suppose, is to be courageous
& kind.

By the time we got to the California border—I'd been reading by flashlight since the middle of Nevada—Berryman had transitioned from self-aggrandizement that was more or less indistinguishable from self-doubt to a professed letting go of the ego, the better to praise our Lord and maker, *Master of beauty, craftsman of the snowflake,* and my voice was shot. Sadie mused about Berryman's sudden religious conversion. It was just another way to be seen, she said. *Love and fame*—both were ways to be seen, but both distorted as much as they revealed. Only God could see us perfectly. "Unfortunately, God doesn't exist," she said.

"Which is why Berryman jumped off a bridge," I offered.

At the checkpoint a bureaucrat confiscated an orange, and soon we were climbing the Sierra Nevadas. We stopped for a bathroom break at a rest area near the top, and I took us down the other side. As I switched lanes to pass a semi I told Sadie about how when I was a kid, I understood turn signals not as signals but the actual mechanisms by which cars switched lanes. "One of those childhood causality mistakes," I said. A few minutes later she said, "I want to tell you something." I think this was the first time I'd heard her say that. Go ahead, I said, and Sadie said, "I've really enjoyed this. Am really enjoying it. I hope we stay friends after this is over." I thanked her and said I was really enjoying it, too, and we rolled down the mountain and into the valley through the mild night.

We passed Sacramento, Davis, Vacaville, Fairfield, and finally took our exit. A few minutes later we were driving through dark vineyards. We rolled down our windows; the air was almost warm; we felt as though we'd driven from winter to spring. Soon we reached the base of our mountain and began, once again, to climb. For maybe half an hour we wound up a steep gradient past long gated driveways that led to mansions that shone forth from the darkness. The road leveled out and faded into gravel. The rumble of our tires on a cow grate surprised us. We passed a small pond or reservoir on which I could make out a dock and wooden raft, then curved up through a forest and came to a stop in front of an iron gate in the center of which was wrought a gigantic *D*. Had we arrived? "I don't see a house." "Dave said we'll know it when we see it." I pushed open the gate and held it open while Sadie drove through—it was cooler here than down in the vineyards—and then we continued climbing, climbing. We entered into a series of switchbacks. The gravel faded into dirt. We hit an enormous crater of a pothole and Sadie slowed our pace to a crawl. An animal—coyote? raccoon? bobcat?—scurried out of the headlights and into the trees, leaving an afterimage of its eyes. "This is insane," Sadie said and I agreed. The trees became sparser, then disappeared, and we rounded a bend that felt like a ridge and then we *knew* it was a ridge because on one side of the road instead of the darkness that indicated Earth's reassuring solidity we saw, or seemed to see, spread out against the sky, the yellow and red and whitish blue lights of an entire city. "Fairfield," Sadie said. "Incredible," I said, and we drove on at an even slower pace until Fairfield disappeared behind a tree.

Then more climbing, no signs of human life, only the darkness of mountainside and sky, which was clouded over, starless.

We didn't speak. Dave had told us his house was on top of a mountain, but I think we'd both imagined it as more of a hill. It must have been well after midnight by now. We hit a fork in the road, the first since the gate, and chose what we decided was the "main" road, slightly wider than the other. After some time we reached another gate, this one chain-link. I got out to see if it was locked; it slid open. "Keep going?" "We haven't reached the top yet, so . . ." More climbing, a level section through treeless plain, more climbing, one of us let out a laugh, which made the other laugh, too: what were we doing here? A bit later we passed what looked like a water tank, surrounded by a bunch of metal boxes, pipes. A low stone wall ran alongside the road, which turned back into asphalt. We were close. The last stretch was the steepest of them all; it felt like the first slow ascent on a roller coaster. I was still wondering if the Volvo would make it up when I realized it had.

The headlights lit up a two-car garage door. Sadie found the opener Dave had given her; she pressed the button a few times before it took. The "tricked-out Jeep" was parked in one spot; we took the other, closing the door behind us. As we got out of the car Sadie gave me a look that said, *We made it,* and *I'm scared,* and *This is very strange,* and *I hope you'll be okay here,* and possibly other things. On the concrete wall, next to the door to the house proper, was a panel of maybe fifty buttons. Light switches. We leaned in close to make out their labels: Living Room, Pool, Kitchen 1, Kitchen 2, Library, Guest 1, Guest 2, Atrium, East Balcony, Entrance, Living Area . . . Sadie's finger found a button labeled "All." She looked at me. I nodded. She brought the house to light.

What our eyes saw, our minds could make no sense of: a dizzying array of lines and light; light from a thousand sources or just one, but infinitely mirrored and refracted, fractured; rooms made of light; light audible, like bells; pools and showers of light, fields of light; light shifting, light shimmering, light within light; light shattering in fugal, in centrifugal shards. Impossible constellations flickered and dissolved. Lines met, or failed to meet, at odd angles, a collision of incompatible geometries. Reflections dissolved in reflections of reflections. Someone had poured a cup of stars into a bowl of broken glass. Room spilled onto boundless room; we moved or were moved through them. Rooms? Or was the structure one big room? And was that a tree growing out of the floor? Is that a ceiling or the sky?

Gradually the place resolved itself into familiar substances: glass, stone, wood, concrete. Reflections peeled away from their sources. Lines combined to form planes: floors and ceilings. The floors were slate, the ceilings wood; they floated at slight angles from the horizontal, unsupported by walls. There were no walls, only windows, or the windows were the walls. The house was two stories and hexagonal, more or less, not octagonal as Dave had said. At its center was a roofless atrium with a pond, beside which grew three Japanese maples. We walked around and around, gawking. Each "room" could have fit five or six of the rooms in Sadie's Des Moines, in my childhood house. In the kitchen were four sinks, two ovens, three stoves, and two gleaming granite-topped cupboarded islands. In the living room, two midcentury-modern-looking couches faced each other across a big orange block of a coffee table, on top of which Angelina Jolie looked out from the cover of a *Vanity Fair* from four years ago. Other than some wooden chairs and a few built-in desks, this seemed to be the extent of the furniture. The indoor/outdoor infinity pool was lit from within.

Some of the planes of glass had locks and handles; we unlocked one and pushed and were outside. The balcony, whose floor was the same slate as the interior's, stretched around almost the entire building. Its parapet was made of glass. We walked along the rectangular pool to the edge of that side of the balcony and looked out. At a slight angle to our left: the swimming lights of a city, the same we'd glimpsed on our way up, Fairfield, if Sadie's internal compass was correct. A grid of slowly blinking red lights, windmills, floated just outside the city. To our right, dark masses of land, and beyond, part of a slightly more distant city—Napa? We could make out a line of traffic on I-80 winding its way toward San Francisco. I'd only ever experienced nighttime aerial views from planes, which may have been why I felt a sudden sensation of motion, or maybe it was an effect of the wind, or maybe my body still thought it was in a car, but in any case Sadie said she felt it, too, and we returned to the other side of the glass.

Perhaps because we'd just been outside, it occurred to me now that though we couldn't see out, those outside could surely see in. Was there anywhere in the house to hide? Another lap revealed a bedroom—small, relative to the house's other rooms; cavernous, relative to the bedrooms I'd known—half-hidden behind a wood-paneled partition. In the center of the room was a large, made bed. The windows in here, though enormous, seemed slightly smaller than the windows in the rest of the house. (They were, I later realized, for the simple reason that the ceiling was slightly lower in here.) What we assumed was a light switch turned out to call down translucent black blinds from a slot in the ceiling. After failing to find any other switches or buttons, Sadie turned off all the lights from the garage and returned to the bed, which I'd already climbed into. Neither of us reached for the other, but there we were. "Jess won't mind?"

she whispered as we kissed. I laughed into her mouth. "She'll be furious," I said. Then added, "Just promise not to tell my mom." And I remember feeling as I pulled her closer that we'd done this many times before, as though we were entering a memory of the world into which we stepped at that moment through each other, where aspens grew in place of pines, fall leaves yellow against the sky.

10

THE BACHELOR RISES BEFORE SADIE, PEES, PULLS ON A hooded sweatshirt, Keurigs a cup of "Dark Magic" coffee, pushes open with all his weight one of the enormous glass doors, steps barefoot in his boxers onto the balcony, and shuffles past the two gas fire pits and the hot tub to the far end of the pool, where he leans somewhat tentatively against the parapet and tries to perceive his new world into existence. Below, as advertised, the morning clouds extend toward the horizon. Their dark-light surface is broken only by the occasional brush-covered hilltop or ridge, an archipelago of uninhabited islands. A waxing moon hangs in the western sky, bathing everything in bluish light. A delicate fragrance he can't identify—herbs? fruit? flowers? trees?—rises from the earth and mingles with the smell, so foreign to him still, of saltwater. The pool reaches out from the house like a diving board, and he feels an urge, familiar from window seats when he was younger and also not much younger, to leap onto the clouds and bound off across them into some better, softer life. The winter air's coolness holds a secret warmth. Birdsong amplifies the silence beneath it. He stands there for some time with his awful coffee before realizing the clouds are moving, receding steadily toward the moon, the invisible Pacific pulling them like a tide. Their motion is a species of stillness. They *flow.* He watches them caress the contours of the land, gradually revealing folds of oak savanna, a patch of suburb, a golf course, as if the air is drawing back a blanket, startling the sleeping landscape into consciousness.

The balcony's slate is cold against his feet; he goes back inside and finishes his coffee while walking slow laps around the gradually lightening atrium, then returns to bed, where he and Sadie again have sex as the rising sun filters through the translucent shades.

Sex was what anchored us on top of that mountain; without it we would've floated away. In the light of day we realized the house was almost certainly far enough from other human dwellings that no one *from outside* could see us, no matter where we were in it or on its balcony, and we fucked on the living-room couches, the kitchen countertop, the islands, the library floor, in the shower, the atrium, the pool, on the edge of the hot tub (the glass people couldn't make it today), light-headed from the heat of the water that clung to our exhausted and happy bodies. I told Sadie I was a little scared. "Of what?" "Of my own desire." "What is it, exactly, that you desire?" she asked, and I told her, and we did that. Then I asked what she most wanted to do and we did that, too. There was, in general, more biting than I was used to, a stronger undercurrent of violence. I was surprised at how comfortable I felt inflicting pain on someone I liked and esteemed.

As we lay on the sun-warmed slate of the balcony letting our bodies dry, we heard what sounded like an approaching helicopter, and then it was no longer approaching, it was here, it circled twice close around the house and flew off into the horizon. Whoever was inside must have seen us there, but by this point we didn't care. Let them look. We stood naked at the parapet beyond the pool, gazing out on our kingdom. We laughed. Think of all those poor people not us. We returned to bed, fucked, slept. We awoke and ate granola bars and potato chips in bed. We allowed our bodies to become objects of study; Sadie photographed us with her disposable camera. "Just don't post these on the Internet," I said. The Internet? What's that? She'd never heard of it. Didn't I know moms didn't use the Internet? "Am I the first mom you've ever slept with?" she asked later. I pointed out that was a complicated question and she pretended to disagree. We reveled in the unlikeliness of our coupling to the point where it no longer seemed unlikely.

Then Sadie flew back to New York and I was alone, looking through windows, seeing her. I saw the skin, lightly creased, in the hollow of her neck and shoulders; her brown eyes flecked with yellow and green; the tattoo of a falcon on her ass. When I closed my eyes she became more vivid. I spent hours just walking around the house. She'd been here only one full day, but every room held some memory of her. It took a while before my mind had the strength to push remembering into narrative or analysis. What should I *do* with my experience with Sadie? Where to put it, how to arrange its moments? We hadn't talked about what came next, whether, or to what extent, we'd stay in touch. In the days after she left, we G-chatted a bit—my phone didn't get service inside the house—mostly, or so it seems to me now, to express and re-express our mutual gratitude. "I keep thinking of what a lovely time I had with you." I think we were both wary of shading or complicating what had been for both of us "a simple, fun thing" (as she'd later put it). Then at some point—Sadie suggested this—I discovered that our time together could be both that and something slightly more, something useful, a transition into a new era for me, a sort of welcome, or a door.

I only felt alone in the house at night. During the day I was too amazed to feel alone. I couldn't stop taking laps around the house, letting view give onto view, as the sun projected its daily light show onto the house's surfaces—not only the usual light shapes migrating almost imperceptibly across the floor, but light reflecting from the pool, from the atrium's pond, shadows of birds and planes, little rainbows; all recurred with such regularity that I began to feel as friendly toward particular effects of light as I did toward certain corners of my mind. Then I'd lift my eyes to the windows and words like *friendly* lost their meaning as my boundaries expanded to the surrounding hills and cities and the horizon beyond. I'd never known how much space I could fill. Sadie's house, without furniture, had seemed huge; this house simply was. It was more than huge. Its windows were what made it limitlessly big; they opened the house up to the world in all directions so that inside overflowed into outside, or there was no outside, or outside leaked in. For a long time I struggled to get my bearings. When you're above that which is normally above you, it's hard not to feel like the world is upside down.

Dave assigned me little tasks by email: water the trees in the atrium, clean the fire pits, check the salt level in the water salt container, pick up the third garage door opener from Dave's wife's sister in Vacaville, update passwords, put chlorine tablets in the pool; buy padlocks, flashlights, houseplants, lightbulbs, the biggest flat-screen TV Best Buy sells; clear stray branches from beneath the pool area, install the motion-detecting camera by the water tank, post NO TRESPASSING signs. Many days, too, contractors came, not only the glass people but the elevator guy, the floor guy, the roof guy, the pool guys, the window washers, the landscapers, the housekeepers, the plumbers, the gas guy, the alarm guy, who was also the sound system guy, though Dave was convinced he could get a better deal on speakers from some other sound system guy. They'd call me when they reached the wrought iron gate and I'd give them the combination to the lock I'd installed, knowing to expect them half an hour later. When they arrived they'd express disbelief at the house and I'd take them on a tour around the hexagon, first inside, then on the balcony. "On a clear day you can see the Golden Gate Bridge," I'd say, if that day wasn't clear. Many of them told me they'd often looked up at the big glass house on top of the mountain and wondered what it was like inside. A few told me they'd been up here before the house was built; there used to be miles of hiking trails, they said. All of them asked me how much the place cost and I quoted the figure Dave had bragged to me about (without my having asked): twenty million. "The windows alone must have cost a million dollars," they said, under the spell of the word *million*. "Are they bulletproof?" I forget which contractor asked me that but I remember assuring him they were. Probably they were. At least one contractor did a double take as he saw me emerging from the house, I guess because I looked young or poor or both, and said, "You *own* this place?" Not technically but in a deeper sense the house was mine: *I* was here, not Dave. *I* paced its rooms, *I* lost myself in its reflections and views, which were mine just as million-dollar paintings are yours for those moments you stand before them in museums.

The alarm guy who was also the sound system guy started

coming up almost every day. The installation of the alarm system and the rewiring of the sound system were both more complicated than he'd expected, or so he claimed; I suspected he just liked being up here. In any case we became friends, sort of. I gave him beers and we sat drinking by the pool. His name was Oscar and he was from Colombia; he showed me photos of his life there on his phone. He'd been an outdoor adventure guide, and his photos were mostly of himself and his clients on horses, mountain bikes, whitewater rafts. He'd been in California seven years and planned to stay for seven more before returning to Colombia with his wife and kids, one of whom was born in America and barely knew a word of Spanish, Oscar lamented. "Colombia is home," he said. "Will always be. America is where you go to make money," and he waved his hand at the ostentatiousness that sheltered us. Another day I lent him my binoculars, which were actually Sadie's, and he called me over to look at something on a grassy rise a little ways down the mountain: "These big things—they are guns?" he asked, handing me the binoculars. They did look like cannons but what they were in fact were sections of a life-size fiberglass tyrannosaurus. I'd seen it once from the road on my way up, just beyond a copse of oaks, and Dave had told me it belonged to the only previous owner of the house, who'd planned to populate the top of the mountain with dozens of fiberglass dinosaurs. But then he went bankrupt and lost not only that dream but the house he'd spent a decade fighting to get built. He and his wife had only lived there three years. Now they lived in a normal-sized house not far from the broken dinosaur, and, as Oscar and I stood on the balcony, I could just make it out through the binoculars.

One day, not long after I arrived, the man, whose unlikely name was Ward Druthers, invited me over for dinner. His present house was probably a mile away, but, by the winding dirt roads down the mountain, it took me twenty minutes to get there in the Jeep, in which I felt invincible. This house had two bedrooms and a large living room with big windows and would've worked well as a walk-in closet inside House Above the Morning Clouds. But whatever tragedy I'd been hoping to have elaborated soon dissolved in Ward Druthers's stoicism, which seemed to be underwritten by his wife, Lynn's (he did most of the talking). He and a partner had started a chain of convenience stores—he'd coined that term, *convenience store,* he said—when he was young and stupid and had no idea what he was doing and for some reason the stores took off. They became billionaires. He and Lynn traveled everywhere, he said, they saw the wonders of the world, Timbuktu. "We've been together over fifty years," Lynn chimed in. (She was a stewardess, I learned a bit later, but had to quit when she married Ward because stewardesses weren't allowed to be married back then.) Then he got sued by Big Tobacco—all this he told me without any prodding—for selling gray-market cigarettes. The Supreme Court declined to hear the case, and he lost almost everything. "But we're fine. We liked living up in the house you're looking after and we like living in this house. We're used to hardship." I nodded but inside I was laughing—hardship! I thought of Oscar and his wife and kids, thousands of miles from home.

Anyway, he went on as I endured the roast beef, coleslaw, mashed potatoes and gravy, there was a lot about that house they didn't like. Sure, the sunsets were spectacular, but just wait until the winds came, he said with grave eyes. The winds should be starting up again anytime now. Lynn, in response to this, gave a little shiver and brought her arms in close to her torso. "The winds!" she echoed, and shook her head. "You're lucky you missed the rains," she said. "That's what drove the woman before you out. But the winds . . ." Again she shook her head.

Over "banana split" ice cream with brownies, Ward told me they'd wanted to have the house designed by a certain protégé of Frank Lloyd Wright, but he died so they'd settled for a protégé of the protégé. It took four years to get the permit and six years to build. He took a lot of crap from the neighbors, he said, but look at it now: it was beautiful. "Beautiful. As long as you can forget about the wind," said Lynn. "It's beautiful to people who aren't in it," he said, "and they don't have to deal with the wind. Let's have a look." We followed him outside, to a little hill that rose behind his house. From there we had an unobstructed view of House Above the Morning Clouds. It jutted from the mountain like a frozen flame, straining toward some gaudy ultimate. The only way it would ever disappear, I found myself thinking, was *upward,* in an explosion—either that or it would take flight like the spaceship Dave was right to say it resembled, and return to whatever planet it had come from. We all agreed it was beautiful.

"Have you come across the plane crash yet?" Ward asked as I was walking toward the Jeep. Apparently a bomber had crashed into the mountain on its way to Hawaii during World War II; the wreckage was fifty yards from the house: Ward told me how to find it.

Next morning I searched for it and there it was—a patch of dirt and loose gravel underneath which the remaining debris lay buried. I unearthed a mangled set of earphones, two buttons, a belt buckle, several rusted scraps of steel, a shard of glass, and what looked to be a layer of ash. Later a bit of research revealed the names and ranks of the five crew members: Capt. F. S. Nelson, 2nd Lt. E. W. Sell, T/Sgt. Phil Zeik, T/Sgt. Richard Kinney, and Pfc. Evan Phillips lost their lives on December 21, 1941. I wondered if they left behind children, wives.

The Bachelor had never given much thought to the question of what would happen to his body after he died. Shawntel, who thought about it every day, wanted to be cremated: that way she could avoid the chemical resurrection she inflicted on Chico's recently dead as embalmer at her father's funeral home. "I don't handle death well," the Bachelor said as she gave him an exclusive tour of the place on her all-important hometown date. "I don't handle saying goodbye to people well." Shawntel walked him through the mausoleum (two caskets per crypt, one for husband, one for wife), demonstrated the crematory ("PRESS FOR FLAME"), and, in the prep room, asked him if he had any interest in lying down on the embalming table. Not really, he said, climbing onto it. Fluorescent light blasted the white walls and ceiling and glared off brushed-metal surfaces. "So what happens is I would take a scalpel," she explained. "Make an incision. And then what I would do is I would take an aneurysm hook, and this would be going through your incision and finding your carotid artery and your vein . . ." She laughed. "Are you, like, creeped out or what?" He was, but at the same time he respected what Shawntel did—not only the hooking people's veins part or whatever, but, in all seriousness, having conversations with those poor people who'd so recently lost loved ones. "I could not do it," he said with intensity. "No way. I'd cry with the families."

Sadie and I agreed that comment almost made up for the odd furtive behavior he uncharacteristically displayed during the rest of the date. "Shawntel is right," Sadie wrote from the other coast. "We *do* live in a death-denying society. I knew she wouldn't get a rose; she's too real for the Bachelor to handle": words I could hear Sadie speaking, see her writing, before I read them in her letter—one of our first—since by this point when I watched *The Bachelor* I experienced Sadie's reactions at least as fully as my own, whether she was sitting next to me or thousands of miles away.

Our progression from G-chat to letters had been swift, bridged by a single postcard, hers, a reproduction of the cover of *Rock Me Baby!,* a 1962 pulp fiction by Greg Randolph ("Bop king Dickie Wild was the idol of millions of screaming teenagers . . . but his private love life would have made even Casanova blush!"). "One thing we've sacrificed in our age of electronic immediacy," she wrote near the end of her second letter, in the elegiac mode that I was coming to realize characterized so much of her writing and thinking, "is the ability to just settle with one's thoughts, to think both broadly and deeply. I've noticed it lately because in our G-chat habit I push myself away, somewhat, from really thinking about you. It's a paradox." Mail wasn't delivered to House Above the Morning Clouds, so every few days I'd make the hour-and-a-half-long drive to Fairfield's nearest post office, where I'd drop off a letter and, more often than not, find one waiting for me. Sadie wrote on soft, thick, cream-colored stationery in small, distinguished cursive. Later I'd learn she used a $500 fountain pen her stepfather had given her when she was ten. "So I write this letter," she wrote, "to allow my thoughts to settle on you, your hand, your neck, your mouth against mine, my lips moving slowly up the edge of your ear, my tongue tracing its way back down. . . ."

From the start, we were almost reckless in our intimacy. We recounted our last day together in as much detail as we could muster, letting fantasy and projection take over whenever memory failed. And yet while I was interested in all aspects of her life, which seemed so far away from mine, I can't deny I was particularly interested in the details of her open marriage. Making sure to get across that I approved of the arrangement, and not for selfish reasons alone—"It must take a lot of courage," I wrote, "to opt out of the prescribed ways of ordering your life"—I prodded her, gently I hoped, with questions. How were things with Ryan? Did he know about me? Did he have a girlfriend? How did the whole thing *work*? It worked by communicating about it every day and meeting its difficulties and awkwardnesses head-on. Ryan knew about me but didn't have a girlfriend, though he'd had a few since they'd opened the marriage. He had rheumatoid arthritis and often lacked the energy for anything outside of work and family, both of which he was passionately devoted to and together seemed to provide what pleasures he needed. He loved exploring New York with Ethan, visiting galleries and museums and parks. "They like it here more than I do," Sadie wrote. "For them it's a vacation, for me—I was going to say a nightmare, but that's probably a little too strong."

Only a little, though. Committed to a six-month vacation from work (after working for two decades without more than a three-week break, even when Ethan was born), she spent her days wandering the streets and buildings so familiar to her from her childhood. It seemed impossible that so many places—and not only places but views, smells, sounds, architectural details—could have been holding for all these years scraps of Sadie's life. It was overwhelming. The world seemed alien in the sheer intensity of its familiarity. One day she found her feet had carried her without her permission to Gramercy Park, and she didn't even make it to the iron gate before nausea overtook her. She tried to seek out new experiences, but even in places she'd never been she found herself thinking about the ruin of her family, how cut off from each other they'd always been, even before they cut each other off in the biggest, most final ways. "How little experience I have of *gathering,*" she wrote, "and trusting in the ways such an activity might nourish one." All the walking made it easy to fall asleep at night, but once asleep she was visited nightly by dreams unsettling and worse. In one, she dreamt that two of her teeth fell out into her hand, "a classically horrible dream, of course," and then, on the street, people kept asking for her ID, and she could never find it. "My therapist suggested that my chronic jaw clenching, which I've always taken to be related to anger, might also be interpreted as a kind of subconscious effort to hold myself together."

Beyond Ethan, who was a "constant delight," bird-watching in Central Park, "and, it goes without saying, *you,*" her only reliable source of solace—one completely new to her and that took her by surprise—was (could I believe it?) karaoke. She loved watching other people, especially, that volatile mix of embarrassment and exhilaration, aloneness and togetherness, irony and sincerity. She liked the most nervous ones the best, she wrote. It was as though all the hardest parts of their lives showed up on the features of their straining faces, either to be muddled through for the length of the song or transformed into a sort of redemptive joy, and because you never knew which direction the performance would take, there was this wonderful, awful tension. "Our own hang-ups get to be so boring," she wrote; "other people's: endlessly interesting."

"You should have seen me when I got your letter today," she wrote in another letter. "I shrieked like a little girl. It would've embarrassed you if you'd been there. Then I took it to my bed and read and reread it, then put it aside and started touching myself, all the way aroused, when Ethan got home from school and ran down the hallway and into my room and jumped into bed and lay down on my chest and wrapped his arms around me, then started kissing me up and down my legs and telling me he loved me. Being a parent can make a person's head explode sometimes." Most of the time, though, it was a consolation. She tried so hard to be a mother for Ethan in all the ways her mother never was for her. "I pulled him next to me against my pillow and read to him for a long time from the sci-fi talking-cat series he's obsessed with, even though I hate, hate, hate reading those books—the language sticks so badly in the mouth—and when I stopped he looked up at me, his face just totally glowing, and said, in a voice so serious and hushed, 'Mom, I love this book.' And in that moment I was so, so happy. I remembered being his age and getting lost in books, that overwhelming feeling. And then I thought, Damn, that's exactly how this whatever-we-have—you and I, I mean—is going to go, isn't it: we can't be together even in my imagination. Which I guess is my way of saying, again, maybe we should stop corresponding?"

"Again": the written record is full of other instances of what I took to be Sadie's fatalistic attitude toward us. But this attitude proved to be just the spark we needed: if she hadn't insisted on our imminent decline, I doubt I would've fought so hard against it; if she hadn't deemed a long-term relationship with me impossible, I never would've thought to imagine a future for us.

Sadie accepted my invitation to return to California; she'd arrive one month exactly after she'd left, and we'd have three nights and two full days to celebrate our anniversary. A few days before she was due to arrive, I picked up from the post office a small padded envelope that turned out to contain a mix CD from her. I listened to it on the way back to my mountain: sad pretty songs about heartbreak and loss that sounded like they came from another era, an era when men rambled and women pined and everyone was on closer terms with death. Scaffolds littered the countryside. Ghosts were real. There was a tremendous and general yearning for home, which was synonymous with Heaven and sometimes Mother, sometimes also Kentucky or Virginia. People were weary, unspeakably weary. The living slept on straw-covered pallets and the departed slept on our Savior's breast. Murderers drew daggers that flashed in the moonlight, then fled for California or Chicago, leaving brides behind. The wildflowers their children saw in dreams were windows onto eternity.

When I got home I read the note Sadie had enclosed. "I've been thinking about you," she wrote, "and the sadness you carry without acknowledging it, perhaps even without realizing it's there, and I've been wondering how much of it has to do with your having abandoned the activity that once held such a central place in your life." The letter went on in this vein for a while. "Forgive me," she wrote three times. She suggested I direct my "energy and talent" into some sort of long-term project. Had I ever tried my hand at nonfiction? Memoir? "I know you don't think your life is interesting enough to write about, but maybe there's some other subject out there calling for your sustained attention."

That night, in the enormous bed in the enormous bedroom that was nonetheless smaller than the enormous rooms surrounding it, I lay awake thinking about Sadie's note. That she clearly knew I would find it annoying ("Forgive me") didn't make it any less so. I resented what I shuddered to (but couldn't help but) think of as her *motherly concern.* She was projecting her sadness onto me. I wasn't sad. I was fine. I was. The CD full of sad songs was a trap; I wouldn't allow myself to fall into it. How dare she try to lure me into the suffering that constituted her life. It had been a mistake to invite her back, we were incompatible. Suddenly the difference in our ages represented an insurmountable gulf.

And yet, the more I considered her suggestion, the less repellent it became. Laura had made a similar suggestion earlier in the winter, I remembered, and a few days earlier my agent had emailed, asking when I thought I might have some pages to send. It would be nice if I could truthfully report that I was at work on something. I still had enough money to live on for a while, but I'd been spending more on gas here than I'd expected (the drive up and down the mountain burnt so much), and it was becoming more dispiriting by the day to watch my so-called savings drain away. More than that, even if I wasn't as sad as Sadie presumed, I was growing, I had to admit, a little restless. *What are you doing with your life?*

I got out of bed and wandered around the house, trying to think of a subject to write about. I brainstormed in my pocket notebook:

—panoramas
—clouds
—the Bulls
—*The Bachelor*
—documentaries
—the pine beetle epidemic
—pineapples
—music playing from other rooms

—the pleasures of reading aloud
—the history of flight
—reading after watching TV
—mass extinction
—owls
—apocalypticism

I had wandered into Dave's wife's library. Built-in bookshelves lined the walls, which with the entrance formed a massive hexagon covered from floor to ceiling with books. Entering it was like being swallowed by a monster whose stomach was lined with all of literature. I made my way slowly along the shelves, vaguely searching for potential topics, when my gaze caught on a series of books whose author called out to me like a long lost friend: *Henry's Fate; Recovery; 77 Dream Songs; His Toy, His Dream, His Rest.* Next to these was a copy of the biography I'd stolen from Maria, and I could almost taste the blueberry-banana smoothie, almost hear Maria in the shower, almost see the books and bottles of wine that lined her room, and it was in that moment that I decided my destiny would be to write a new biography of John Berryman.

I went upstairs and Googled "Berryman archives," and discovered that the bulk of his papers were kept at the University of Minnesota: I would go there the first chance I got. Maybe I could combine it with visits to my parents, whom I hadn't seen in ages, and to Laura. Meanwhile, I would finish reading his published work, and reread what I'd read already with renewed purpose. Rather than telling "John Berryman's story" I would tell a story about John Berryman. Taking my lead from Berryman himself, I would be transparent about my limitations. I would make clear, through subtle tactics, that I was writing from a particular point of view. But I would also—how, I wasn't sure—transcend this point of view. I would enter into Berryman's life as though it were my own, and maybe in the course of inhabiting it I would discover something about myself, and in making that process of self-discovery visible on the page, the book would also be an invitation for readers to discover things about themselves. That I didn't know how to write a biography was hardly a reason not to try: I hadn't known how to write a novel before I wrote one of those.

It took me a long time to fall asleep that night, and I woke up the next morning full of purpose. A new beginning.

In February 1937, John Berryman attended a Cambridge performance of *The Revenger's Tragedy,* a Jacobean play full of sex and violence probably written by Thomas Middleton, though for many years it was attributed to Middleton's contemporary Cyril Tourneur. Its opening scene features a young brooding man holding the skull of his murdered lover, almost certainly an allusion to *Hamlet,* in whose plot Berryman recognized parallels to his own life. But his attention was soon diverted from his sad past toward an actress with large, dark, passionate eyes. She was playing the role of the brooding young man's mother. Berryman couldn't stop thinking about her long after the play had ended.

A few weeks later he attended a lunch party thrown by an American friend. There she was. *I couldn't drink my sherry,* he'd recall or invent or half-invent in a poem more than thirty years later, *I couldn't eat.* Her name was Beryl Eeman and she was a student of modern languages who was also interested, she told Berryman, in theater and ballet. He couldn't bring himself to talk with her much, and then the party was over. He doubted he'd ever see her again but promised himself that if he did, he'd ask for time alone with her.

He ran into her a few days later on a Cambridge quad. They chatted until he worked up the courage to invite her to his apartment, where he made tea and they sat on his bed sipping it and talking about themselves and literature. She claimed to prefer Racine to Shakespeare. Berryman, incredulous, tried to change her mind by reading to her from *All's Well That Ends Well.* The Shakespeare seems to have had its effect: *By six-fifteen,* Berryman would write, *she had promised to stop seeing "the other man." / I may have heard better news but I don't know when. / Then—I think—then I stood up, & we kissed.*

He forgot about the girl he'd left behind in New York, the Jean or Jane to whom he may have been engaged, and began writing a play about Cleopatra, a vehicle for Beryl. That spring, they spent most of their free time together. By June, she'd put down in writing that she loved him. Shortly thereafter, he reciprocated, with the difference that his letter was addressed to his mother.

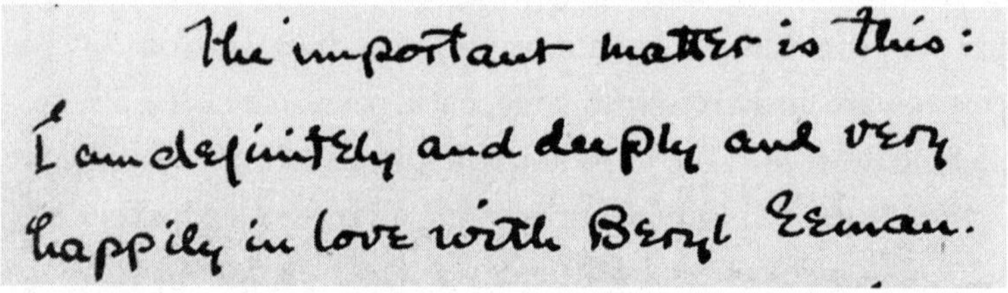
The important matter is this: I am definitely and deeply and very happily in love with Beryl Eeman.

He was making his case for not returning to New York to be with his mother for the summer. Knowing from experience—he'd had a few serious girlfriends—his mother would be suspicious at best of his love for any woman other than herself, he enumerated Beryl's best qualities for her with swift and cunning precision. She was "physically beautiful and vigorous and graceful," he wrote,

> *with a strong, direct, skeptical intelligence, no sentimentality, but a powerful emotional nature held rigidly by will and self-examination. She came slowly and profoundly to love me—she is tender and lovely beyond telling, Mum. Neither of us is primarily interested in how long it will last—for each, the present is rich and valuable when we are together and would be intolerable if we were not—that is the point. But we do, in fact, feel married now—without any adventitious strain on "forever."*

For their summer vacation, Berryman and Beryl decided to go to Germany. She would learn German and he would study for the Charles Oldham Shakespeare examinations: the top performer would win a scholarship of seventy pounds, which, if he had it, would not only ease his living expenses but prove to his mother, after all these years, his worthiness as a son. The couple spent most of their time in Heidelberg, from where Berryman sent his mother a series of letters and postcards. He saw everything through the gauze of new love. "You cannot believe a place can be so lovely," he wrote, "with its heavenly hills & woods & river & shops & people & food & coffee & beer & the Schloss & plays & Beryl & Shakespeare." Berryman and Beryl read *Romeo and Juliet* together in three stretches, in preparation for seeing a production that was part of the *Reichsfestspiele* organized by Goebbels, himself a poet and playwright in the Romantic vein. "Magnificent production," Berryman reported to his mother, "several hundred actors storming in from four angles, brilliant lighting, fireworks at the banquet . . . drums &

swords & dances & a 20-minute wordless procession to lay Juliet in the tomb." A few days later, he and Beryl happened to come across the actor who'd played Capulet, and Berryman saw in him a manifestation of Aryan perfection—"possibly the most satisfying human being I've seen ever, large, powerful, open, brilliantly alive, laughing, magnificent." His shoulders were broad, his jaw square, his eyes an intriguing silver-blue. . . .

The Germany vacation affirmed what Berryman already knew about Beryl. She was his "one chance for a full and rich and permanent (if, necessarily, desperately partial) human happiness," he wrote his mother. "I find capacities I had not dreamed of, never admitted the existence of, and derided even in art."

As for me, there was no question of telling my mother about Sadie. It wasn't that I feared she'd disapprove, exactly, but that such transgressions of societal convention weren't spoken of in my family. I had no interest in upsetting the smooth surface of the early part (I hoped) of my parents' old age. Sadie, though, wanted to tell my mom. Her own mother's lies had taught her to hate deception of any kind. I argued that some forms of deception were benign, and that in any case everyone was always deceiving everyone else, we didn't go around baring our souls to everyone we met. She accused me of lacking courage. Chastened, I told her we could tell my mother eventually but I needed time, secretly suspecting the relationship would end before we revealed our secret.

The tension that had begun to cloud our correspondence in recent days, though, seemed to dissolve the moment I saw her. We embraced, kissed, held hands to the Jeep, and drove back from the airport to my mountain listening to a mix I'd made for her the night before. "It's so great to *see* you," she couldn't stop saying, as if the words were what kept me from disappearing. "It's so great to see *you,*" I said. It was. The day was bright and warm. As we passed through the vineyards of Suisun Valley, the pleasing rhythm of the passing rows of grapevines was interrupted by a flurry of digital chimes, and when we reached the base of the mountain I asked Sadie if she'd mind if we stopped so I could check my phone before it went out of service. "You mean before we enter the Void?"

The texts turned out to be from Laura. Today was the day of her sister's wedding, and Laura was giving me a running commentary of the reception: her mother was getting drunk, her mother was drunk, her mother was whisper-yelling about her sister's dress, her sister was talking shit about her mother, the reception was fast turning into a "disaster"—a disaster I knew Laura was sort of enjoying even as it appalled her. *Keep the updates coming,* I texted. *Will respond more fully later.* "Just a friend with a crazy mom," I said, not wanting to invoke an ex-girlfriend at this moment, and Sadie and I, still dazed by each other, ascended above the clouds.

Reunion sex with someone you really like is the best sex not only because the pleasures of rediscovery are overlaid on the more immediate pleasures of touch, almost as though you're reenacting your first time, but also because, as in a suspenseful book or movie, you experience equally and simultaneously anxiety and its assuagement.

Next day was the warmest since I'd arrived and so clear we could see not only the Golden Gate Bridge but downtown San Francisco. I let Sadie press the button that retracted the glass doors suspended half an inch above the pool, while I inflated the floating chaises longues. We spent the day getting in and out of the pool and sometimes lounging beside it. The pool was warm; the wind was cool; the sun was warm then hot. Sadie had a higher tolerance for the hot tub than I did (more than five minutes at a time made me light-headed). The chaises longues' cupholders didn't support our mimosas, so we drank them sitting on the edge of the pool, legs suspended in the water. We tossed quarters in the deep end and dove to retrieve them. Sadie swam like an Olympic champion, so I was embarrassed, but also not, when it was revealed I could barely swim the length of the pool. Sadie asked if I'd taken swim lessons when I was a kid, and I told her I had but they never took.

"Water isn't my element," I said.

"What is?"

"You," I said ridiculously, kissing her.

"You're ridiculous," she said, pulling me toward her.

"Where did you learn to swim so well?" I said into her mouth.

"Ocean," she said into mine.

Ocean.

Later, or earlier, we watched a pair of eagles circle the house and then swoop through the valley.

"Golden," Sadie said.

We ate strawberries for lunch.

We ran laps around the house till we worked up a sweat, then dove into the pool and got out and did it again.

All day we did whatever felt good. I have a photo of Sadie on the edge of the pool, legs in the water and sunlight streaming through the pane of glass behind her onto her naked and gleaming body, a look of contentment on her face that consumes all other contentment in the world. For a long time we sat in folding chairs on the balcony, reading our respective books (hers:

the latest Didion; mine: Berryman's *Collected*), and I thought, *If happiness exists then here it is: two naked people reading silently together on top of a mountain in the sun.*

We'd planned to descend into Napa the next day, maybe visit a few wineries, but we awoke to find ourselves not above the clouds but in one. "I think it's raining," Sadie said. "I think we're inside the rain." Purple-gray fog pressed against all windows, bathing the house in an alien light that didn't change as the day progressed. It was crepuscular, the light, but also bright, as if combining the softness of twilight with the clarity of midday sun. It was lovely. Without clocks, it would've been impossible to guess with any accuracy the time of day.

"Fuck time."

Beads of water ran down the windows. Swirling eddies appeared here and there before losing themselves in the cloud's near solidity. There was no question of going to Napa now, not because we didn't want to drive through the cloud but because we wanted to stay inside it, to see what effect it would have on us.

We spent the morning replacing lightbulbs. Dave had ordered 950 "cool blue" bulbs to replace the ones that had come with the house, less because he disliked their quality of light than because he could afford it, I sensed. Sadie and I quickly developed a routine. We took turns on the ladder, unscrewing and replacing, while the other tossed up new bulbs, caught old ones, and made sure the ladder didn't fall. We worked in near silence, honing our techniques. We aimed for, and achieved (we decided), "maximum efficiency." The work required just enough attention to keep us from thinking of other things. Our minds relaxed almost into mindlessness. I want to say we entered a *trancelike state,* but I was too aware of being with Sadie for that to really be true. What is true is that beyond her and the lightbulbs I was aware of little else, and I felt a new quality settling around us, and sensed she felt it, too.

I didn't expect to feel this way.

That's a good thing, right?

Every time we fall in love, we imagine that all the other times weren't real, our new love's authenticity exposing the hollowness of our previous love. Such an intuition is as necessary as it is illusory. Sadie and I knew not to trust it but did. The visit had initiated something, we both felt that, and our drive back down the mountain the next day was permeated with that certainty-in-uncertainty that accounts for the terror and joy of such beginnings. As we neared the bottom my phone went crazy and I pulled into a driveway to check its messages: ten or twelve more texts from Laura completing the tragicomedy of her sister's wedding and one from the day after that read, *Sorry for bombarding you. Everyone fine. My sister is a wife!* Then there was one from a few hours later—*Are you there?*—and another that seemed to answer it: *I'm here,* and it took me a few moments to register that the last one wasn't from Laura but Maria, sent that morning, a little after six, her first response to the email I'd sent what must have been only a little more than a month earlier, and it's strange to remember thinking as I stared into my phone of Michael Jordan's 1995 fax announcing his return to the Bulls from minor-league baseball—strange to remember he'd ever left, strange to remember remembering faxes—which said simply, "I'm back."

Where's here?

11

"THE HOUSE IS OLD, RAMBLING, SO OVERGROWN WITH flowers that it seems rather to have grown with them than to have been built before or after the lovely half-wild garden in which it stands," wrote Beryl to Berryman on June 18, 1938. She was staying at a friend's house outside London as an interlude between university, which she'd completed, and her summer job as tutor and au pair in Italy. Berryman, also through with Cambridge, had returned to New York to live with his mother. The past year had been a difficult one for the couple, newly engaged. The moment they got back to Cambridge from Germany, Berryman had thrown himself into his Shakespeare studies in preparation for the Oldham exam. "I've been puzzling pretty steadily now for a week on 'Most busie lest, when I doe it,' he wrote his mother, "and a certain baffling gem in *Romeo and Juliet* which turns on a single word in the phrase 'that runaway's eyes may wink.'" Also, he added, he'd grown a beard. "Delicious not shaving, my sole object; the necessary result I don't mind, scarcely know I have it, and it's generally admired;

will have a picture taken and send you one; may keep it permanently or may take it off next week."

He sat for the Oldham Shakespeare exam and proceeded to worry about its results. Beryl alternately eased and tormented his mind, impeding his progress toward the literary immortality he planned to attain through poems inspired by her. His diary from the fall of 1938 maps out his central preoccupations. October 1: "Very happy doing nothing at all with B." October 7: "Uncertainty kills me as finality kills most men." October 10: "Brooke approved my beard." October 11: "More anxious about the Oldham than I tell even myself. . . . Seeing Beryl every day is heavenly, but I'm not able to work very consistently." October 17: "Up in Beryl's room all day. Rather than begin revision of Cleopatra in the evening, I read two meaningless plays." October 25, his birthday: "Mainly music and very gloomy thinking about all kinds of things—*Hamlet,* survival . . . Ezra Pound, the critical labor, possibilities of greatness. Again and again, the meaning of life and its negation. I must go deeper before I leave." November 2: "Beard trimmed extensively." November 5: "Beryl in during the evening. I've seen her every day since term began; it may be bad for us under the circumstances Cambridge imposes." November 10: "I wonder if I shall live long enough to write the great poetry I know I can." November 23: "I have the Oldham."

The Oldham didn't solve any of his problems. The irrelevance of his chosen field, for one: "I wish I could believe people read poetry, but they don't and it doesn't much matter." "Stupid insipid" people "who asked for opinions," for another: "I must stop telling people who are of no sensibility what I think, and my useless rages must stop." Another: making art was incompatible with living life. Yet another: his fiancée was pregnant.

Beryl wanted the child; Berryman didn't: he had no money or job prospects. He endured weeks of worry before Beryl reported that the positive had been false. "Not our fault," he wrote his mother, "a mechanical slip, but sufficiently harrowing."

After that, he and Beryl agreed it would be best if they saw a little less of each other for a while, which gave him more time to sit alone in his apartment, blurring the worlds of art and all that isn't. He bought a gramophone he couldn't afford and listened obsessively to the Fifth Brandenburg Concerto, with its driving strings and leaping flute and harpsichord that plucks your nerve endings. "Blake born 180 years ago today—where now?" he wrote in his diary. He slept in his clothes and let his beard grow long and scraggly. In a fit of self-analysis he summed up his character: "a disagreeable compound of arrogance, selfishness and impatience scarcely relieved by some dashes of courtesy and honesty and a certain amount of industry." "The central difficulty," he explained to his mother, "is that of being certain one will be able to write well. More than ever before, the world is full of men who have given their lives to literature and have achieved nothing: humiliation to eternity. I have only contempt for such men, they clutter the horizon."

As his time in England drew to a close, he wrote Beryl a letter about their engagement, which he was trying to honor in spite of creeping doubts. Her brave, beautiful, heartbreaking response is dated April 26, 1938:

> *I too have been thinking about our marriage. I too love you devotedly and believe you love me. And I too think we have been happier than most men seem to have any right to expect. But, as you say, there's more in it. . . . If you are best pleased that we see each other for the next six weeks and then no*

more, I shall have strength to be so too. I cannot see to write this. . . .

As for the artist in you, you are as you are, and I shall love you as long as I am not hurt beyond your healing. "This one difficult life is all we have, and being so is precious, and is so quickly gone away." I have no desire, no hope or expectation of living happily; life and happiness contradict each other as I understand them. But I have a most passionate desire to live fully. *To do the work I must do, I must live, and sweet or bitter, the taste must be strong.*

She asked Berryman to tell her how she hindered him. Did it bother him that she was financially independent? That she was English? That she loved him so intensely? "Finally," she concluded, "do you wish to marry at all? and is marriage of vast importance anyhow?"

Berryman's answer to this interesting question is buried in a letter he wrote around this time to his mother ("Dearest little angel mum"): "Life for the artist is a single moral act of vision. . . . He works only for himself, perhaps for a few friends, for the recognition and establishment of a relationship with God. What the world gets is its own affair, not his. There is something peculiarly terrifying in his solitude."

Sadie didn't react well to my proposal that Maria stay in her house for a while, I told Laura on the phone a few days after the conversation in question.

"How did you expect her to react? I mean, unless I'm misunderstanding, you were basically asking one girlfriend if another could stay in her house."

"I don't know. She's in an open marriage. I thought she'd be more . . . open." Instead, I told Laura, she was upset. She accused me of taking advantage of her. She had no idea who this Maria character was; why should she trust her with her house? It wasn't until I relayed a version of the story Maria had told to me—edited to blur the edges of our relationship and make her as sympathetic as possible—that Sadie grudgingly allowed her to stay in her house through the end of March: twelve days. After that, she said, she was putting it on the market; she didn't expect her presence would be needed in Des Moines much after spring. I thanked her. I apologized. I told her a partial truth: that I'd been moved by Maria's story and wanted to do what I could to help.

Maria's story (from her narration of it on the phone when I called her from a Dunkin' Donuts parking lot in Oakland after dropping off Sadie at the airport):

Sam and Jo, Maria's newly married housemates, abandoned their South American honeymoon after falling sick in the Peruvian rain forest. The day after they returned to Detroit, she developed symptoms identical to theirs but stronger: fever, loss of appetite, localized paralysis, and a nausea that resolved into stomach pain just sharp enough to make the slightest exertion unthinkable. Her father drove up from Indiana and took her to a hospital near his house, where she drifted in and out of pain and sleep for three and a half weeks. It turned out some gnarly equatorial caterpillar had laid its eggs inside her, and her doctors, who'd never seen such a case, tried two treatments before the third one took. Back in her father's country house—which had undergone so many renovations in the past decade that it barely resembled the house she'd grown up in—she rested, ate, watched TV, and started piecing her life back together. When, sifting through the correspondence she'd missed, she read the email in which I declared my love and invited her to live with me in Des Moines, she didn't know how to begin to respond. "I really appreciated what you said," she said; she "felt it deserved a thoughtful response." But the prospect of explaining her long delay had filled her with an anxiety that bordered on dread. She still felt so weak from her illness, she said, and the medications were making her light-headed. And so, she told me, her voice faint and tinny, she'd decided to wait to respond to me until she felt more herself.

Meanwhile, she was determined to use her illness as a means of escape from the house in Detroit. She drove back up, packed her stuff, and returned to Indiana. It felt so freeing to abandon that life, which had never stopped seeming, she told me, like an interlude, though between what and what she couldn't say. As her health slowly improved, however, and she became more aware of her surroundings, she began to be troubled by a growing sense that her father's mind was going. He seemed alternately withdrawn from the world and totally bewildered by it. One moment he'd look lost in dark daydreams or memories, and the next he'd be laughing at the strangest things—the sudden appearance of a stinkbug on a window, a commercial for agricultural fertilizer, a ringing phone, the lighting of a stove. Several times she saw him standing in front of a door, looking down at its handle for what seemed like minutes, as if unable to remember its function or afraid it might burn his hand. Also, his speech was faltering. He often trailed off in the middle of sentences, sometimes frustrated that he couldn't find a word, other times appearing to lose interest in the thought. And he'd started saying aloud, in a barely audible voice, what he was doing as he did it: *locking the door, peeling a banana, opening my inbox, watching*

TV—as though if he stopped narrating his life it would cease to be real.

The day before she texted me and I called her, Maria said, she'd yelled at him for interrupting her reading with this constant self-narration. He yelled at her for yelling at him, and in the midst of the ensuing fight he said that a family friend had recently died, a man who had been like an uncle to him during his years in Argentina, thus severing the last of his remaining ties to that country, and, he said, to his youth. "I knew about this guy," Maria told me, "and had even met him once, when I was very young, on a family trip to Buenos Aires. All I remember of him is that he was obese, and that he spoke Spanish with a German accent so thick I could barely understand him. Anyway, I was almost certain he'd died when I was a teenager. I called my sister, and she confirmed my memory. The next day I accused my father of lying, and he just completely exploded. I felt so bad. I decided I had to leave that night, so I did, I wrote my father a note, and since I didn't know where to go I went to you. I drove all night. But you're not here, you're there."

I told Laura I found it hard to assimilate all the elements of Maria's story. I was disturbed almost to the point of nausea by the thought of a caterpillar laying its eggs inside her, troubled by the news of her father's apparent degenerative disease, and equally troubled that Maria had abandoned him in his vulnerable state. And yet the moment I heard her voice, I felt the same tenderness I'd felt before she'd fallen out of touch, as though the events of the past month and a half had never really happened—the concert with Jess and Amanda and friends; the retirement party back in Des Moines; my move to House Above the Morning Clouds; my fling with Sadie that had, behind my back, developed into something more. All the affection and fellow feeling was still there, the sense of being intimately and inextricably—and happily—bound up in her thoughts and feelings. I'd told Maria I was falling in love with her, it was *on the page,* there could be no question of taking it back. I asked Laura what she thought I should do.

"Ugh. You're really in love with both of them?"

"I don't know—in love, falling in love . . ."

"I'd start by trying to figure that out."

"How do I figure that out?"

It worried her, Laura said, that I hadn't told her about Maria until now. It was like I was trying to keep her secret; it suggested I was ashamed. I told her the whole thing had taken me by surprise. Everything was happening so fast, I said.

"And Sadie," Laura said—"I don't know, she's an *adult.* And she lives in New York. You live in California."

"*We're* adults. And I don't live here."

"Tell me this: How much do Sadie and Maria know about each other?"

I felt unfairly cornered. "I mean . . ."

"Okay, right, well. I wish I were surprised. You haven't changed at all, have you?"

It took me a moment to understand she was referring to Ellen, the coworker at Sheep's Head Mountain Ranch I'd kissed while Laura and I were still together. But I'd told Laura about the kiss immediately afterward, and Ellen knew all about Laura, as I remembered, so I didn't see how that situation had much in common with my current one. Also, by the time Sadie and I got together I assumed I'd never hear from Maria again, so I hadn't felt the need to explain to Sadie everything about her. Even as I defended myself against Laura, though—"Can we not relitigate the Ellen thing?"—a part of me trusted her judgment so completely that I wondered if I had fallen prey to a pattern that was destined to play out again and again in my life, to the detriment of those closest to me, and to my discredit and shame.

"Anyway, shouldn't you still be getting over Ashwini?" Laura asked.

"Who?" I was trying to make a joke.

Laura stifled a sort of admonitory sigh. "You ask a lot of me, you know."

"You have answers."

"Not all of them, friend."

"Almost all."

"If you say so."

I began to feel a creeping desperation. "So, no consolation? No advice?"

"Meditate. Do yoga. Listen to music."

I told Laura I was already listening to music and had tried yoga and meditation many times.

"Jesus, I don't know. Date them both."

"Right. Okay."

"Marry them both. That's legal in some places. Move to Utah or Afghanistan or wherever."

"Okay, I'm sorry. I'm sorry I brought it up."

"Look, you know I love you—"

"No no no, it's fine. It's fine. I understand. I'm sorry I missed your sister's wedding."

"What? That's not what this is—whatever, it's fine."

"It sounds like I missed out on quite a performance."

"My mom's *life* has been quite a performance. There'll be more. I'll make sure to invite you to *my* wedding."

"With Dan?"

"Things are going really well!"

"I'm glad to hear that."

"You don't seem glad."

"I've never been good at expressing my emotions."

"They get expressed. Just not always in speech."

"I'm glad, okay. I'm glad!"

"All right, well."

"Well," I said. Ending the call meant I'd have to return to the solitude of my big glass house.

"Here's my advice," said Laura. "Be honest. With yourself, and with Sadie and Maria."

I said I'd try.

It was June and Berryman was back in New York, pondering glory, looking for jobs. He wanted to make enough money to move out of his mother's upper Manhattan apartment, and to provide for his future wife, in spite of her stubborn insistence that she was capable of providing for herself. He was rejected from positions at Princeton and Queens College, but set up an interview for a teaching position at St. John's College in Annapolis. He inquired about reviewing opportunities at the *New York Herald Tribune,* but was turned away. He tried *Time* magazine even though it was beneath him, but even *Time* wouldn't hire him. It was the Depression and the job market was pinched. "The city is killing me," he wrote Mark Van Doren: "heat, strain, anxiety, loneliness." He was, he said, "at absolute ebb." Van Doren invited him to spend a weekend in the Connecticut countryside, where Berryman wrote poems and Van Doren praised them. Privately, though, Van Doren wondered what had become of the Berryman that had left two years ago; this new version spoke with an English accent, and affected aristocratic mannerisms, and had a beard. Maybe that explained why he couldn't get a job.

The interview with St. John's seemed to go well, but a few weeks later Berryman was rejected. He tried interviewing with some of his mother's contacts in the business world, but they were all "stupid" and "parasitic" and "vain," possessing "a kind of practical shrewdness and self-absorption hideous to see." He considered trying to get in touch with Orson Welles—maybe he could work as some sort of assistant—but the impulse passed and he brooded his days away at his suffocating mother's little apartment, lamenting "the whole complicated business of my return: mental adjustment, a terrible strain, which was unavoidable but which I had in no way foreseen." The separation from Beryl compounded his nervous exhaustion. "But," he wrote, "in any case I should be thankful: the energy released has given me half a dozen poems." Already, then, so early, he was moving toward the theory he would articulate most memorably in a 1970 interview. "My idea is this: The artist is extremely lucky who is presented with the worst possible ordeal which will not actually kill him. At that point, he's in business."

The sadder your story, Berryman believed, the better your chances at winning the whole thing.

Dave hadn't installed a printer in his house, and so, until I finally bought one myself, I had to read Maria's emails on my laptop, doubling the font size and closing my eyes once in a while to stave off headaches and floaters. Our correspondence that early spring was much the same as it had been before—warm, enthusiastic, mutually appreciative—and yet it felt subtly different. There was a new softness to Maria, I thought, a new vulnerability, a meekness almost. I connected it rightly or wrongly with her convalescence, whose progress she reported on regularly. She still felt, she wrote, not quite herself. She oscillated between periods of not unpleasant fatigue, during which she flickered in and out of sleep, in bed or on the couch or living-room floor, and a sort of heightened wakefulness that made the world seem incandescent. "You never told me how lovely Des Moines is!" she wrote. The snow melted except for a few rogue clumps (armored with thick layers of dirt and dead leaves), birdsong woke her before dawn most mornings, green had begun to infiltrate lawns, little red flowers were pushing forth from the outermost branches of silver maples. More than anything, though, what she noticed and loved was the silence and the space. People moved about quietly in Des Moines, as if not wanting to disturb even the air. "That's because they're ghosts," I wrote, but Maria saw in their uncertain movements, and in their abstracted, unreal faces, a resignation indistinguishable from contentment, which held within it some ineffable saintliness.

And so we kept asking each other what we were doing and thinking and reading and writing. I told her about my Berryman biography, an idea she enthusiastically supported. I presented it as a project I could begin to ease into as I finished "Grandpa." At this point I was still in the very early stages, the *preliminary stages,* as I put it in an email, establishing an intimate knowledge of Berryman's work, making plans to visit the places he'd lived, or at least those in New York and Minneapolis. Also Tampa. Rereading the biography Maria and I had hated, the biography Maria had taught me to hate, I began to wonder if it might be possible that Berryman's father actually *didn't* kill himself, if in reality it was Berryman's mother or stepfather who had killed him. Berryman himself entertained this hypothesis in a late journal entry. Plus, there were all kinds of holes in the various accounts, most of which in any case came from Berryman's mother, and I wondered if a little sleuthing in Tampa might uncover the truth. Oh yes, wrote Maria, you must go to Tampa. We must get to the bottom of that.

She decided to stay in Des Moines for at least a few more months; it wasn't hard to find a downtown sublet, she said. Also, she'd started writing poetry again: reworkings of poems she'd translated from the Finnish, filled out with new material and stitched together into an ever-expanding narrative poem, the Finnish-Midwestern epic the world was waiting for, she joked, though I could tell she was only sort of joking. It was just such inventions, Maria never stopped believing, that the world needed above all else. For such beliefs, I loved her. Did I love her? In those days, as in these, it was so hard to separate what I said from what I felt.

Meanwhile, Sadie's letters seemed increasingly full of bad news. "I'm in the ER with my son and husband," she wrote, "who's being treated for severe intestinal pain likely caused by a new medication he's been trying. It's 2 A.M., I'm tired, Ethan is also sick (just a cold, we're hoping, but it seems to be getting worse), and all I can think is *I wish I were with you.* I know this must make me sound like a monster."

"It makes you sound like a person dealing with some difficult things," I wrote, grateful for an opportunity to demonstrate wisdom and compassion and maybe a certain stoicism that I hoped stood in for my lack of life experience in the face of Sadie's excess of it. So often my life felt small next to hers. I wondered if to Sadie that was part of my appeal, if to her I was a sort of refuge of relative uncomplicatedness. The thought of her sitting there in the hospital with her son and husband, thinking of me, moved me. It made me want to be worthy of her love. But it also scared me: was I? "You shouldn't feel guilty for a feeling," I wrote. "And it makes me happy that you're thinking of me."

But she was also thinking of other things. For example: the earthquake and tsunami that had taken so many lives in Japan the previous month, and that, along with the subsequent Fukushima meltdown, had made refugees of so many families. A friend of hers, an artist who lived in Tokyo, was hosting a mother and her two young sons who'd fled their home in a Fukushima prefecture village when the nuclear reactors began to explode, Sadie wrote. The mother's parents, who'd lived closer to the coast, had been swept away by the tsunami. Her husband, risking nuclear contamination, had stayed behind to take care of the house and tend the small farm and apiary that were the family's only sources of income. In the days after the earthquake and tsunami, the Japanese government had repressed information about the extent of the fallout, and the family had at first fled directly into the path of the most potent radioactive cloud. Now the mother blamed herself for the thyroid cancer she was sure would afflict her children in time. The family had lived just outside the so-called Exclusion Zone surrounding the nuclear reactors, so it seemed unlikely they'd get anything from the energy company or the government. Their village was practically deserted, they couldn't go back, and yet remaining in Tokyo indefinitely seemed impossible.

What was most appalling about the whole thing, Sadie wrote, was that Japan wouldn't even be so dependent on nuclear power if it hadn't been for the active encouragement of the American government. As part of its attempt to restore relations with Japan in the years immediately following World War

II, Eisenhower had initiated a secret plan—did I know?—later pursued by the CIA, to help build the Japanese a nuclear reactor. In this way the Japanese people, it was surmised, would come to see nuclear power as a creative, rather than a destructive, force. "Now, instead, it's like we've dropped another bomb on them, half a century after the war ended," Sadie wrote.

It could all seem very far away, she continued, until we remembered the hundred-plus nuclear reactors scattered throughout our country, most if not all of them as unprepared for natural disaster as Fukushima's had proven to be. The Indian Point plant, for example, twenty-five miles north of New York City, had recently been discovered to lie at the intersection of two very active seismic zones, one of undoubtedly countless crucial facts unknown at the time of its construction. If its reactors melted down, Sadie wrote, the fallout would make a ghost town of New York City and likely kill tens of thousands of people. Even the U.S. government acknowledged this internally. And so she'd started volunteering for an advocacy group that opposed the plant's imminent bid for relicensing, even though she suspected her efforts were doomed to failure.

I didn't know what to do with that. What was I supposed to do?

Decent, patient, passionate Beryl was lonely in her friend's old rambling house. "Dearest heart," she wrote her fiancé, "I am lying in a little white bed beneath a pink coverlet. On my right is another bed exactly like the one I am in, only no one will sleep in it. And inside and outside the little room is space and stillness."

For the past year and a half she and Berryman had been together or at least in close proximity; letters seemed "unreal, such poor substitute for your dear presence." Alone in a strange, unfamiliar place, she began to experience others' pain as her own. "The suffering cannot be believed, John," she wrote. "That men should be turned penniless into the streets, thrown into concentration camps, beaten—often to death, turned out of cinemas, starved by financial restrictions, and degraded in every horrible way, because they believe in Socialism or happen to be Jews is unbelievable enough. But I heard things so agonising that only by causing myself physical suffering can I find ease from prayer."

A young socialist couple from Vienna had passed through the house and told their story. The husband, foreign editor of the *Daily Herald*, had been forced out of Austria by the Nazis that spring. His wife stayed at home to care for their eighteen-month-old baby. Soon after her husband left, though, an informant warned her a Nazi official would be coming at any moment to apprehend her. She fled immediately, leaving her child in care of her grandmother, and made her way to England to join her husband. Now the couple couldn't go back to Austria, and couldn't risk having anyone bring them their baby, since in that event the Nazis had threatened, plausibly, to cut off the grandmother's already meager pension and send all remaining male family members to camps. "Yet this couple," Beryl wrote Berryman, "knowing they cannot hope to see their child again except at the expense of the lives of almost all their relations still alive in Vienna, consider themselves fortunate and less deserving of pity than almost any of their fellows. I cannot understand how any man can cause such suffering."

Berryman, meanwhile, resigned to unemployment, burrowed deep into his poetry. He wrote a poem based on his reading of Herodotus, one dedicated to his brother about "the violent world our fathers bought," one called "Accident" inspired by a news item about a window washer who'd fallen from a skyscraper to his death. "I am beginning to feel in me a kind of authority which I trust and must follow," he wrote. His poems were rejected by *The New Yorker* and *The New Republic*, but *New Directions* accepted a few. When Berryman sent in edits to them, though, he was told they'd already gone to press. "I've no readers," he wrote Van Doren, "but I feel as if I've betrayed them all." The episode compounded his general melancholy. His relationship with his mother went from strained to confrontational; he escaped for a few weeks to Allen Tate's house in Connecticut. There, he continued to work on his poetry, and wrote his mother several letters. "Fortunately I miss [Beryl] less here than I did there, though I become daily more convinced of her value as a wife."

By this time Beryl had left England for Cortina, a resort town in the Italian Alps, where she hunted and fished and went on long walks and picked flowers and "fascinating beard plants" that reminded her of Berryman. She promised him she'd come to New York as soon as possible, maybe sometime around Christmas, maybe earlier. She cursed "the tyranny of time and space" and gazed up at the surrounding mountains, "great projecting masses of black and tawny rock that seem engaged in a desperate struggle to defy the limits of the earth, and indeed to have defeated the sky when they prevail upon the clouds to cover their passionate longing. . . . Hour after hour I can stand and watch them, for they are never the same from one moment to another, and never acceptable as real."

. . .

The gun club halfway down the mountain inaugurated its season toward the end of April, around the same time the winds I'd been warned about by the Drutherses began to blow. The shooting typically began late in the morning and lasted through late afternoon or early evening. Weekdays often brought long stretches of silence, but weekends the noise was almost continuous. Each gunshot produced three distinct echoes, so that at times of high activity the valley rang with braided thunder. Once in a while the racket gathered itself into a rhythm that could've been mistaken for intentional, and after some time these random orderings were all I heard, the general cacophony having worked its way beyond hearing into my nerves and bones.

Most days, the gunshots began to subside just as the wind began to rise. The latter arrived at the mountaintop daily neither at full blast nor in a gentle crescendo; rather, it announced itself with sudden, brief gales, some of them strong enough to knock you off balance, which interrupted intervals of relative calm that grew increasingly loud and portentous. If you were on the balcony, these gales were the signal to go inside. Close the doors over the pool if they're open. Stuff folded up cereal boxes into the cracks between doors and windows, windows and floor. Make a bowl of pasta or a toasted cheese sandwich and take it to the bedroom to eat in bed while you watch a Bulls-Pacers playoff game and try to ignore the banging and shrieking coming at you from all six sides. There was no question of reading while the winds blew, much less of working on my Berryman project, which, if I were to do it justice, would require ultimate concentration. Because of this the coming of the winds coincided with a general ebbing of my scholarly efforts, as if the wind were blowing away the sense of purpose I had only just discovered, and so for the time being my biography would have to remain in its preliminary stages.

The winds seemed to blow from all directions, due to what accidents of atmospheric conditions and topology I could never determine. I never got used to it, but I learned some coping mechanisms. Besides the cereal box trick, which really helped, the main one was going to bed early, with earplugs. Then, if I was lucky, the sounds would wake me only three or four times before dawn, by which point the winds had almost always subsided, at least a little. If I was unlucky, I'd be awoken seven or eight times, including once or twice by the alarm system Oscar had finally succeeded in installing.

The alarm accomplished its purpose admirably. Every light in the house flashed on and off, to a just-out-of-rhythm accompaniment of a madly pulsating electronic honk that must have been audible throughout the valleys. The scene into which I awoke at these times was as terrifying as any nightmare. Usually the assault of sound and light would paralyze me in bed for several moments, until I gathered my senses and sprinted in my boxers to the garage, where I could enter in the code that ended it. Then the house would be all lit up, and silent. I'd call the alarm company on the newly installed landline, and the representative would ask if I'd like for him or her to stay on the line while I checked for intruders. Yes, I'd say, that would be nice, and I'd move slowly through each room of the house, checking closets and bathtubs and drawers until I could be reasonably sure I was alone. Then the representative would ask if I'd like the police to be notified, and I'd say that wasn't necessary. I figured it would take the police at least an hour to get up there, plenty of time for an intruder to kill me and bury my body in the atrium or beneath the cantilevered pool.

But the only intruders I ever saw—beyond the ubiquitous contractors, who continued to come up in a never-ending stream, making improvements to the windows, the floor, the plumbing, the peeling strips of wood on the eaves—were the flies that seemed to be breeding in the kitchen, the frogs that occasionally made slapping sounds in and around the atrium pond, the songbirds that entered through the opened pool doors (two sparrows and a yellow-breasted warbler of some sort), the juvenile red-tailed hawk that got stuck in the atrium for most of a misty night and day (a woman from animal control came up, tossed a towel over it, took it outside, and released it), the pair of mating quail that didn't make it out alive, and the little clay-red and dusty green lizards that scuttled past my feet with increasing frequency. The motion-detecting cameras a little ways down the mountain picked up bobcats, coyotes, deer, foxes, and raccoons.

It was during this period that I got an unsettling update about Maria. It came from Sadie—in an email, not a letter. She had recently arranged for a realtor to start showing her home, and she and Ryan had hired a stager to clean the interior and fill it with furniture. The day that the staging was set to take place, Sadie got a call. The staging team had found the house unlocked, and when they went inside they discovered someone there: a young, very thin dark-haired woman who appeared to be asleep on the living-room floor. She was surrounded, Sadie wrote, by empty and half-empty bottles of wine. When they woke her up, she claimed to live there; she was renting from the house's owners, she said. No one was renting from her and Ryan anymore, Sadie told the man on the phone. He asked if he should call the police. No, Sadie said, she'd take care of it. She'd arrange for them to come back another day. She asked me in her email to drive into cell service and call her as soon as possible.

On the phone, her voice was calm, but I could tell it held an anger.

"What are you going to do? This is *your* problem."

I apologized several times. Maria told me she'd found a sublet, I said. I'd been under the impression that she'd moved out at the end of March, as she'd agreed to do.

"She's *troubled*. She's clearly a very troubled person. I'm not about to kick her out on the street, but I'm also not interested in extending her any more charity than I already have."

I told Sadie I'd get in touch with her. I'd figure it out, I said.

"Please do."

"I will. I promise. I'm really sorry."

"It disturbs me that you'd allow yourself to get involved with someone who exhibits this kind of behavior."

"Believe me, I had no idea."

"Do you know how stressful it is to try to sell a house *without* some transient squatting there?"

I didn't.

"Of course you don't. Of course you don't. You're a child. What *do* you know?"

As soon as the conversation ended, I called Maria. She didn't pick up. I left a message. I texted her: *Please call.* When after five or ten minutes I didn't hear back, I called a mutual friend in New York. Jack hadn't heard from Maria in a long time, but he was in touch with one of her housemates, he said. I told him they weren't her housemates anymore but it might be worth trying to connect with them. Maybe, even if they hadn't heard from her, they'd have her father's contact information. After I hung up with Jack I didn't know who to call. I sat there in Dave's ridiculous Jeep, staring at a McMansion, trying to fend off a rising dread when I thought of someone else.

"Didn't expect to hear from *you,*" Jess said.

I apologized for being so out of touch, said I would explain later, and asked if she'd be willing to do a weird but important favor.

The house was locked and all the lights were off, she reported back twenty minutes later. There were no cars either in the driveway or on the curb in front of the house. I thanked Jess, who sounded annoyed, said we should catch up later, and hung up.

The sky had begun to darken. It was almost seven, nine in Des Moines, ten in New York, for Sadie. My next move, I decided, was to call her back, to talk through possible next steps. It didn't matter that she'd said this was my problem, it didn't matter if it would make her more upset with me; I trusted her, more than anyone else I knew, to know what to do in a difficult situation. Still, I didn't look forward to the talk. I decided to give it ten minutes. Fifteen. After twenty minutes I got a text. Maria: *Driving to India*—she could only have meant Indiana—*talk tomorrow.*

I put my phone to sleep and cried for a minute, mostly out of relief, I think, but also worry, shame, regret, and more than a little anger. I wanted to *do something* for Maria, but what? I hoped she was okay to drive. I wondered what, besides the sublet, she had lied to me about. I thought about the changes I'd noticed in her since we renewed our correspondence, and about how much she liked to drink, and about how often she talked of escape, she was always escaping. (Did I recognize myself in the impulse? Was that part of our connection?) Why couldn't she have texted or called or written about her mysterious sickness earlier than she did? (On the other hand, why hadn't I followed up on my email after a few days?) If there was a perfectly good explanation for her long silence, why had she felt for such a long time she couldn't explain it to me? The caterpillar story, on reflection, was far-fetched at best.

That night I got drunk for the first time since I'd come to California. I blasted alternative rock from my childhood, went for a probably ill-advised night swim, and sat in the hot tub in the violent wind, watching the red lights flash in the distance, until I got light-headed and went inside. I brought my laptop and another beer to bed, where I sat watching YouTube videos, first of Daniel Day-Lewis interviews and then of early Stones performances, Mick Jagger was a miracle of a man, the charisma, the squirmy joy. I checked my email, nothing new, found myself typing into a window I must have opened a moment before.

ME: *you up?*

The response was almost immediate.

ASHWINI: *hi it's been awhile*

It was almost three A.M. in Halifax, but she often kept very late hours.

ME: *no kidding. how are you? how's your semester going?*
ASH: *i got fired*
ME: *what really?*
ASH: *for sleeping with a student*
ME: *ha, right.*

ASH: *hahahahahahaha*
ME: *i liked your book.*
ASH: *thx*

(I still hadn't read her book.)

ME: *does it feel good to have it out there in the world?*
ASH: *are you kidding*
it feels fucking terrifying
ME: *haha*
ASH: *my dad's reading it right now*
he's going to hate it
ME: *you think?*
ASH: *i killed off the dad in the book!*
ME: *oh right, haha*
ASH: *haha*
ME: *remember when he told me i looked like robert redford?*
ASH: *all white ppl look the same to him*
ME: *ha*
ASH: *ha*
how's dm?
ME: *actually i'm in california. i'm housesitting a glass-walled hexagonal mountaintop mansion w/ wrap-around balcony, open-air atrium, hot tub, and indoor/outdoor infinity pool cantilevered over napa valley.*
ASH: *when can i visit?*
ME: *ummmm. . . .*
ASH: *relax i'm joking*
sounds like a nice gig
you always seem to luck into nice situations
ME: *haha thanks.*

ASH: *yr welcome*

ME: *i mean, do you want to?*

ASH: *hahahahaha*

ME: *just a thought.*

i miss you.

it'd be nice to see you.

i'm sorry for how things ended.

you there?

ASH: *are you drunk?*

ME: *no.*

ASH: *i appreciate the apology but i'm in a good place now*

as they say

i've been seeing a therapist

i started swimming

ME: *that's really good to hear!*

i'm in a good place too.

i've been swimming too.

ASH: *that's great*

what you can't swim.

ME: *i've been teaching myself.*

ASH: *that's great*

ME: *so do you feel like you've been experiencing less anger than you were in the fall?*

ASH: *excuse me?*

ME: *nevermind*

ASH: *i wasn't angry, i was STRESSED*

i was starting a new very stressful job and editing proofs of my novel.

ME: *ok, sorry.*

i mean, you threw a chair.

ASH: *i accidentally tipped a chair over.*

ME: *haha, right and broke a lamp*

ASH: *i was upset and grabbed a chair and when i let go it fell over and hit the cord attached to the lamp*

ME: *ok, we'll go with that*

ASH: *and what did you do that night?*

ME: *i went for a walk*

ASH: *you FLED*
and you weren't there for me the rest of your time here

ME: *i wanted to be there but you wouldn't let me.*

ASH: *you CLOSED DOWN*
you stopped trying
you're unreliable
and impatient
and inconsistent

ME: *anything else?*

ASH: *yes*
you're always floating away
you're not able to deal with reality

ME: *i deal.*

ASH: *someday you'll have to face it*
someday you'll have to come down from your castle

ME: *it's a house*

ASH: *and join the rest of us in the real word*
world

ME: *right.*
i'll be sure to say hello if i ever go there.
i want to end this conversation but no doubt you'd interpret that as proving your point.

ASH: *i don't need you to prove my point*
you've already proven it to me.

ME: *well, nice chatting with you.*

ASH: *:)*
ME: *good night*
ASH: *night*

I quit the browser, turned off my computer, and went out to the balcony. The wind hit me. The lights of Fairfield twinkled below. I closed my eyes, then opened them: the city was still there. I stripped off my clothes and dove into the water and stood on the floor of the pool for a long time. Finally I needed to breathe. The wind against my dripping face was painful. I stayed in the pool for a while, treading water. Why had I agreed to come back on this show?

After the Final Rose

Then came a departure.
—JOHN BERRYMAN, "Dream Song 1"

THE BACHELOR CHOSE EMILY. HER STORY WAS TOO good; the other bachelorettes never stood a chance. When he visited Emily in Charlotte on hometown week, he was very sweet to little Ricki. He gave her a kite. He understood Emily was a package deal. "Sitting here playing board games with Emily and her daughter was like the perfect image of what I want my life to be." Riding elephants in the South African veldt next week was cool, but to the Bachelor the most important thing was Emily's company. That night, in the Fantasy Suite high above the plains, she finally accepted her fate and told him she was falling in love with him. The next episode was the most emotional two-hour finale in *Bachelor* history.

Thirty seconds later, a few months had passed, and Emily and the Bachelor were trying to explain to the host and studio and television audiences that yes, they were still together, contra the tabloids, though they had broken up once since filming ended and there was no wedding date. (Were they engaged? America wanted to know. He was pretty sure they were.) The trouble had begun when Emily saw the Bachelor on TV with all those other women. She couldn't bear to watch him saying almost exactly the same things to them as he did to her. "Going through it, everything was so real to me," she said, significant candles flickering in the background. "Watching it, I'm trying to figure out what's reality TV and what's my reality." The Bachelor assured her: this wasn't some fantasyland. Emily would always have his heart.

By the end of the next month they'd broken up for good. Less than a year later she was the Bachelorette. Things didn't work out with Jef with one "f," the pompadoured, boyish CEO of a bottled-water company who beat out race car driver Arie in the two-hour finale, but she applied a lot of what she learned from that relationship to the one she's in as I type these words, with a man she met while volunteering through her church as a teacher for a middle school jewelry-making class. Emily and Taylor's engagement was brief; finally, Ricki has a father in her life.

Emily isn't the only bachelorette whose failure with the Bachelor made possible lasting love. Chantal, the runner-up, had already found her soul mate, a marketing consultant for a money management firm, by the time "After the Final Rose" was filmed. Meanwhile, Ashley H., who came in third, beat Emily to the punch as Bachelorette, stepping out of one show and into another as if from dream to dream. Her season gave the franchise one of its few success stories, and ABC televised her wedding with the winner, kind-eyed construction manager J.P. Their first child, Fordham, was born two years later: 7 lbs, 2 oz; 18.5 in.

Thus *The Bachelor* partakes of the eternal. It transcends history, politics, work, society, family, calendar time. Neither real nor quite unreal, it submits reality to formal pressures in order to forge new things, new feelings, then releases them into other worlds, where only usually do they dissolve.

Sadie had volunteered to put me up in her guest room, I told Laura. It was July, and we were sitting on a couch in her gorgeous condo in the warehouse district of Minneapolis, sipping whiskey and admiring the view of the Mississippi from her living-room windows, which took up most of the north-facing wall and let in late afternoon bluish light. I'd spent the morning in the Berryman archives, my fourth day in the company of John and Beryl, and their story of love won and squandered was still running through my mind.

"Do you really think that's a good idea?" Laura asked. I'd been staying at her condo since I arrived in the city, but she'd been away the first two evenings and spent the third practicing a mournful, foreboding piece I didn't recognize—she played the same phrases over and over—which turned out to be a suite by the twelve-tone Austrian composer Alban Berg.

"We'll see," I said. "Things have been going well lately." This, I felt, was more or less true. Two months had passed since the Maria incident, and Sadie's anger toward me had subsided after a few days. Still, I felt vaguely embarrassed for a while longer, and I tried to compensate in the ensuing weeks by being an especially good listener to Sadie, who seemed to be growing more and more melancholy. She wanted to talk on the phone more often, and so most days—and some days twice—I made the half-hour drive down the mountain and talked to her in the Jeep. One day, as gently as possible, I suggested that she start looking for jobs. It might help to have a sense of purpose, I said. Look at you, giving advice, she said. But three weeks later—

Sadie moves quickly—she accepted a position raising money for the Whitney. It started in June.

First, she visited me one more time at House Above the Morning Clouds. This time we left the mountain once a day, spent afternoons in the valleys below. We tasted wine, went to fruit stands, bought eight-dollar cups of coffee. We walked through vineyards and along coastal paths and through dappled patches of oak savanna. There were new moments of friction between us but we worked through them, and that made us feel proud. These ventures into the real world, besides breaking up the pleasant monotony of our days, also brought us the pleasure of seeing our coupledom reflected and legitimized in the eyes of other people. "I love young love," an old woman said as we walked past her arm in arm on a Napa street, and the rest of the trip we repeated it to each other as a sort of mantra or spell. Sadie, who had recently turned forty-six, loved that she'd been called young, and so did I, but I also wondered if our attachment to the woman's comment belied an unspoken insecurity about our age difference. Why did we need other people to affirm what we already felt so strongly?

I got used to life on top of the mountain. After a while you can get used to anything, as my mother often told me when I was a kid. The enormous rooms, which were gradually filling with furniture and art Dave's wife had ordered—emerald chandeliers made from Mount St. Helens ash, a zebra-print rug made from real zebras, a classical landscape from the workshop of Titian—had come to seem normal-sized, almost cozy. The winds and gunshots faded into ambience. I'd become an almost competent swimmer. Even the security cameras Oscar installed, which allowed Dave to monitor my comings and goings, brought me a certain amount of comfort. And yet I was growing tired of being a house-sitter, of not having a home. I started to think about moving back to New York, reuniting with my friends, dating Sadie. Maybe I could get a job at a magazine or something.

My out materialized just a few days later, when Dave showed up at his house unannounced, setting off the alarm. He and his wife had been fighting more or less continuously for the past few months, he explained almost jovially after I got off the phone with the security company, and he'd come to seek refuge above the clouds. I moved into the guest room on the lower level, and for several days Dave and I were uneasy housemates. I forced myself to sit at a desk all day, to prove to my patron that I was making good use of the space he had so generously granted me, but with Dave either watching TV at high volume or yelling into his satellite phone (sell this, buy that, hang on to this), I found it hard to concentrate on the selection of Berryman's letters to his mother that I'd recently ordered. Evenings we descended in the Jeep, Dave singing along to the classic rock station as he took hairpin turns at 40 mph, and dined at the finest restaurants in Napa Valley, five-hour dinners at which we both got smashed well before the arrival of the olive oil gelée; the Reblochon; the chocolate crémeux with whipped Manjari anglaise, muscovado crumble, and peppermint sponge. Of our conversation I remember nothing, save for Dave telling me with apparent glee that all he'd really cared about his entire life was money, money money money money money money money, and he was right to, you couldn't argue, he said, look at where we were right now—that and his pitch for a reality TV show (apparently he thought I could help get it made) about middle-aged divorcées reconnecting with their prom dates at dances organized for that purpose. He had the structure of the show all worked out: the first third would be devoted to the women's tragic backstory and documenting their preparation for the dance; the second would be the dance itself; and the third would be the drive home, the kiss good night, and, maybe, if things went well—here was the climax—the invitation inside. He even had a name for the show: *Prom Moms.* I told him it sounded like a great idea.

When it became evident in the subsequent days that he and his wife weren't about to reconcile, I started making plans to move out. I'd fly to Minneapolis, where I'd spend a week at the Berryman archives. Then I'd spend a couple of days with my parents and continue on to New York, where I'd stay in Sadie's guest room and look for a place to live.

"And Sadie's husband and son know you're coming?" Laura asked.

"They're excited to meet me, according to Sadie."

"And you?"

"I'm excited, too! Terrified, but excited."

"What will you talk about?"

"I don't know, what do people talk about? Sports? Ourselves? John Edwards's indictment?"

"Oh, that's perfect, you should definitely bring that up."

I promised her I would.

What I didn't tell Laura was that I'd been harboring a fantasy—one I recognized would likely remain a fantasy—in which Sadie and Ryan invited me to become a permanent member of their family. I'd hit it off with Ryan and Ethan and become a sort of stay-at-home dad. I'd clean, do the laundry and dishes, buy groceries and cook elaborate dinners. I'd write little notes and stick them on the fridge. I'd take out the garbage. I'd water the plants. I'd pick up Ethan from school and walk him home or to a café or park, and most days I'd supervise while he did homework or read but sometimes we'd play games we invented or collaborate on a story. And I'd feel I was contributing not just to the household but to the world's sense of what was possible. Meanwhile, I'd finish my Berryman book, then write another, and another.

"Anyway," I said to Laura, "I've gone on way too long about myself." Night had fallen suddenly, without my noticing. No lights were on inside the condo, but there was enough light from the moon and/or the city to illuminate our portion of the room. "What's new with you? How's Dan?"

"Dan's great! You guys should meet. You'd like him. He's a big Bulls fan."

"That's all I need to hear."

"And he likes Woolf."

"Hey!" Laura loved Woolf. We'd fallen in love with her together.

We sat for a moment watching moonlight on the river, then "Can I tell you something?" she asked.

"Of course."

"A few days ago I told him I love him."

Maybe it was partly the whiskey but I felt tears welling in my eyes. "And?"

"He told me he loves me, too!"

I told Laura that was amazing. Nothing was better than being in love, I said, and how could she disagree?

It was spring, 1940, and John Berryman found himself once again all alone. Beryl's visit to New York had not gone well. They'd fought. Beryl had threatened to leave him. The war in

Europe hung over all they did. Back in England, Beryl wrote him a series of letters in which she enumerated their essential differences: she was active, he was passive; she was an optimist, he was a pessimist; she needed people, he needed solitude. Of course, she still loved him more than ever. What exactly was she trying to say?

Late that summer he began teaching literature at Wayne University in Detroit. He had 131 students across four classes and spent thirteen hours a week in the classroom. "I am as busy as death," he wrote his mother. "Wayne will leave me in the hospital shortly." He'd chosen Wayne over Columbia because Wayne offered him more money, which meant he could afford to pay for Beryl to rejoin him in America sooner. The Battle of Britain had broken out, however, and Beryl told him she'd remain in England for as long as she could be of service to her country. She was training to become an Air Raid Precautions warden, dusting off her German and Italian. Berryman was stuck. "Disfigurement is general," he wrote.

By day he drank coffee and smoked cigarettes and taught and graded papers and met with students. By night he took long walks and visited bars. He went days at a time without eating a real meal; he went from gaunt to gaunter. He had a few flings, but they meant nothing to him. He almost never spoke to his fellow professors. "It is mainly the fatigue, and the terrible sense of waste I have, that makes me a spectre and a sad spectre," he wrote. In December, after four straight days of grading, he collapsed. The diagnosis: "nervous exhaustion." Try reading Dickens before bed, the doctor wrote.

The Luftwaffe dropped bombs on London for fifty-seven consecutive nights. Air raid sirens echoed through the city. Smoke rose from the East End, obscuring St. Paul's Cathedral.

Almost twenty thousand civilians were killed, many in deliberate acts of terror. Beryl was tasked with administering first aid to injured victims, as well as with helping to recover bodies. During calmer moments she patrolled the streets to make sure no one was violating the blackout. Hurricanes and Spitfires roared above her. She wrote Berryman about the sky: "Still light out at 11 with our double summer-time . . . dirty blue, and dusty pink; slate clouds, white gold distance where the sun had sunk, silhouetted purplish trees and fantastic searchlights dazzling the rising stars."

His second semester played out much like the first. Class prep, classes, grading, student meetings. Late-night walks, poems begun and abandoned. "Violent headaches, insomnia, fatigue." Collapse. A new diagnosis: epilepsy. That made Berryman feel a bit better. He started a poem about death and destruction and "heartbreak as familiar as the heart is strange." He felt himself receding into the background again. When the phone rang he'd pick it up and slam it down, over and over again until the caller hung up. "I have been reading some notes by my dead self," he wrote in his journal. "Of course it is not dead, I am depressed to say." Not long after his best friend died of cancer Berryman got a dead-end teaching appointment at Harvard that left him no time to write. He lived with his brother and his brother's fiancée in a run-down apartment near Harvard Square. If you pulled the blinds shut, his brother would later write, "you could look out through the walls." Berryman taught, graded, met with students. His brother's fiancée became his brother's wife. "I hope they will be happy," he wrote in his journal. "So much works against happiness now. For B. and me I see nothing—whatever might be is too long in coming." Nine days later he was more optimistic: "I work and postpone my disappointments, delay my terrors—if she comes, I think forever. If not, they come and they will be more than I can bear." Beryl never came.

The final chapter of the Berryman-Beryl story is written in unsent letters. I found nine in the University of Minnesota archives, some handwritten, others typed, ranging from two to eight pages in length, the first one dated January 9, 1941, the last August 9, 1942. All of Berryman's longing and self-loathing and generosity and self-delusion and excuse making and brilliance seemed distilled in these letters, elusive artifacts that inhabited some hazy territory between journal entries and letters mailed and received. "Dearest Angel," they begin, or "Dearest Little Angel," or "Dearest adorable blessed little Angel"—as if Beryl were a denizen of another realm. "It is impossible for me to live without you—without you is alone, is to be worthless and ill and empty and without faith or strength for anything, is not to exist or to exist only as a wound exists, is to be sorrowful and insane and angry." He was always "insanely busy," always sick, never had enough time for his poetry. His memories of good times he'd had with Beryl only increased his sense of detachment from her. "You are in my mind constantly." Meanwhile, the Japanese had bombed Pearl Harbor, America was at war, the world was disintegrating every second. "We picked, you and I, in history," Berryman wrote, "a poor scene for our love; that it continues at all is a miracle." There were moments of hope, of happiness even, but it was best, Berryman argued, not to write about these moments, lest they vaporize in their articulation. "When you come the actual life begins." Words not quite addressed to no one.

When I held those unsent letters on my last day in the reading room, in the company of twelve or fifteen other researchers, I felt more acutely than at any other point during my project a sense of the onrushing moment-to-moment reality of Berryman's life as he lived it. If he had sent those letters, I couldn't help thinking, he and Beryl may well have gotten married, and if he and Beryl had gotten married, he never would have had the affair with Chris, never would have started seeing Dr. Shea, never would have written—though of course this can't be proven—the Dream Songs that in large part emerged from those sessions. And what then? And what then? And what after that? When I'd first come across the Beryl correspondence, I barely remembered her from the biography I'd read; she had been one in a seemingly endless stream of women that flowed through Berryman's life. Now, though, after a few days with her, she seemed like the key to his artistic development, the hinge on which his life turned. More than that, she was clearly an extraordinary person. Her writing was unfailingly lucid and direct, with moments of virtuosity. Even through the war she remained alert to moments of tenderness and beauty. And she seemed so *good:* honest and kind and shrewd and passionate and patient almost to a fault. She deserved posterity, I felt, as much as Berryman, whom she loved so well.

Eventually her concern and annoyance and anger resolved into resignation. Her letters became less frequent, then stopped. She quit volunteering for the Air Raid Precautions to take a job working for the Foreign Office, then quit that job for one with the BBC. In February she wrote Berryman a letter effectively breaking off the engagement: "I feel and know now that our happinesses do not lie in each other's hands." Taking a page from him, she didn't send it. Then, in July, she returned to the letter, framed it with a few further thoughts in the same vein—"I don't think I shall fall in love again. I don't particularly want to"—and mailed it.

On the one hand, Berryman was devastated. "I was in a heart- and brain- and body-stupor of grief and desperation unspeakable," he wrote in his penultimate unsent letter. On the other hand, now he was free to ask Eileen Mulligan, an aspiring psychiatrist, to marry him. Eileen was friends with a college friend of Berryman's. He'd been dating her for the past year and a half. He'd wooed her on long late-night walks through Manhattan during which he'd talked about art and the death of poetry and his own shameful lack of accomplishment and his potential to write great things. He showed her his poems and she liked them. She liked his smile. They went to movies at the Forty-second Street Apollo. They danced the boogie-woogie on rooftops. After he went back to Boston to teach, he wrote her long, passionate letters. He sent them. She visited. They called each other "Broom." His romance with Beryl he dismissed as a "phantom relationship." Then Beryl ended it and it was the phantom of a phantom.

While it's true that Berryman was full of doubt about Eileen for much of the two and a half months of their engagement, and found himself reading Beryl's last letter over and over, and confessed to feeling "terror" on his wedding day, and later called the October of his marriage "the most racking month of my life," once it was over he settled into a new kind of contentment. Eileen moved into his Boston apartment, and the newlyweds stayed up late by the fireplace drinking hot chocolate and listening to Mozart. Life would be like that now—warm and rich and sweet and full of beauty. "How I lived unmarried I hardly know," Berryman wrote in his journal. He felt reborn.

Now teaching would cease to be a burden and he would write the great poems he knew he could and Eileen would be his muse and helpmate and partner in all of life's joys and pains and sorrows. "I am certain that I will be happy with her," Berryman wrote Beryl.

At the lockers outside the reading room, a woman I'd noticed earlier—her desk had been a couple of rows in front of mine, and my eyes had found rest from time to time on the nape of her extraordinarily long neck—struck up a conversation. It turned out we'd been sharing the Berryman archives all day; Deirdre was preparing a paper on his Shakespeare scholarship. Wasn't it sad, I suggested, that Berryman had spent so much time on Shakespeare—years and years of his life, I'd read, much of it on arcane folio analysis—without completing any of the many books he'd planned to write on him?

"I don't think it's sad," said Deirdre. "He took so much from Shakespeare. Look at the Dream Songs; Shakespeare's everywhere: in the form—the songs are basically exploded sonnets—the syntax, rhythms, the range of registers. I'd argue that the Dream Songs never get written without those years of Shakespeare study. Plus he made important contributions to the field, he gets cited all the time. And his essays are really good. Have you read them? Have you read 'Shakespeare at Thirty'?"

I hadn't.

"Read it. It's a very strange, very revealing essay. Berryman reads Shakespeare as a proto-confessional poet. 'When Shakespeare says, "Two loves have I," reader, he is *not* kidding.' That's a quote."

"That's a good quote. I'll read the essay."

"Do. So what's your story? What are you up to here?"

"Well"—I felt embarrassed to say it—"I'm considering a new biography."

"Of—Berryman?"

"Who else?" I said.

"I don't know, I thought maybe, like, I don't know, JFK. Don't you think you'd better read his essays on Shakespeare?"

"I didn't realize JFK wrote Shakespeare essays."

She started to laugh but caught herself. "Oh yeah. He wrote a great one on Hamlet's soliloquies."

"His answer was 'Not to be.' "

"Exactly. Lee Harvey Oswald took it very seriously."

"The conspiracy theorists need to know this."

"I'll send out an email to their listserv."

"You're well connected."

"I've always made friends easily."

"Crazy friends."

"Everyone's crazy," said Deirdre.

"Not me. I'm the only one. Anyway, I'm still in the early stages of my project, obviously. But I'm interested in Berryman's relationship with Beryl Eeman. Do you know of her?"

"The name sounds familiar. Remind me, though?"

I explained who Beryl was and we chatted awhile longer, then exchanged email addresses, shook hands, and parted ways. In the hallway I bought a pack of peanut butter crackers from a vending machine and checked my phone: a call from Sadie. No message. I sat down on a bench in the atrium and texted Laura that I'd see her in half an hour. It was my last night in the city and we'd planned to have dinner with Dan and see a movie. Then I checked espn.com—the NBA lockout had entered its third week—and called Sadie back.

"My mother died."

I don't remember most of what I said in response. I didn't react well, I think. How could I say what was actually true, that I hadn't known her mother, up until yesterday, had still been alive? I wondered if I'd misunderstood or misremembered what she'd told me about her. At some point I asked Sadie how she felt, and she said, How do I *feel*? My mother died. I am *in mourning*. That's how I feel. I apologized, then apologized again using slightly different words. I think I'd thought that since Sadie had all but disowned her mother, she might not feel how people usually feel when their mother died. The silences between me and Sadie grew longer as the conversation went on. I'd never heard her sound so distant. I didn't know what to say. I asked about the funeral, it was in France, Sadie didn't think she'd go. More silences, more saying the wrong things, more silences, searching for words. I was running late for dinner with Laura and Dan and suggested we talk later that night.

"Of course. You should go. We can talk later."

"Look, I know I'm not responding well. I'm tired. I have a headache. I just spent five days in the reading room."

Another long silence, then: "You know I love you. But I'm starting to think your coming to New York isn't such a good idea."

Outside, a fitful wind pushed dead leaves across the brick-and-concrete plaza. Students walked past, absorbed in their phones. I wandered around, eating crackers. After some time, as if controlled by exterior forces, I found myself walking toward the bridge over the Mississippi that connected the west side of campus to the east. When I reached it I stood on the sidewalk, grabbed the railing, and looked down. Berryman had missed the water, I'd read; his body was found facedown on the frozen embankment. I had problems, but they weren't as bad as his. I texted Laura I'd be late.

I decided to extend my stay with my parents for a couple of weeks. Then I could recalibrate with Sadie and go to New York—or not. I sensed a finality to our last conversation, and a part of me was relieved. If I didn't feel equipped to be there for her in the way that she needed, I also felt that being there for her was a role better suited to her husband of twenty years. And while there were advantages to returning to New York, even if Sadie and I weren't together, it was also very expensive, and I'd already lived there, and I could go anywhere I wanted.

At my parents' house, though, the sadness descended. Even after just a few days of silence, I'd started to really miss her. I missed her vulnerability and playfulness and sadness and seriousness. I missed how seriously she took *me;* it had made me better, I felt. And I was ashamed that I couldn't meet the gravity of her suffering. To distract myself I spent long hours at a desk in the basement, trying to weave a story from the texts I'd photographed in the archives. This task proved trickier than I'd expected—what were my criteria for selecting what to include? how could I justify excluding anything?—and at moments I felt a grudging appreciation for the work of Berryman's biographer. I thought of Maria, wondered how she was doing—the Berryman biography, as much as anything, had been what brought us together—and I thought of the novel I'd abandoned, the disfigurement of my grandfather's memoirs. While working on it I had felt a gnawing unease, verging at times on disgust—what was the point of distorting reality according to whatever whim?—but now I missed the sense of freedom that came with making things up.

Evenings, I ate dinner with my parents. We talked mostly about their lives—the friends they had made through the Nordic skiing club, their progress on hiking all 310 miles of the Superior Trail, the classes they were taking through a senior program at the University of Minnesota Duluth. When they asked about my life, I said little. I'd told them a while ago about my breakup with Ashwini, and they didn't mention her even once. I wondered if they knew about me and Sadie. If they did, I felt sure, they wouldn't mention her either unless I did so first. That was how it was in my family, and I liked it, it made me feel safe. At the same time it gave me the unnerving sense that the past six months had taken place in another world.

One day, a week or so after I arrived, I discovered Ashwini's novel on a shelf in my parents' office. Of course my mother would have bought and read it, she'd always liked Ashwini. I took it to the basement and started from the beginning. The novel was very good. Like its author, it luxuriated in sensation—fabric against skin, the color of the sky, smells of spices and flowers and rain. The narrator's eye was drawn to well-crafted objects, a mahogany door, a brocade curtain, a rug with a "gorgeous fringe." Paragraphs and chapters tended to land on the striking image, burning banana leaves flaring like fireworks, moths flying away like something shattering. I'd forgotten how attuned Ashwini was to the physical world, so sensitive to it, I used to think, that it was as if she went around without skin, everything pressing against her organs. I remembered how when we first started sleeping together she'd take deep sniffs of my neck and hair, trying to memorize the smell, she told me later, so she could categorize it and store it away (no doubt she can recall it exactly to this day). Or how she ran her hands up and down my face, like a blind person forming an image through touch.

Her novel wasn't about me, as Maria had predicted, but it was semi-autobiographical, as they say, a portrait of her childhood and adolescence and young adulthood as they might have played out if her father had died when she was two or three. The family moves into a smaller home, the mother takes a second job, she's forced to rely more strongly than before on the support of the region's large Indian Canadian community. But the lives of the Ashwini character—whose name is Parvati—and her sister and mother strongly resemble their real-life counterparts. In fact, some scenes and stories seemed directly transposed from life, and I wondered if Ashwini had been trying out anecdotes on me to test them for pathos and humor. Parvati is a book lover and hyperaware of language and seems on track toward becoming a writer, but instead she ends up going to med school and becoming a doctor. In real life, when Ashwini dropped out of med school to go to grad school for creative writing, her father didn't speak to her for three and a half years. Now, in the novel's counterfactual, she had somehow managed to combine propitiation with revenge.

When I finished I sat down to write her an email of appreciation and apology. We hadn't been in touch since our contentious G-chat, and I wanted to reestablish friendly relations. I wrote some sentences praising her book, but when I read them over they seemed insincere, or at least impersonal, as if from a book review, so I started over and wrote some sentences apologizing for not having been a better communicator, but why should I be the one apologizing when she had been as uncommunicative as me? I clicked out of my email to *The New York Times,* and when I clicked back I saw an email from an unfamiliar address. Subject: docs. *Hi there,* it began, *I've been meaning to write. I found a couple documents you might be interested in.* The letters, Deirdre wrote, were addressed to Beryl but apparently never sent. They were dated several years after she and Berryman had broken off their engagement. Deirdre had guessed—correctly as it happened—that these had eluded my attention, since they had been filed in different boxes than the main cache of Beryl materials, and so, with touching thoughtfulness, she'd photographed them for me.

The first letter, from the late forties—after the Chris affair, but well before Berryman and Eileen divorced—is in response to a letter from Beryl that Deirdre couldn't locate and may not be extant. For Berryman, Beryl's letter is like a trapdoor through which he falls several years into the past. It has come "like lightning into a crisis of character, as well as into the pure, neverending, desolate sense of my loss of you." He writes feverishly but without direction, his letter is full of erasures and false starts, he doesn't know what he wants to say. "I have been feeling an atrocious urgency," he writes, "as if, if I didn't hurry, you would disappear again, reject me, not exist." He starts to reminisce about his final years with Beryl, reassuring her that so long as they were together there was no question of marriage with Eileen, but—unable to sustain the lie—he breaks off. "It seems after all impossible to write!" Beryl's letter was so magnanimous, so lucid; why can't Berryman respond in kind? "Perhaps if I had sent the sheets I reserved out of my imagination of your good—but I *dare not* think of this. Only, B., let us not be silent again."

The silence that ensued lasted almost a decade. Then the

second letter, again apparently in response to one from Beryl. The date is July 10, 1956, a few months after Berryman married a graduate student named Ann Levine. "I don't understand yr letter," he writes; "you never did me anything but *good*—only I cdn't receive it, owing to my pa's suicide long before and my own lifelong illness. . . . *I* did *you,* I think, w. grief, only harm—and I have v. imperfectly forgiven my self—or not at all—& yr rather unreal letter I know wishes to help but doesn't."

Deirdre didn't know exactly what to make of these letters, she wrote, but she was moved to find that so many years later Berryman was still brooding on his relationship with Beryl, and she thought they might contribute something to my project. "I guess it's up to you to say what Berryman couldn't," she wrote. I wrote her back thanking her for the letters and suggesting we get coffee next time she was in town (though who knew if she'd ever be back to Minneapolis, or how long I'd stick around). After I sent it an exciting thought occurred to me: Maybe Beryl was still alive. I resolved to track her down if she was. Then, remembering Deirdre's recommendation and wanting to linger a while longer in her presence, I checked out a volume of Berryman's Shakespeare essays from the University of Minnesota Duluth library. Back home, I turned to "Shakespeare at Thirty." "Suppose with me," the essay begins, "a time, a place, a man who was waked, risen, washed, dressed, fed, congratulated, on a day in latter April long ago—about April 22, say, of 1594, a Monday . . . a different world."

A few days later *I* turned thirty, and instead of celebrating with Sadie, as we'd planned, I spent the day with my parents. In the afternoon we went on a short but strangely draining hike in a state park on Lake Superior's north shore, then drank a bottle and a half of wine together on their screened-in back porch. I'd gotten it into my head at some point that I wanted to end the day by myself—taking stock of my thirty years on earth, I guess—and so, though I would have liked to stay with my parents on the porch drinking wine, I told them I was meeting Laura for dinner at the revolving circular rooftop restaurant thirty stories above Duluth. In fact I had made a reservation there for one, and half an hour later I was gazing out its windows, moving almost imperceptibly in a circle. Outside: the dark harbor, the twinkling city, dark harbor, twinkling city, dark harbor. Whenever my parents and I drink together they end up telling stories about their past, and today they had told, with my encouragement, the story of stories, their coming-together story: the friends in common, the college dance, the moonlit walk, and (of course) the kiss—so uncomplicated, so old-fashioned, in their telling, as to be almost as unimaginable as their eventual deaths. I sank into the story helplessly, as into a childhood memory; and in fact it had seemed to me as though the three of us had entered a world akin to childhood—elemental, full of nameless delights, unself-conscious, scornful of time. Maybe, I thought now, that's what love was: two people rediscovering through each other a child's sense of the eternal. Who cared if that sense rarely lasted? You've got to try, as Berryman said. Because the World never stopped showing up at your door with news of pain and uncertainty and loss: loss above all, its animating constant, without which the screen flickers out and dies.

My entrée arrived and Lake Superior edged for the tenth or hundredth time into view, and for a moment I saw Sadie's eyes above it, imploring and vaguely accusatory and sad—*sad and lovely, with bright things in it*—and, though it had been years since I'd read the book, I remembered that this was where James Gatz of North Dakota became, through a feat of imagination, Jay

Gatsby—"the unreality of reality," goes the passage, descending on the seventeen-year-old boy for the first time. Moved by passions I didn't understand, toward destinations I never quite reached, and no doubt under the influence of the wine and my birthday negroni and my parents' story, I felt a connection with Fitzgerald's dreamer and all the American dreamers he stood for—Wounded Warriors, each of us; Bachelors, Berrymans, Henrys. Dad wasn't destiny. Destiny was destiny. Dad was Dad, and I loved him. I was the confluence of a million forces, not quite all of them beyond my bending. Heroic feelings, or almost heroic, gathered and rose within me to an accompaniment (Bach?) I wouldn't be able to hear until months later when I watched this episode. I knew I was supposed to be full of regret (Berryman: "At thirty men think reluctantly back over their lives"), but instead I felt full of gratitude and excitement: gratitude for everything I had ever been through (not much, unimaginable multitudes), excitement for everything that would come. A resolution: sow only seeds of love. Another: read aloud. Time opened up into a panorama that evening in the rooftop restaurant on my birthday, and, ignoring the vibration against my thigh, I saw in a flash of overlaid images Dave in House Above the Morning Clouds, my grandfather flying above fallow farmland, my teenage self typing birth certificates on the thirty-second floor of the Ruan Center, Berryman leaping from the bridge to his death, the Bachelor sitting on the floor of his apartment, gazing out over his city.

He has a twin brother, I recently discovered. They co-own four Austin-area bars: the Dizzy Rooster, the Chuggin' Monkey, Molotov Lounge, and the Dogwood, an "indoor/outdoor concept" named after their grandmother's favorite tree. He still hopes to find the love of his life one day. Maybe she's sitting in the room he's about to enter. No longer young, not quite middle-aged, he'd still make quite a catch for a woman who didn't mind his unconventional dating history. Meanwhile, if he finds himself feeling down, he can always watch the footage of himself watching himself, miraculously sealed as in a magic tank, kneel on one knee and say to the woman who will never stop being his future wife, "You're the one, Em. You're it. You're my once-in-a-lifetime. I'm asking for you to please give me your forever."

Acknowledgments

THIS BOOK WOULD NOT BE WHAT IT IS WITHOUT THE contributions of many people and organizations. Thanks to Brian Platzer, Rachel Monroe, and Greg Jackson for their early readings. Thanks to my agent, Sarah Bowlin, for her wisdom, patience, and textual insight. Thanks to my editor, Alexis Washam, for her excellent suggestions, and to Jillian Buckley and the rest of the Hogarth team for their behind-the-scenes support. Thanks to Salvatore Scibona and Matthew Neill Null for their unwavering advocacy of my work. Thanks to Paul Cavanagh and Molly Schaeffer for publishing an excerpt of an early draft in *Big Big Wednesday.* Thanks to Kate Donahue for granting me access to the Berryman archives at the University of Minnesota, and to Martha Mayou for giving me permission to quote from the archives. Thanks to Brush Creek Foundation for the Arts, the Ucross Foundation, the Anderson Center, the Fine Arts Work Center, and the Corporation of Yaddo for the time and space to work. Thanks to the late Stephen Dixon. Eternal thanks to my parents. And thanks to Liza Birnbaum for her conversation, her encouragement, her countless readings, and everything else.

ABOUT THE AUTHOR

ANDREW PALMER's writing has appeared in *Slate, The Times Literary Supplement, The Paris Review Daily, The New Yorker* online, and *McSweeney's.* He has been a fiction fellow at the Fine Arts Work Center in Provincetown and a resident at Ucross, the Anderson Center, and Yaddo. He grew up in Iowa and lives in Seattle with his partner and their dog. *The Bachelor* is his first novel.

ABOUT THE TYPE

This book was set in Dante, a typeface designed by Giovanni Mardersteig (1892–1977). Conceived as a private type for the Officina Bodoni in Verona, Italy, Dante was originally cut only for hand composition by Charles Malin, the famous Parisian punch cutter, between 1946 and 1952. Its first use was in an edition of Boccaccio's *Trattatello in laude di Dante* that appeared in 1954. The Monotype Corporation's version of Dante followed in 1957. Though modeled on the Aldine type used for Pietro Cardinal Bembo's treatise *De Aetna* in 1495, Dante is a thoroughly modern interpretation of that venerable face.